"[*In a Dark Dream* is a] nifty little exercise in surreal spookiness [by] one of the genre's more literate practitioners."
— *Kirkus Reviews*

"Grant's style of horror takes hold of your spinal cord and plays it like a violin. His books are addictive."
— Charles de Lint in *Mystery Scene*

"There are few pleasures as delightful or rare as an exciting and well-written horror novel. Charles L. Grant always provides that pleasure."
— Whitley Strieber

Charles L. Grant

IN A DARK DREAM

A TOM DOHERTY ASSOCIATES BOOK
NEW YORK

IN A DARK DREAM

Copyright © 1989 by Charles L. Grant

A TOR Book
Published by Tom Doherty Associates, Inc.
49 West 24 Street
New York, NY 10010

Cover art by Lee MacLeod

ISBN: 0-812-51844-6

Library of Congress Catalog Card Number: 88-29167

First edition: February 1989
First mass market edition: April 1990

Printed in the United States of America

0 9 8 7 6 5 4 3 2 1

This is for Jill,
Through the Looking-Glass,
With love

In a dark dream
There was sunlight and laughter
And moonlight and shadow;
While Sleep crooned with Screaming,
Love waltzed with the Dead.

I

The dream when it comes . . .

. . . the spectered shadow of a cloud crawling westward off the summit of a dark forested hill, sliding down the slope where it deepens the shadows and stains the bark and swings the leaves to a deep deathly gray, causes birds to stir and huddle, a raccoon to hiss and snap, then slips across the road and through trembling bushes to the surface of a lake where ripples abruptly calm and reflections no longer matter; it bulges; it shrinks; it moves to the opposite shore and through the trees again, and the road, and up the blunt wedge of a high rock, pausing at the edge, shifting slightly to one side, shifting again and sliding on, filling the cracks with black, covering a hunched man with winter, and taking the upward slope, leaving the black behind . . .

the shadow of a cloud in a cloudless blue sky.

ONE

THE outcropping was massive on the side of the hill, and rose a straight and full hundred feet above the road that followed the contours of the lake. Even in the clear light, the morning's soft and warming light, the rock was deep black, the leading edge of a prow, a petrified galleon forever trapped in escape. And a squint of an eye caused the striations and cracks to reform into timbers, the moss and clumps of grass into seawater stains, while embedded strips of ore reddened and ran into strips of dried blood. Its top was flat and angled slightly lakeward, its sides thrusting from the forest floor to bull the trees aside.

But not the trees behind it.

They rose thickly and darkly to the top of the uneven ridge that formed a semicircle rim around the lake's deep basin; and when the foliage was thick, the summer wind still, the water calm and empty, it was easy to imagine that no one lived there on the slopes, and no one lived along the shore, and there was no town to the south, beyond the sagging stone bridge that spanned the creek the lake fed. There were too many leaves and too many gullies and too many dips where a house could be hidden and lie unseen from the road.

From the rock.

The black rock where Glenn held his breath and concentrated on a stone loosely cupped in his left hand. He blinked against the water's glare that only moments before had made him think there'd been a cloud, then dropped the stone and watched it wobble away. His right hand snatched at it. And missed. And he lost it over the edge and groaned.

A mild gust pushed him gently.

He shifted.

Slow; he was getting slow.

In days past he would have grabbed it without looking, tossed it once, and grabbed it again. Big ones. Small ones.

Slow; he was getting slow.

He shifted again, wondering what it was that made him sit on his heels instead of his rump, as if his legs wouldn't protest and his knees pop when he moved. The perversely tempting feeling, perhaps, of falling, nearly falling, because of the angle, and because of the trees that poked their way up from the narrow shoulder below, tops straining, boles twisting, leaves hissing at him to come on, come on, it won't hurt if you jump.

Hypnotic; it was hypnotic, and sounded perfectly reasonable—like standing on the edge of an impossibly high cliff and thinking you had wings unflexed but ready.

Come on, Glenn, come on; it won't hurt; you can fly.

From the rock.

To the ground.

He shivered and sank back until his buttocks touched the ground; he stretched his legs out and his arms out behind him. His hat, a western hat battered and grey and long without form, prevented the sun's water ricochet from blinding him directly; his jacket, dark denim, was zipped to his neck, collar snapped up, the too-long sleeves rolled back at the cuffs; and his jeans almost too snug, flaring to slip over the tops of black boots.

"You know," his wife had said the night before, for at least the hundredth time since the beginning of the year, "you really ought to live in Montana or something."

It wasn't the way he dressed, clearly not an affectation; it was, he was told, the attitude he no longer had the patience to hide—too damn many people and too damn little land and too damn much government and too damn little time.

"Right," he'd answered. "And would you come with me?"

"Are you kidding?" Marjory said, one hand waving his attention to the mess in the kitchen. "And leave all this?"

They had laughed, and had made love, and when he woke up this morning his hat was on the bedpost and his boots were on his chest.

He lowered his chin and stared at his lap. Then he yawned and laughed aloud, and suggested he best get on his horse and ride into town before someone got the idea the bad guys had nabbed him and had chained him in a cave.

Or onto the rock.

The laugh drifted away with the breeze when he rose and dusted off his legs, his smile replaced by a slight puzzled frown as he slipped one hand into a hip pocket and stared out over the water. The shadow of the hill to his left slipped back toward its shoreline as the sun rose toward nine, letting loose the green and the blotches of flower color.

Hunter Lake was a surprise for most visitors to the county. Most of the others were blobs and circles and ovals and blots, half of them manmade. This one resembled nothing more than a bloated horseshore, the black rock dead center on its upper rim and visible all year round. From where he stood it was almost exactly two miles down to West Point on his right, and another two miles to East Point by the twisting road. The land that split the water into its uneven arms came to a virtual point and rose two dozen feet above the surface, poor land for a lawn unless you wanted to mow straight down.

Despite its length, Point to Point, the lake was only a few hundred yards across at its widest—from the shore below the rock to the land that he faced.

And beyond, due south, was the village.

Once, it had been only a few houses, a general store for the local farmers, and an inn that had provided rooms for travelers who'd gotten lost and were too weary to complain and move on; the houses along the shoreline had been merely cabins and cottages for fishermen and hunters and a handful of the wealthy who didn't want company.

But that, he thought sourly, was then; unfortunately this was now, and the village of his childhood was a village no longer. There were streets and sewers and reservoir water, a high school, a junior high, and a grade school that was demanding either a twin or a huge addition.

And on the lake . . .

He couldn't help grinning again—too damn many people and too damn little land and too damn little time left to stop the place from exploding.

You, he told himself, are getting too damn cranky for this job.

A shrug. It was a fact, unfortunately, that some of those people living down there, hidden under the trees and hiding in town, would just as soon see him vanish into the woods, or wander into a desert, if such a thing could be found in this part of New Jersey. They didn't care about the way he dressed; they just wanted to replace him with someone who liked the way the community was growing.

Glenn Erskine, he was positive they said in quiet corners and whispers, was a reactionary, not a progressive; he couldn't handle the job anymore.

And there on the rock, mist sculling over the lake and the morning sun promising July heat as June set to pass, he almost wondered if they were right.

"Sure," he said to his shadow as he moved. "Sure."

A steep narrow trail led down to the blacktop road where he had parked his car. He took the way slowly, cautiously, mindful of the afternoon three years ago when he'd tried to impress Marjory with youth no longer his and had tripped over a root and rolled the rest of the way. Two broken ribs, scratches all over his lean face, thick brown hair crusted with dirt, and embarrassment so broad he could have built a house on it. Marj hadn't laughed; she'd only given him a look.

When he reached the bottom, a jay screamed at him. A squirrel sat up on the white center line and chattered at him. He smiled and snapped his tongue against the roof of his mouth several times; the squirrel quieted and stared, then wheeled and shot away, tail high and fluffed, its passing into the underbrush as silent as the jay's flight when it darted out of a pine tree and aimed for the water.

A check of the sky.

It was perfectly clear, and had been since dawn.

He couldn't imagine where that cloud had come from, and decided that he'd probably dozed off for a few seconds. It wouldn't be the first time, up here in the new sun. The rock was his thinking place, his pouting place, the not-so-very-secret place that had heard all his anger, all his depressions, all his occasional bouts with self-pity.

All his fears for his family, for himself.

This morning had been no exception.

The difference, however, was that talking it out to the air, the water, the chipmunk that had taken the peanut from his hand, had done him little good.

Old.

Getting older.

An excuse, nothing more, because Susan Leigh was coming for her first visit in three years. His wife's younger sister, not so recently widowed, and the only woman he'd ever met who could, if she tried, tempt him into another bed.

And if that wasn't enough to nudge him off balance, summer vacation was only a week away, the Fourth of July three weeks later, and already the more rambunctious younger natives were getting anxious to party. Late nights and long days and the unmistakable smell of trouble that kept his sleep too light. Not to mention the someone who had evidently decided to supplement his income by engaging in a little breaking-and-entering while the houses' owners were out. Seven in twenty days. And nothing stolen but petty cash lying in drawers and on dressers and not so cleverly hidden in cookie jars and bread boxes, plus a few apparently worthless items of costume jewelry, hair brushes, and vials of not terribly expensive perfume. The effort involved seemed hardly worth it, but the grief it brought him made the burglaries seem like murder.

"If I quit . . ." he'd said to Marj only a few days ago.

She'd hushed him with a wooden spoon that cracked across his knee.

"What the hell'd you do that for?"

"Quit and do what? Hang around here all day? Drive the kids nuts?" She scowled; no mirth in her eyes. "What? Work in the garden? Paint the house? What are you going to do the second week, huh?"

Wincing, he rubbed his knee. "I don't know. Help you at the office?"

Her hair, blonde and long and bobbing as she bobbed her head, seemed suddenly sparked with red. "You stay the hell away from me, Glenn Erskine. I have enough trouble selling houses without you tagging along."

"You don't think I could do it?"

Her smile was gentle. The spoon whacked his shoulder. "You probably could. But that's my territory, pal. You want to stay married, you stay the hell out."

He'd run from the kitchen then, yelling at his four children to pack their bags and get out, find a bomb shelter quick, their mother was planning to take over the world. The spoon hit him between the shoulders. When he turned, red-faced from laughing, her lips were grinning, her eyes telling him to knock it off.

Another check of the sky.

A chill on the breeze.

He slid behind the wheel and pulled the keys from his jacket's breast pocket.

The car was dark brown, or had been at one time, before the summer's sun and dust, the claws of low branches, had faded and scratched it to a shade no one could name. He loved it. He'd had it for six years, and the driver's leather seat had finally conformed to every sag of his spine, every bulge of his rump. Like slippers that looked as if they were ready for the trash, and couldn't possibly be that comfortable.

He switched on the ignition; the engine coughed worse than a dying man. He waited for it to settle, the patience of experience. And when it did, after flirting with a stall just to annoy him, he pulled onto the road—all curves and sharp bends, rising and falling as the land rose and fell. The houses on the slopes above and below it were widely separated by wooded lots, mailboxes in clusters on cleared patches of level ground, oak and caged birch and hickory and pine that hid much of the sky and most of the sun, railroad ties and whitewashed stones to mark driveways.

Even in the afternoon it was like driving through evening.

But the more houses there were, the less trees there would be, and the less—

"Cut it," he ordered, left hand on the wheel, right hand on his thigh. "You're beginning to sound like an old man."

But he had missed the stone.

And there'd been a shadow without a cloud.

And as he swung around a bend forced by a huge boulder, there was a body in the road.

Oh great, Nancy thought glumly when she recognized her father's car; great, wonderful, swell, shit. I'm dead. Aw shit. I'm dead.

"Hi, Dad!" she called brightly when Glenn pulled alongside her bike and braked sharply enough for her to wince. She leaned over to peer through the open passenger window. "I thought you were going to work."

A moment passed without an answer.

Please, she prayed; God, please let him be in a good mood.

Then she panicked, fought it back, because her shorts were too tight (he would say), her thin white t-shirt too revealing (he would say), her hair, thick and brown and inherited from him, long and almost frizzy, which would make him ask (as always) if the humidity was too high, maybe she ought to get it cut so she didn't look like steel wool.

With exaggerated caution that made her add an earthquake to her prayers, he slid out and rested his arms on the roof, rested his chin on one wrist, and said, "Nancy, who the hell is that?"

Oh hell. But at least it hadn't been a crack about the way she was dressed.

The body stirred.

"Dad, look, I can explain—"

He turned his head; she couldn't see his eyes. "Is that Thorny?" His voice deepened, and a chill settled beneath her breast. "Tell me that isn't Thorny."

The body rolled over, and she closed her eyes briefly, thinking that being grounded for a year was probably the best she could hope for if that idiot tried to stand.

"Morning, Mr. Erskine," Thornton Ollworth said, sitting up and wrapping his hands around his knees. He wore faded cutoffs and a rugby shirt, and no socks with his sneakers, his red hair laced with dead grass and a single leaf.

Nancy pointedly refused to look at him when he nodded to her and tried a smile that was more sickly than friendly. Instead, she wheeled her bike hastily around the front of the car, as much to get closer to her father so she wouldn't have to talk over the running engine as to keep him from seeing how drunk the jerk still was.

"Nancy," Glenn said, "I thought we had an agreement about that young man."

"Dad, it wasn't my fault," she answered truthfully, keeping her voice down so it wouldn't shake so badly. "He was just there, that's all. I was riding to work and he was just . . . there."

"Lying in the middle of the road."

"Yes."

"Where anyone could run over him."

She glanced over her shoulder. "No such luck."

He pushed away from the car and started toward the boy, and she snapped a hand to his arm. "Dad," she said. "Please."

He looked at her, and she didn't smile. When he was in this kind of a mood, that would only stir his temper to the boiling-over phase and she'd end up caged in her room, spending the rest of her life counting lily pads and dragonflies. But she did give him her best *let me handle it* look, one so intense that she couldn't help smiling anyway when the corner his mouth began to twitch and he couldn't meet her stare.

"We had an agreement," he reminded her.

"And I've kept it, haven't I? Until just now, I haven't seen him in two weeks. I swear."

Grudgingly, he nodded. Then he said to Thorny, "You been drinking, Ollworth?"

"No sir," the boy answered quickly, shaking his head slowly, crossing his heart. "No sir."

Nancy backed away as her father returned to the car, closed the door, and looked up at her.

"He lies like a rug," he told her, and drove away, veering widely around the boy, speeding up only when he neared the next bend in the road.

She sagged for a moment, then swung back onto the bike.

Thorny tried twice to stand, twice fell on his rump, finally made it unsteadily to one foot before yelping and toppling sideways off the road. He sprawled under a tangled laurel that dropped a web onto his chin, a leaf that wedged behind his ear. He swore, pushed himself to his hands and knees, and said, "Nance, I think I'm gonna throw up."

"Just don't lie on your back, Thornton," she said as she rode by. "You'll drown."

She sensed him struggling back to his feet, heard him call her name hoarsely several times before she was around the bend herself, and out of sight. Where she slowed and blew out a relieved breath. But she didn't stop; she didn't have time. She had to be in Hunter in thirty minutes, out of her shorts and old shirt and into that dumb pink-striped white dress with the stupid cutesy ruffles, ready to take orders from the world's greatest grump. If it hadn't been for the money, she would have quit months ago. As it was, every dime and every tip was a dollar closer to getting the car.

And once she had it, once the bike had been shoved into storage and lost forever, she wouldn't have to depend on anyone anymore. No begging transportation from her parents, no making deals with her brother just to get her out of the house, no having to ask creeps like Thornton Ollworth to give her rides to wherever she wanted to go.

Which was anywhere but here.

Anywhere.

Period.

And that, she admitted as she swerved around a fallen branch, wasn't strictly exactly true, not really. Hunter wasn't all that bad, and would get better once summer was officially here and the city people came and there was *life* again on the streets. Otherwise, unless you were a gopher, it was like living in a haunted house.

What was bad was the way her father kept looking at her when he thought she didn't notice his attention. It made her feel strange, and she didn't know why. She couldn't ask her sisters, of course, because they were only children, and her mother was definitely no help these days. Hardly home, practically living in her office selling what seemed like half the Garden State every time she turned around. Rushing like she had electric wires attached to every joint in her body.

Definitely no help there.

And Aunt Susan wasn't here yet, to offer her the shoulder, and the advice.

But a car . . . that was a different story.

Her father had sworn she could have one the minute she had enough money to pay for it in full. He would take care of the insurance and incidentals. That deal had been made two years ago. And now, after working after school and on weekends, saving her birthday and Christmas money, and keeping on her father's good side—most of the time—she was only six weeks away from the big day, and the idea of having to waste half the summer without one was making her crazy.

Bern thought she was nuts, but what did he know? He was going to college in California in the fall, never had a car, and didn't seem to want one. He didn't understand because he was a man, and a brother, and half the time he didn't know she was around anyway.

Someone called. She waved with her left hand. Then her grip tightened around the handlebars when she thought of Ollworth, charging out of the woods in front of her, nearly driving her into the lake. Scaring the hell out of her while he screamed about love and dying and swearing that his family's fortune would be hers if only she'd give him the time of day.

Ten seconds. Ten lousy seconds before her father had come down the road. Ten shitty seconds that had almost ruined it all.

"I'll kill him," she told the shadows that flicked over her. "I'll kill him if he's wrecked it. The son of a bitch."

Up over a rise that banked sharply to the right, and the houses now closer together, more of them, older, with kids in the wooded yards and dogs barking as she passed and cars backing into the road and making her swing around them.

By the time she reached East Point she was scowling, and when she reached the fork she had a good mind, as her grandmother used to say, to swing off to the right, cross the high stone bridge that connected the two halves of Lake Road, and head straight back home.

Before the day was over, Thorny the creep was sure to come to Vorssen's, sober or not, sit at the counter and drink milk shakes until he popped. While he stared at her. Smiled at her. Winked. Made suggestions that would make her stomach flutter.

The car, she reminded herself.

Her father would come in for lunch, and not take his eyes off her.

The car.

And with a loud martyred sigh that startled a half dozen starlings into chattering zigzag flight, she veered resignedly left instead, paying no attention to the way the trees abruptly fell away from the road, giving way to a large well-kept field on the left where a dozen redwood picnic tables had been set up, and a baseball diamond, wooden bleachers four rows high, two small buildings back near the woods that were supposed to be restrooms though she'd rather die than use one, no matter how badly she had to go; and a smaller field on the right, badly overgrown, pine saplings dotting the weeds, a worn and weathered sign announcing, for the fifth year in a row, the imminent construction of Hunter Lake Plaza, a small shopping center whose backers had gone bankrupt.

The sun was hot here.

She pedaled more slowly.

And after not quite a mile the fields gave way to houses, most of them low and neat and yard-wise, most of them packed to the brim with children and housewives, most of them with boats or canoes on carriers in the side yard, fishing rods propped against the side wall, beach towels on clotheslines getting their first airing.

There would be regular blocks now. Street signs. Traffic lights. Noise. Sidewalks and hydrants. Fire alarm boxes beneath blue lights on telephone poles, and trees so old they were old when she was born.

And her father waiting at the second corner, leaning against a fender, jacket off, arms folded across his chest, chin pulled in to his neck.

Oh shit, she thought; why doesn't he just take a hike?

There were times—just about every minute of every day lately—when Glenn wanted to grab his eldest daughter and lock her in the cellar, bury the key, and pretend she didn't exist. She was too beautiful to be seen in public. She was too old to be his baby. And by the look on her face, as lean as his but without the sharp angles, she was mad. Even the handful of pale freckles across the bridge of her nose seemed to be accusing him instead of turning his heart to jelly.

He wondered what he'd done this time.

She swerved sharply and braked, hopped the bike over the curb, and walked toward him. Long strides, and he wished to hell she were knock-kneed or something. Legs like that reminded him of her mother, and it was Marjory's legs that had trapped him in the first place.

"Dad," she said, giving it two syllables, the tone not quite disgusted.

He smiled and tossed his hat into the front seat. "I wasn't waiting for you, Nance, really."

She didn't believe him, with one eye partly closed. "You just hanging out?"

"I got a call from Robbie, if you want to know. He wanted me to meet him here."

Her eye opened; the doubt was still there. "I'm gonna be late for work."

He shrugged. "Okay. I'm not keeping you."

Doubt in the way she almost frowned. "Dad, that"— she waved vaguely behind her—"wasn't my fault."

"I never said it was."

"He just jumped out at me, that's all."

"Okay, okay."

She grabbed the bike as if she were going to throw it. "You don't believe me."

"Hey." He spread his hands. "I said I did, didn't I?"

"You never believe me," she muttered, and crossed

the street to head for the center of town. "God, sometimes I think I live in one of your damn cells!"

He didn't move. He didn't change his expression.
When she behaved like this, and increasingly so lately,
there was no sense trying to prove himself innocent of
whatever she'd already tried and convicted him of; it was
hopeless. He prayed it was a phase. But he didn't stop
watching her, couldn't stop, until she was at the second
intersection and wheeling herself onto Springwood Avenue, Hunter's main street. She was a ghost in all that
shadow, a sprite in the sun, and he had a feeling that
her wedding day was going to be the worst day of his
life.

Ah well, he thought, shifted gears, and looked up
the street, hoping to see Roberto Sandera. He was a
good man, Robbie was, five years on the force down in
Philadelphia before his father had suffered a mild but
frightening heart attack and could no longer run his
thriving shoe repair shop here in town. Without being
asked, Robbie had quit and came north. And once the
old man had been settled, the house mortgage paid off,
Sandera asked Glenn for a job because though he could
do it, he couldn't see himself fixing soles and heels for
the rest of his life; when Glenn said yes, the shop was
sold.

Eager, street-wise, and perhaps a little too anxious to
find city-style crime in a place where the last murder had
been nine years ago.

A blue-and-white cruiser swung onto the street several
blocks away.

He straightened.

The patrol car eased through the intersection, made a

U-turn, and parked facing the wrong way behind his car. Then Sandera climbed out, and Glenn couldn't help shaking his head in both amazement and mild amusement at the size of the man. He himself was just six feet tall without his boots, shoulders and chest wide enough to be intimidating when they had to be, but Sandera was unquestionably huge. A full six inches taller, a good fifty pounds heavier, and his Zapata mustache combined with his dark skin to give him a presence that was, Glenn knew, downright terrifying at night.

There was no official uniform in Hunter, but Glenn, despite his own preference, tried to keep his men at least looking like police: grey shirts, sharply creased grey slacks, enough brass and badge and gunbelts to keep civilians alert. They all, however, wore western hats—they were comfortable, provided shade, and provided an image no tunic or cap could deliver.

Sandera's was dark brown, with a black-and-gold band around the crown.

"I'm not going to like this, am I," Glenn said with a grin as the younger man stepped over the curb.

Sandera grinned back, white teeth lightly stained, irregular enough to be devilish. "I don't know." He looked back the way he had come and pointed to a small, blue Cape Cod four houses along. The front yard was shaggy, the concrete driveway pitted, an American flag hanging from a canted wood pole over an aluminum screen door. "Iroquois called me a bit ago, said he needed to talk."

Christ, Glenn thought sourly; this is not the way to start the day.

"What'd he want this time? Someone step on his precious grass again? Or did someone look at him cross-eyed?"

Sandera laughed without a sound, and Glenn moved to his side as they started for the house. "No, I don't think so. But he was pretty damn upset."

"He's always upset," Glenn grumbled. "He's upset at the Fourth of July parade, at Christmas carolers, writes letters to the paper about his neighbor's radio being too loud, and he probably sets traps for the Easter Bunny in his spare time." He raked a finger through his hair, scratched the back of his neck. "It's rotten, but there are times when I wish the old fart would just give it up and go to hell."

Sandera tsked.

Glenn didn't care, and felt no guilt for it. Iroquois Trace, once his wife had died and his granddaughter had moved to her own apartment on the other side of the county, seemed to have only one goal left in life, which was to pack Glenn's workday with as much petty nonsense as a single human being could generate, or kill himself trying. And yet Glenn didn't dare succumb to the "cry wolf" temptation—one of these days something really might be wrong.

They trudged up a worn and buckled brick walk and heard a large dog barking furiously inside, stepped onto a water-stained concrete stoop, and Glenn knocked on the screen door. He couldn't see inside; all the shades were drawn, there were no lamps lit, and when Trace finally appeared out of the dark, Glenn stepped back, suddenly uneasy.

"Good morning, Mr. Trace," Sandera said.

Trace cupped his hands around his eyes and leaned against the screen. "What do you want?"

"You called us, Mr. Trace, remember?"

The old man shook his bald head. "Never did."

Sandera was patient. "You wanted to see the sheriff."

Glenn nodded to him, said nothing, scanned the empty yard instead. He couldn't understand why he felt so peculiar. But today Trace wasn't a nuisance in torn sweater and baggy trousers; he was different, almost menacing, the bark of his face like rock instead of rotted wood, the twisted lumps that were his knuckles like stone instead of knots. He had the feeling, no more, that Trace was gathering his strength to reach through the screen and tear his throat out.

He took a slow deep breath and looked back.

"What's up?" he said politely.

Trace glared and lowered his hands. A loose bandage flapped across the broad bridge of his hooked nose, and even in the screen's shadow Glenn could see that his upper lip had been split, a scab already forming.

"Someone take a swipe at you, Mr. Trace?" he asked.

"Fell," the old man said gruffly, a palsied hand pressing the bandage back into place. "Go away."

"Now wait a minute," Sandera said, patience gone. "You called, we came, and now I think—"

The old man slammed the inner door.

The bolt turned over.

Sandera lifted his arm to knock again, and Glenn shook his head. "Don't bother."

"But Christ, did you see him?"

"Sure. He said he fell."

"Right."

Glenn turned and walked away. "Robbie, maybe he did."

"And maybe," the young man said, striding angrily beside him, "some punk shit tried to mug him. Maybe it was our midnight bandit, huh?"

The thought had occurred to him; he dismissed it with an abrupt wave. "With him still in his house? And with that dog?"

Sandera opened his mouth to argue, closed it and clamped a palm around the butt of his revolver. "I didn't see any dog," he muttered.

"Be glad," Glenn told him. "I have. Some kind of hound out of the Baskervilles."

A silence until they reached their cars.

Glenn felt his unease lift and scatter. He rolled his shoulders to be sure it was gone, then told Sandera to get on with it, whatever it was. He made it clear he wasn't going to brook an argument, neither was he in the mood for gossip and chatter. The man looked at him sideways. Glenn smiled. Sandera gave him a lazy salute and left.

And when the cruiser was gone, not speeding but fast enough to make Glenn smile, he leaned back against his hood and gazed up the street.

It wasn't right, that feeling back at Trace's.

He scratched the side of his nose.

No. It wasn't right.

It had been, now that he thought about it, the sort of instinctive reaction he had just before a drunk threw a punch, or a wiseass pulled a knife. Intuition that he imagined came from two years shy of two decades patrolling this town, honed by the last eight when he'd

23

worn the sheriff's badge. But this time that was as far as it went. He had suspected something was going to happen, but he hadn't known what.

And still didn't.

And it bothered him.

Slow; too old; oh, shut the hell up.

TWO

SPRINGWOOD Avenue ran in a long curve east to west that bowed toward the lake, splitting the town in half, split itself by Midrow Bridge that took the street over Marda Creek running from the lake. It had once been a scenic way for drivers to get from New Jersey to Pennsylvania without having to use any of the major, crowded highways; then trees had been leveled, land had been leveled, sidestreets formed blocks that formed neighborhoods, and a business district along Springwood soon enough found itself working twelve months a year instead of just through the summer. The newest homes were at either end and below it, styles that marked them new, styles that had glared uncomfortably out of place until the trees had regrouped and the lawns had settled in and owners had decided to add on, to paint, to give their homes a difference more than just a number. They were pleased that the lots were large, gloated over how small the lots were in the two developments west of town, and paid little attention to Hunter's growth until taxes made them realize they had a problem.

"It's dumb," said Hugh Frennel, his voice deep and slightly hoarse. "You got your schools, you got your cops, but what you don't got is your basics."

The afternoon was warm, the southern breeze humid.

"Your amenities, if you know what I mean. You know? The things that make living out here worth leaving the goddamn city in the first place."

He sat on the raised redwood deck behind his house, a cedar shake Dutch Colonial not quite two miles east of the center of town. He had few close neighbors, the nearest some kind of intellectual who lived across the road and fifty yards down. Hugh didn't like him. The guy lived alone in an undistinguished boxy place that had more trees than decent grass, and no back yard at all—just woodland that stretched all the way over to the lake, woodland that began again at the eastern edge of Hugh's property and didn't break until it reached a county highway, three miles away.

His own two acres had been carved from the back of John Wortan's dairy farm, and the apple trees and two willows he'd planted in the back yard were just now beginning to provide enough of a screen to hide the damned cows that wandered over the pasture rising beyond the fence he'd built the day after he and Loretta had moved in.

Beside him, his wife lay on a chaise lounge, an amber glass of soda in one hand, a fan in the other.

"I mean," he said, scratching idly at his bare chest, "we haven't got a single mall within twenty miles, not to mention one of them five- or six-store shopping center things, you could die for a decent meal when you want to eat out, and don't hit the bees with the fan, Loretta. You leave them alone, they won't bother you."

Loretta swatted at the bee again and said nothing.

He smiled at her. He shifted in the lawn chair and reached over to touch her arm. Warm sun. Warm skin. Fine dark hairs from elbow to wrist that just about drove him crazy. Married twenty years, he thought, and she doesn't look hardly a minute older than the day he married her. Hair still black, no gray, her stomach flat and her breasts still not sagging, and a way of shifting when she lay down that made it look like she was dancing.

Proud of her was what he was.

Next to using his hands, bringing her into the city to show her off at dinner was the greatest joy he had.

With a loud sigh as proof of his content, he settled back and clasped his hands over his stomach. Then he looked down and smiled again. Not too bad for a guy stomping flatfooted through middle age. The gut could still be sucked in, the muscles of his arms were still well-defined, and the legs that poked out of his shorts were ample evidence of strength. He'd built the deck himself, the garage, had laid out the yard and its rose garden, and had converted the attic into an office for himself, when early retirement from his construction firm had driven him nuts and he'd wanted a place to work without bothering his wife.

"If you ask me," he said, "that so-called planning

commission this burg's got couldn't plan its way out of a wet paper bag."

"Crime," Loretta said.

He frowned. "What?"

"Crime," she said. "We don't have any."

"All right." Sometimes it took him a while to understand where she was going. The way she said things, he didn't know if she was making fun of him—his lack of formal education and his manners, which didn't always sit well with what she called the horsey set—or if she was just letting her mind wander from the topic at hand to something she really believed had a point.

He just didn't know.

And these days it was worse.

He didn't know why, but since the middle of the week things had been a little fuzzy around the edges. Blurred, like the way his glasses got when he kissed her cheek and her makeup smeared the corner of a lens.

"Okay," he agreed. "So we don't have much crime. You gonna give the credit to a guy like Erskine? Shit. What the hell kind of crime could we get anyway? A break-in here, a drunk lying in the gutter there. Shit, we've seen worse. Loretta, you know that."

"I know," she said.

So stop your bitching, the tone added.

A grunt, a palm slipped over his chest to wipe off the sweat, and he stood and padded to the deck's edge, looked down at the brick barbecue pit he'd finished only last week with some help from old Trace, and suddenly grabbed the railing when the ground spiraled sharply away. He clamped his eyes shut. Bile lined his mouth.

And for a moment, just a moment, he was sure he tasted blood.

"Jesus," he whispered.

"Hugh, you okay?"

He nodded. He swallowed. He straightened and breathed deeply. A man his age, a year off from fifty-three, he had to take better care of himself.

"Time for my walk," he announced, turning decisively, rubbing his hands.

She opened one startling blue eye and smiled, the dimple in her right cheek the only line on her face. "It's hot."

"There's shade on the road, don't worry."

"Watch out for the kids," she said as he moved past her. "They drive like jerks around here."

He reached down and touched her shoulder, leaned down and kissed the top of her head. It was warm. He could see droplets of perspiration in the gap between her breasts, and the faint flush of pink that would turn dark before she peeled. Just like him. By summer's end their friends would think they'd been months in the Bahamas.

"Just a mile today. To the old well and back, all right?"

"All right." The eye closed. "Be careful."

He nodded, made a sound to let her know that he had, and hurried inside through the sliding glass door. The kitchen was chilly but not too cold; nevertheless he adjusted the thermostat downward to keep the air conditioning from switching on again too soon. He grabbed a short-sleeved shirt from the newel post, slipped into worn sneakers kept by the door, and hurried out the front way before he changed his mind.

The front yard was large, blocked off by a split-rail fence he'd painted white the first warm day last April, and as he headed for the road along the inlaid brick walk, he squinted, trying to imagine just what shrubs should go where when he plotted the landscaping next fall.

A glance to his left, to the intellectual's dark green Cape Cod diagonally across the street, and he swung his arms to loosen his shoulders, picked up his knees to loosen his thighs, and started up along the shoulder. Marching. Gazing straight ahead. Hoping that his wife didn't have plans for tonight.

Hoping that the dizziness wouldn't return.

And once his stride had been set, he smiled, and even flicked a friendly hand at the intellectual, who drove past him in the opposite direction, in a station wagon that was, to be kind, more rust than metal.

Nate was almost too surprised to return Frennel's sudden wave, but he managed it without making it seem as if he would have avoided the gesture if he'd been able. Then he checked the man's shrinking figure in his rear view mirror, grinned, and headed on toward town.

To stop at home would be too tempting.

Loretta would be on the deck, or on a blanket in the yard.

If he hurried over, she'd tease the hell out of him, kiss him, and offer him a cold shower.

That he didn't need. Hugh wasn't going to be gone for very long.

Besides, one of these days his luck was going to sour,

and the former contractor was going to beat the living hell out of him, probably leave him crippled, and then brag about it for years while Loretta played recluse in her bedroom, nursing a perpetual blackened eye.

You, he told himself as he switched on the radio, are a jackass.

You, he said two miles later, are not stupid, just horny.

A laugh. A shake of his head. An automatic glance at the hunched Bait Shop bar on the left, the Clearwater Restaurant on the right—the landmarks that signaled Hunter's true beginning. Beyond them were a handful of wooded lots with For Sale signs on the trees, and beyond them the businesses that commenced without interruption, none of the buildings more than two stories, most of their facades brick or white clapboard. Many had signs on white posts instead of neon in windows; more than a few had been set back a few feet from the pavement to provide for a patch of grass, a flower bed or two, every so often a plaster figurine to help identify the shop or office more clearly.

He parked at the curb two blocks later and sat for a minute as the station wagon's engine coughed itself to silence.

The sidewalks were busy, the weekend traffic heavy.

The sun that at last drove him out of his seat was only partially blunted by the fat-crowned elms and maples that lined the curbs and speckled the pavement with dark.

With hands in his pockets he walked quickly past the town hall—which looked no different than the shops around it—crossed the street and passed the sheriff's office, where he waved vaguely at a shadow waving inside, and at the corner turned into Duke Massi's Diner, a small place just wide enough for booths along the left-hand wall, and a counter on the right; the aisle between was only wide enough to walk if someone wasn't coming the other way. At the front there was barely space for a cashier's register and a tall rack for magazines, the hunting and fishing ones at eye level, comic books below, men's magazines along the top where everyone could see when you had to reach up to grab one.

It was hardly the most elegant place in town, but he didn't care. Even with the summer prices posted, it was the cheapest, the friendliest, and it had the best smells—hamburgers and bacon forever spitting as they cooked, ice cream in sodas, wax on the speckled linoleum floor, the old leather on booths and stools, cheese and pickles and catsup and eggs and the grease that held it together. Handwritten menus high on the wall behind the counter. Duke at the grill and Cornelia Bonne in her too-tight white and black uniform, too pretty to stay in this town for very long, too sad with herself to look for something better in a place that mattered.

All the booths were taken, the noise level high, but most of the stools were empty and he sat at the first one, propped his elbows on the counter, and wondered as he waited for service how the hell he was going to explain to his ex-wife that he had no more money, that she'd be getting no more checks.

He had a terrible feeling that "robbing a bank" wasn't just a phrase anymore.

Two books published, and four short stories.

The last time his name had been in print had been two

years ago, and the last time he'd seen a decent check from his agent had been last October. Barely enough to get him through the winter. And he knew the next one wouldn't cover a cheap breakfast.

If it hadn't been for Loretta, somehow smitten by the image instead of the man, he would have frozen to death when he couldn't pay for heating oil.

Robbing a bank.

Damn, he thought, and wondered, not for the first time, if he really did have the nerve to rob a bank. Or a store. Just once. Just to get him by. Someplace in another county, isolated, old folks behind the register, or a teenager too dumb to play hero. What would it be like? Who would suspect him?

Then he wished himself instantly invisible when Robbie Sandera took the stool beside him, dropped his hat on the counter, and let out a sigh that almost blew the napkin dispenser away.

"You know, Pigeon," the policeman said wearily, "I could have been in the FBI, wearing good suits, guarding presidents, stuff like that. I really could have."

"Right," Nate answered quietly.

"But no, I gotta stick around here. You know why?"

He did. Everybody did.

"Because," said the man, picking up a plastic menu and squinting at it through his dark glasses, "I am a jerk."

"Right," Nate said, smiling this time.

"You order yet?"

Nate pointed with a nod down the row of customers, to the redheaded waitress making her way slowly toward them. "Corny doesn't love me anymore. She wants me to starve."

"You call her Corny to her face," the cop said, "she'll make sure you're dead before you ever starve."

He laughed without a sound, tried to relax and tell himself he wasn't arrested when a light hand rested on his shoulder. He turned slowly to his right, blinked once and felt a familiar false smile cut his face in half.

"Hi, Kim."

"Hi yourself. Where've you been, working?"

He nodded easily, turning partway to the woman. Her hand stayed where it was, her forefinger lightly scratching the side of his neck. "Gotta pay the bills," he said, giving her a shrug, *you know what's it like.*

She leaned closer. More smells—sun on her dark hair, sweat on her arm, the musk of high summer as her other hand gestured vaguely and swept across his thigh. "I have a better way," she whispered quickly, and drew back. Drew away. The hand stayed on his shoulder; the finger still scratched.

"I'll bet," he said, the smile game now.

"Come and see us," she said, her eyes smiling at Sandera, her lips moving slowly, double messages only a deaf man could miss.

"I just may," he answered, and saw the eyes narrow, the prey sighted and sized and found needed and needing.

At that moment a teenaged girl rushed in, grabbed Kim's arm, pulled her to one side with only a *hello* look at Nate.

"Mom," she said, "are we gonna go or what?"

"Beverly, you're being rude."

Beverly Raddock groaned without making a sound. "I'm sorry, Mr. Pigeon," she said automatically.

"That's better."

"No problem," Nate said quickly, winking. "Take her for every dime she has, Bev. Tell her you'll pay her back when you're forty."

"Gross," Beverly said. "I'll never get that old."

"Beverly!"

Nate laughed.

The girl rolled her eyes, almost stamped a foot. "Mom, please, huh? Can't you see the time? I'm supposed to meet the guys at—"

Kim hauled her shoulder bag around and pawed through it for her wallet, out of which she counted four bills and handed them over. "Then go. Just don't blame me when you can't find a bargain."

Beverly kissed her cheek quickly, waved a finger at Nate, and raced outside again, hesitated, then ran to her right across the street, dodging and skipping through slower pedestrians until she reached the next corner where she slowed, touched at her auburn hair, crossed again and walked into a restaurant decorated red and white, wire-backed chairs, square tables by the calico-curtained windows that overlooked the street. Prints of hunting dogs and ducks on the walls. A long counter across the back, for the ice cream and snack crowd. Luckily, old man Vorssen was in the kitchen, and she hurried over to the register, stuffing the money into her jeans. She hadn't counted it. Whatever it was, it was too much.

It was always too damned much.

Nancy Erskine scribbled something on an order pad,

erased it, wrote again. Bev shook her head at the tight fist her friend's family had over finances. Nance could have had her car for Christmas if the sheriff hadn't been so goddamn cheap.

"I'm going," she said as soon as she reached her friend.

Nancy looked up, momentarily startled, then grinned. "You're kidding. No shit?"

"Got the stuff right here," she said, patting her pocket. "It's okay, I'll be alone. Mom's at the diner, making eyes at the birdman."

"Oh Christ." Nancy rolled her eyes. "My father thinks he's a dealer."

Bev shrugged. "So we should care? Look, I gotta go. Just wanted you to know. See you tonight?"

Nancy nodded, then stiffened when a hoarse bubbling voice called her name from the back. "The trolls," she muttered angrily and, out of sight behind the register, gave the kitchen the finger.

Bev grinned, touched her arm in sympathy, and hurried out to fresh air as fast as she could without running. She hated Vorssen's. Everything was so clean, the table-cloths practically starched, the food so tasteless, she couldn't understand how Erskine had managed to stick it out all this time.

The car, she reminded herself. What else? What else mattered?

Another block west brought her to Springwood and Grange, where she crossed over to the municipal parking lot behind the department store and brownstone bank. Her own automobile, small enough for her to afford the gas, large enough to enjoy Thorny when he was in the mood, was under a dying chestnut tree at the back. The windows were down. The handle when she touched it was hot enough to make her swear. And the front seat made her raise her buttocks, press back and hiss.

She hated summer.

She hated Hunter and the lake.

The only thing she could stand were the Saturday night parties on the Spit. Luckily, few parents bothered to make it past eleven, and the nerds and the braces not much past midnight. Which meant that those who counted would remain to enjoy what was left of the night.

People like her.

She grinned as she eased her rump back down, rolled up the windows, and switched the air conditioner to "on" before she started the engine. And only when she was out of the lot and crawling east on the main street did she let herself think about Bern.

And wonder why there wasn't any pain.

After all, she had loved him for nearly two years. She had let him take her to the senior prom only two weeks ago. And she had let him know how much she'd loved him in the cabin on the west ridge, when all the parties were over, breakfast served in houses and at Duke's, and she had stood in front of him, gown at her feet, her stomach jumping so hard she thought she was rippling right up through her scalp.

"No," he'd said at last.

She had felt like a jerk. An asshole. A whore.

What the hell had he wanted then, taking her up there, kissing her like that, touching her breasts and between her legs and driving her to a frenzy she'd never felt before? What the hell did he mean, no? And when he pointed at the ruins they were standing in, some hunter's place hardly anyone knew about, when he pointed at the mildewed mattress on the dusty, warped floor, at the cracks in the panes, at the cobwebs swaying from the beams, she'd told him it didn't matter, Jesus Christ, he was driving her nuts and she was *ready*, couldn't he see that, and he'd said no again and looked so miserable she'd wanted to cry.

Then he'd left.

And she'd dressed.

And on the half-collapsed rough timber porch told him she never wanted to see him again.

Her senior prom, and he'd destroyed it.

The son of a bitch. Bastard. Fucking godalmighty fag.

A horn screamed at her.

Languidly, she lifted her right hand from the wheel and gave a slow finger to the driver behind. Then, deliberately cautious, she pulled across the last intersection and sped up, checking her wristwatch, nodding, figuring that unless she ran up a tree or ran into a deer, she'd be able to get to Sparta and back just in time for supper. What she wanted, the kind of bathing suit she wanted Thorny to see her in tonight, she didn't dare buy here. The word would get around, her mother would find out, and before you knew it her father would be driving up from Tennessee for another round of "I may not be here anymore, but by God, Beverly Sue, I am still your father."

Right, she thought as she angrily fumbled a cigarette from the pack she kept in the visor overhead; right. If he was her father, how come he didn't know how much she hated being called Beverly Sue. That she despised Beverly. Jesus. Only four-eyed secretaries and old-time actresses were called Beverly anymore. Jesus. Sometimes she wondered if her mother had been drunk when she named her.

She pressed the accelerator.

Her arms stiffened.

The car gradually took a speed that blurred the trees into a broken wall, the white line into dashes, and the man she passed into an animated scarecrow that whirled and shook its fist while she laughed, rolled down her window, and flicked the cigarette out.

Hugh saw it and ran across the road. Goddamn kids, start forest fires, burn down the houses, every damn one of them ought to be locked up in a private school.

He found it atop a green leaf and crushed it with his heel.

Goddamn kids.

Goddamn—

Abruptly the road rose as if being stripped from its bed, contorting into a spiral that made him drop to his knees, topple to the shoulder where a stone ripped through his shirt, his skin, burned its way toward bone.

The road, twisting, and the trees caught in it, toward him and away, toward him and side to side, spinning the sky beneath his feet and the ground above his head until he slapped the heels of his hands hard over his eyes and curled his knees up, rolled to his back, to the other side, where he groaned and threw up.

And tasted blood.

And felt the chill of a winter shadow rest for a moment on his neck.

THREE

THOUGH the office walls were paneled and polished in light pine, there was nothing else remotely comfortable about the room or its appointments. The square desk was dark metal, the three squat filing cabinets were scratched and dented, the three visitors' chairs were ladder-backed and wood and scraped harshly on the hardwood floor whenever they were used; there were several shelves on the left-hand wall, but aside from a handful of law and statute books, they were empty and always had been, and the fluorescent ceiling light was forever spitting and threatening to give up its job.

The only personal touch was a triptych of family photographs propped on the desk.

Glenn preferred to call it spartan; his wife told him

that not even a masochistic monk would give odds he could last in such a cell.

He sat there now, gazing out the window overlooking the tiny parking lot. A tree in its center dropped shade and leaves, and a squirrel chased itself around the trunk before vanishing into the high branches.

A check of his watch: it was just past three.

He sighed, swung around, looked through the open door to the larger room beyond. No one there that he could see. The blinds on the front window were partially lowered, cutting off pedestrians' heads as well as most of the light. The surface of the counter that cut the room in half was unbroken save for a clipboard where his men signed in and out. Somewhere out there he could hear a typewriter working, Audrey Cray heroically trying to keep up with the files and the reports, and no doubt planning to take over the department so she could run it the way she ran her yearly campaigns to find a husband; the radio buzzed, and he could hear Pete Gorder dispatching one of the patrol cars to the bus station behind the Elks lodge, to hang around and see who got off the afternoon's last run from New York.

Another sigh.

Another glance out the window, and he remembered the August morning Susan had climbed that tree with Cheryl and Bern, her hair bobbed, her long legs bare, and he knew damned well she had known he'd been watching. It was in the way she made sure that everything she did gave him all angles, all views, every chance to begin daydreaming about the woman he'd not married for the woman he had.

The dumbest part was, he'd had no idea Susan felt that way about him. Not that he was surprised—it wasn't until Marjory had done the proposing herself that he realized how much his wife really cared for him.

It had taken a number of years for him to learn what he assumed every other high school kid in the country already knew.

And it had taken longer for him to understand that Susan didn't love him. All she wanted was a guiltless place in his bed now and then.

He stared at the telephone near his left hand, saw the hand move toward it, saw the hand draw away. It wouldn't do to call Marjory, not now. She was at work. That was sacrosanct. He would see her at dinner. But the hand strayed again, and this time he was amused, fumbling like a lovesick (guilty, he suggested) kid, after twenty-two years.

His eyes widened.

Twenty-two?

He counted backward quickly. Someone as young as he couldn't possibly have been married to the same woman for that long. Two decades plus? Hell, twenty-two years at any one thing and he should be ready for the old folks home, the old rocking chair, the—

Funny farm, he thought. God, what the hell's the matter with you today?

The street door opened.

He heard Pete call a greeting, heard a child giggling, and looked up just as his two youngest daughters hurried through the door, jeans and t-shirts and tennis shoes less than white, eyes bright, hair windblown.

"Dad," cried Dory immediately she crossed the threshold, "it isn't fair!"

"Mommy *said*," Cheryl told her primly, plopping on one of the chairs, swinging her legs back and forth.

"Big deal."

Cheryl pursed her lips in a whistle clearly disapproving.

He didn't have to ask what it was Mommy had said. Marj had put Cheryl in Dory's exasperated care until their father got home from work because she thought she would be late tonight, a customer who wanted to see some lakeside property her office was holding. When Dory, with an expression of disdain and lost patience for grownups, had tried to explain that turning fourteen did not mean the house automatically had a free babysitter and especially not her, Marj had walked her into the kitchen. Five minutes later the child had returned alone, disgruntled, dark eyes narrow, telling her ten-year-old sister that she'd better, just better do what she was told for destroying her Saturday, or Dory was going to take her over the hill and leave her to the wolves. She'd stomped out of the room before Glenn could scold her.

"It's all right, Daddy," Cheryl had told him patiently. "I don't care. She's just mad because I hit a home run in gym yesterday and she struck out."

Glenn had decided to let the storm just pass by.

"Dad," Dory pleaded now, leaning over the desk, her hair well on its way from blonde to his brown, bangs matted to her forehead, a stray looping around one cheek toward the corner of her mouth. "C'mon, please?

Do I gotta? It's Saturday, Dad! The whole day's already dead."

Cheryl pulled a pigtail over one shoulder and studied it, lips pursed in a silent whistle.

"Please? Can't she stay here for a while? I have things to do, really."

Glenn clasped his hands on the desk. "I believe you and your mother had an arrangement."

Dory rolled her eyes. "Some arrangement."

He cleared his throat to kill a grin. "She laid down the law, right?"

The girl nodded dolefully.

"The law's the law, sweetheart." He tapped his chest just below his badge. "Remember who you're talking to."

Dory's face darkened but she said nothing until she wheeled about and headed for the door. "I'll be outside," she barked at her sister. "I want to go home. Now."

As soon as she left, Cheryl tossed her braids back and jumped to her feet, made a great show of sticking out her tongue at the doorway and walking around the room, and he knew then why they had come—something was wrong. None of his children ever came to the office on their own, just to visit, just to say hi; somehow that had become one of the house rules, and considering the garbage he had had to put up with lately, he didn't mind at all.

He turned his chair and waited.

Cheryl studied the bookshelves.

Pete walked by the door, chewing on an unlit cigar, muttering to himself.

"I had a dream," the little girl said at last, coming around the desk, ignoring the blatant offer of the comfort of her father's lap.

"A bad one, huh?"

She nodded. "I almost cried."

"So why didn't you come in? You know I don't mind."

She looked at him the way her sister had, and he gave her an apologetic wave for being so grownup dense. Climbing into bed with one's father, the expression tolerantly suggested, wasn't what a future major league baseball player did just because she had a nightmare.

She scratched the side of her nose.

"Monsters?" he asked.

"I don't know."

"You don't?"

"I don't remember."

"Ah."

"But it was scary."

He leaned forward and took her arm gently. "And it was a dream, Pint."

She was obviously torn then between scolding him for the nickname she'd declared out of bounds six months ago and telling him that just because it was a dream didn't make it any the less scary. He could see it all in her eyes—pale blue, like her mother's—and the way her lips jumped, then quivered, then tried to form words she wasn't sure she knew.

He pulled her to him.

She wrapped her arms around his shoulders.

For a minute, the only sound was the spit of the radio in the front office.

"A dream," he whispered, "only scares you if you let it."

"You didn't have it," she whispered back.

He thought of the cloud.

"No, I guess not."

"Besides, it wasn't nice."

Nice, in this case, meant the plans she had devised for herself and for the world; it meant she'd seen things she hadn't wanted to, things that threatened to capsize her carefully and earnestly made boat.

Her persistent optimism sometimes unnerved him; Marj told him more than once not to knock it, the child would learn too soon already.

"Oh well," she said at last, pulling away without releasing him, "I guess I could always beat it up, right?"

"Black its eyes," he agreed.

"Bust a nose?"

"Break a leg."

Her grin was broad and she kissed him, punched him twice on the arm and raced out of the room, shrieking for Dory to take her home before Daddy got mad and threw her in a cell for the rest of her life. Dory shouted something back and the front door slammed, and a moment later Pete leaned on the jamb and folded his arms across his chest, a sheath of papers in one hand.

"Sheriff," he said, "when those kids grow up, you're going to be in one hell of a lot of trouble."

Glenn agreed with a grin. "One thing for sure, I'll be broke before I get there."

Gorder, as tall as he and half again as wide, took the cigar that was his trademark from his mouth, stared hard at the tip, and stuck it back in his mouth after blowing smoke into the outer room. "What I think is," he said, shifting so he could scratch his back on the jamb, like a bear, "that we could deport them teenagers to Russia or something. The Commies would either kill 'em all or go so damned crazy they won't be able to take over the world."

Glenn held out his hand for the afternoon reports, knowing they'd be right because Audrey had typed them, knowing too that Pete had pulled rank so he could bring them in.

"Thing is, y'see," the dispatcher continued, crossing the room, feet heavy and loud, "them Commies, the Russians and all them other guys, they got all these spies right here in the States, right? Secret weapons, shit like that. We could do the same. All the kids between fourteen, say, and eighteen, all them creeps. Either way we win."

"I guess," Glenn muttered. He took the papers and scanned them, and groaned loudly when he saw a budget notice from town hall that reminded him of the four new men who'd be joining the force at he end of the month.

"I know," Gorder said, leaning over, reading upside down. "I'll take care of them."

"Thanks."

"No problem."

And he knew it wouldn't be. The man had been on the force nearly long enough to qualify for monument status, but after his first five years had never wanted to do anything but train the rookies and work the radio. Manning the airwaves was, he claimed, the only way to keep the Commies and the UFOs from taking over. Glenn didn't care what the excuse was—Pete was unquestionably the best man Hunter's police force had; that Glenn also thought him more than a little crazy had nothing to do with Pete's skills as a cop.

"Damn," he said then, reading the hospital summary. "Hugh had a heart attack?"

Gorder shrugged his disinterest. "Don't know. He was found on the road not fifty yards from his house. Wife brought him in, I think."

"I'll look in on him, on the way home."

The rest was routine, and as soon as he'd initialed the ones that required it, he stacked them, smoothed them, and handed them back. When the deputy didn't leave right away, he looked up, saw the scar that kept the man's right eye half closed, and looked away again.

"What is it?" he said. "It's Saturday, Pete. Have mercy, okay?"

Gorder held the reports in one nail-bitten hand, smiled dutifully, and said, "I heard a new preacher's coming to Christ Church next Sunday."

He shrugged. "So?"

"You check him out?"

He frowned, not quite believing. "Do what?"

"Check him out." The deputy waved vaguely behind him. "Get his picture, I mean, stuff like that. You don't want no impostor coming in, screwing around with the kids, bringing in Satan, shit like that."

Glenn bit the inside of his cheek. "I hardly think the new minister's a ringer, Pete. And I'm positive he's not a Satanist."

The big man hitched up his belt as he walked to the door, then turned around and held up the paperwork as if it was his proof. "He's Episcopal, Sheriff."

This time the laugh had to be swallowed, and it was several seconds before he could say, "Yeah, so?"

Gorder's expression was hard, almost ludicrously so in a face round and jowled and gleaming pinkly as if freshly scrubbed with sand. The face of a man nowhere near fifty; the face of a young man who'd been slashed with a razor from right eye to right ear when he'd been in high school.

Gorder took the cigar from his mouth and aimed it at the front door. "They go around dressing like priests, hearing confession, using incense, stuff like that. You can't tell the difference between them and the real thing, y'know?"

Call, Marjory, Glenn pleaded then; please, call, get me out of here.

"Without getting into a theological debate, Pete, I think we'd best leave the reverend's qualifications to his church, okay? It's really none of our business."

Gorder rubbed his chin with the papers. Then he nodded and left, and popped right back into the doorway. "Okay, but don't say I didn't warn you. I had a dream about him last night. He said he was going to kill me."

II

The dream when it comes . . .

. . . on a dark night, no stars, the moon barely a sliver and barely alit, black clouds oddly seen as they lift over the basin, twisting in unfelt wind, settling like fog on the water, in the trees, on the ground, and running like a stream through the gullies, to the house at the end of the road where it slips under the doors and slips around the window frames and slips up the staircase where it sweeps around a corner and into a small room where it smothers . . .

. . . the gentle cry of a baby tossing in its rocking crib, kicking at its blankets until they crumple at the foot and slide into the space between the beveled posts and the mattress, waving a pudgy arm at the darkness in the air, opening one sleepy eye to see the mobile over its head, spinning slowly, turning slowly, winking parrots and rabbits and kittens in starlight while a tinny lullaby begins in a small box near the ceiling, soothing, quieting, dropping a veil of dreams that close the eyes and still the legs and lower the hand to the baby's side while it blows a shimmering bubble and smiles . . .

the gentle cry of a baby in an empty rocking crib.

ONE

ARJORY felt the tears long before she opened her eyes.

And she could taste them.

That they were there didn't surprise her once she came fully awake; that she had the dream that caused them did, because it was the same one she had had each night for a month, before Cheryl had been born.

Cheryl had frightened her.

Cheryl hadn't been expected.

Dory was supposed to have been the last. Two girls, one boy. That had been the plan even before she'd married Glenn, when they'd drifted in a rowboat in the middle of the lake, counting their future on the stars they could see. Two and one. And then, when she was thirty, there was Cheryl, and the dream, and when she was born the dream had vanished.

Until now.

Ten years, she thought, is a long time for something like that to return.

And the tears.

She wondered somewhat grumpily what Susan would make of that.

"An omen, Sis," is what she'd probably say. She was a great believer in omens. She even believed she'd known when her husband Wesley would die, and no one could tell her that cancer was no portent, it was a killer, there's a difference.

Hastily she wiped the backs of her hands over her face as she rolled to sit upright on the living room couch. Susan would have to wait. A scrabble for tissues from the box on the end table—one for her eyes and cheeks, one for her nose. Then she blinked and looked around her, making sure she was awake.

Nothing had changed.

The living room was still the living room, still an oddity among her friends because in the Erskine house, this was where most of the living was really done. Television was watched here when all the arguments had been settled, the stereo listened to, books read, newspapers, report cards, friends and guests led directly in instead of dragged to a basement den as though carrying some invisible, catchable, unnameable shame.

She stretched and cursed herself for falling asleep when there was work to be done.

But the couch had been too tempting. A long one, the longest her husband could find—four broad cushions and rolled armrests and a back high enough so he could rest his head without sliding halfway to the floor. Its back was what people saw when they came in from the foyer, the tables at either end with brass lamps and dark shades, a gap between it and the desk on the long wall. In front of it, a coffee table usually stacked with magazines one of the Erskines was going to read any day now. Beyond that, open space to the far wall, where behind cherry doors a hutch held the TV, the stereo components, and albums that wouldn't go in the low cabinet beside it.

A picture window on the left-hand wall, the draperies open now, a gap in the right-hand wall that led to the dining room. Wallpaper faint and floral; a carpet thick enough to swallow her toes; over by the window Glenn's armchair and god help the kid who was in it when he was tired.

Nothing had changed.

She stretched a second time and lowered her hands to drag them through shoulder-length blonde hair. Not as gold as Cheryl's, not as dark as Dory's. And ready, she thought as she grunted wearily to her feet, for a long overdue slashing. She wasn't about to keep pinning it up, or tying it back, just because her neck was a fertile garden for sweat. This year she was going to get it cut, and if Glenn didn't like it he could buy her a wig.

Absently scratching under her breasts, she wandered through the dining room into the large kitchen, stared at the sink and the dishes stacked there, checked the clock that told her it was going on eleven, and wandered again, this time down the hall to the foot of the stairs.

"Bern!"

She hadn't bothered to look in the back yard. No one

was there. Dory and Cheryl were down at the dock, fishing for sunnies with string, hook, and bread.

"Bern!"

An apprehensive glance over her shoulder and through the open front door, through the screen, across the porch, the yard and the road to the cleared space on the other side. There they were, sitting on the end, feet dangling, a pad between them for keeping score because they weren't allowed to keep the fish.

"*Bern*ard!"

Dory laughed at something her little sister said, threw herself onto her back, kicked her bare feet in the air, and sat up again.

Majory smiled.

Only an hour ago, in the kitchen, Dory, red-faced and quaking, had demanded to know why she had to watch the brat *again*, and on Sunday for heaven's sake Mother, while Bern got to sleep late and Nance got to go to town. God, they didn't do anything in this house anymore. She was, she reminded her mother with quivering indignation, fourteen now (fourteen and eight days, Marjory had thought), and teenagers these days were simply not babysitters for free. It wasn't done. And it wasn't fair.

Marjory had leaned over, took the girl's dimpled chin in two fingers, and said, "I do believe we had this same conversation the other day, didn't we?"

"But Mother—"

"In this house, darling, fair is defined as whatever Mother wants. And Mother wants you to stick with your sister until I'm ready to go to work."

Dory hadn't the nerve to shake the hand off; the dark look was all she had.

"I don't want to stay in the house. It's too nice out."

"Then go fishing."

"Mother!"

A whoop, a splash, and when she looked again, Dory was standing in the water, hands on her hips, hair soaked and dripping, and Cheryl scrambling backward, laughing so hard she could barely move.

"Bernard Erskine!"

She cocked her head. Maybe there had been a reply, but she couldn't tell with all the yelling outside. She took a step toward the door, and changed her mind when she saw Dory grab Cheryl's ankle and drag her toward the water. Cheryl shook her head wildly, pigtails whipping her back, but there was no stopping the dunking now.

Marjory smiled. It would be all right. Cheryl, if she'd wanted, could have easily gotten away. The child, for all her slightness of figure, was much stronger than her sister. She was, in fact, better at most things than Dory except getting along with the other girls at school.

"Don't have to," Cheryl had explained one evening. "I'm going to be a baseball star and make a million dollars a week and Dory can carry my bats if she wants to."

A shuffling at the landing.

She looked up, and Bern stumbled against the railing, hung on, and looked down through a fall of long tangled hair. Marjory said nothing, couldn't say anything until the image of Glenn at eighteen faded and left her with her son.

"It's eleven," she said flatly. "About time you were alive."

"Mom, I'm dying." A deep voice, somewhat rough, and gentle at the same time. "Call an ambulance."

"Call one yourself. I have to get to work. Keep an eye on your sisters while I get ready."

He groaned and sank to his knees, peering at her through the banister. "Aw, Mom, gimme a break."

"It wasn't my idea to stay up until nearly dawn," she said without sympathy.

"I was thinking."

And he had been.

Her eyes had blinked open shortly after three, her breath caught, ears straining—there was something wrong in the house. Without waking Glenn, she'd thrown a robe over her shoulders and checked all the bedrooms, found Bern's empty, and crept down the stairs. He was in the living room. Sitting on the floor, staring out the window at the early morning sky.

From the way his chest had jerked, she'd guessed he was wrestling with the notion to cry.

He hadn't heard her; she'd returned to bed and cuddled next to Glenn, trying not to cry herself.

She climbed the stairs, and as she passed him, rested her hand briefly on his head. "Just watch them," she said softly. "You don't have to talk to them."

He grunted.

She grinned.

The girls shrieked, and she hurried into the master bedroom, stood in front of the vanity's three-sided mirror and wondered what the hell she was going to wear that wouldn't scare her customer off.

It was a problem she hadn't realized she would have when she had begun selling land and houses; it hadn't even entered her mind. Being tall had stopped bothering her the day she graduated from high school. But when a

58

handful of sure sales had turned into unexpected disappointments, Kim Raddock, her partner, had explained that while men liked to think they could pull one over on a woman agent, using superior male guile and incomparable haggling techniques, it was hard to do any of it when the woman agent was considerably taller than he.

"That shouldn't make any difference!" she'd complained. "They're not buying me, for Christ's sake, they're buying a goddamned house!"

"It doesn't make any difference at all to the women usually. Hell, they make the decisions anyway, most of them. But men have their pride, y'know, and that macho crap doesn't extend to not being able to look you in the eye." Kim had grinned then. "If you had big tits now, that would be something else."

Marjory learned. And she sold. And in seven years the Suncrest Agency had become one of the largest in the county, its strongest card exclusive rights to two developments whose homes seldom went for less than half a million dollars, and the same rights now to a much larger place—Hawkwood, a tract of former farmland just west of Hunter. Single-family homes, condominiums and townhouses. The developer was a woman who lived in New York City; her local representative and designer was a man named Grover Pitt, an older man with a full black beard that reached almost to his chest. Award-winning architect. Steam-engine smoker. The man who'd gotten her into selling in the first place.

"You're a natural," he'd told her one afternoon in town. "You ought to give it a try."

"I have a family," she'd answered.

"That make you automatically dead or something?"

Glenn had agreed. The kids were responsible, he was the local cop for god's sake, why should she waste herself cleaning house twice a day?

It had taken a week to find the nerve, two days more to accept Pitt's offer of an introduction to Kim Raddock: "Nice lady, but she's going to starve if she doesn't get a decent salesman soon. Buy into the agency. What the hell. You can write it off if you go broke."

She accepted, but she still didn't understand. The Pitts were one of the oldest families in the area, as were the Erskines; and like Glenn, Grover hated the idea of the place becoming so attractive to tourists, despite the fact that his firm was so involved with the new growth.

Glenn wasn't much help.

He tried in his own way to explain that it wasn't so much that the tourists were unwelcome. He'd be a fool if he thought the town could survive as well as it had without them. The trouble was that increasing numbers of them had begun staying once the season ended. Cottages and cabins had become winterized, land sold and developments dropped on it, and the population was, as he saw it, close to the flashfire point.

Either Hunter had to accept the future and plan for it, and quickly; or it had to dig in its heels and close the place down as best it could, and go slow. Just like always. Just like the way things had always been.

She knew all too well which side he was on.

But never once had they argued about her part in the change.

At least not until the Hawkwood project started and he heard how many families would flood the area when it was done. Since that day something had changed be-

tween them, something she couldn't pin down long
enough to beat into submission. He was still loving, still
loved her, but the way he looked at her sometimes was
enough to make her scream.

As yet there hadn't been the all-out argument she was
expecting.

But when it came, and it would, she knew he was
going to draw a line and demand she stop trying to have
things both ways. *One side or the other,* he would tell her
without demanding; *one side or the other, Marj, right
now, no more crap.*

"Mom," Bern called from the hallway, "Dory just cut
off Cheryl's head. Can I go back to bed now?"

"No," she answered, grabbing blouse, shirt, pumps
from her closet.

"Ma!"

"Do as you're told, Bernard, and—" She stopped midway to the bathroom.

The silence in the hall was decidedly cold.

Damn, she thought, and considered apologizing for
using the boy's dreaded full name. Then she decided this
was no time to coddle him. Losing a girlfriend was a disaster, true enough; but facing an entire summer without
having to work should be a dream for a kid his age;
thinking about leaving home for the first time, in the fall,
all the way to sunny sybaritic California, was something
he had prayed for, she knew it, even though it was rather
unsettling. But there was nothing he could do about his
name now, and he might as well learn to tolerate, if not
actually like it.

She dressed. Brushed her hair. Applied what little
makeup she dared. Checked herself in the mirror and

wished she'd had a few more days to work on her tan. She didn't like ending the summer resembling a well-worn saddle, but color, as her mother said, made her look more healthy.

And despite everything she'd tried, her eyes still had that just-cried look. Not puffy, and not reddened, but a ghost of a tear that wouldn't be banished.

The dream.

An empty crib, a baby crying—losing Cheryl before she was born.

Marjory frowned; she didn't get it.

Nor would she get her commission if she didn't move her ass, and damn all those fussy clients who wanted to take up her Sundays with their carps about attics and furnaces and imagined dry rot in the wall, their snide remarks about previous owners, their suspicious glances at her. It was bad enough Glenn had to work today. Another weekend shot. The kids were going to think neither of them loved them anymore.

In the hall her son was still on the floor, gripping the faceted spindles as if he were a prisoner longing for a pardon. She touched his shoulder as she went by, stopped midway down and looked up at him.

"Don't leave the house without calling me or your father," she said.

He stared at her without expression.

"Dory's friends will be by at noon. Cheryl's going with them. They'll be playing ball at the park. Then you can do . . . whatever."

He said nothing.

She sighed and waved and left, hoping that when her

sister came things would liven up. She hated these days that felt like one funeral after another.

The party had been a disaster.

The morning was already a disaster.

The end of the day was probably going to find him locked in one of his father's cells, the key thrown away, his mail censored, all his food strained in case there were concealed files or bombs or poison gas pellets.

California.

God, he couldn't wait to get to California.

He grabbed the railing and hauled himself up, cocked an ear to be sure the brats were still on the dock, then stumbled into the bathroom where he took a quick scalding shower. He didn't feel any better when it was over. He didn't feel any better once he'd gotten into a clean shirt and jeans and had his sneakers on his feet. And he didn't feel better at all when he took the stairs down two at a time and looked outside and saw the empty dock.

I am, he thought, going to rip off their faces.

He opened the screen door and stepped out onto the porch, clamped his hands onto his hips, and looked around.

The road was deserted. Either side of the Erskine property was nothing but trees; theirs was the last house before the road dodged left to the stone bridge, and the land across the way was too narrow to support any construction other than the dock to which, he noted in relief, the rowboat was still tied. His father owned almost eight acres, much of it stretching up the steep hillside behind the house. It had been in the family for a zillion years, no way his parents could afford that now.

He listened.

Sunday quiet born of warm sun and distant birdcries and leaves talking to the breeze and shouts floating over the water; noontime quiet born of people sitting down to lunch on their porches and patios and talking softly of the game on TV that afternoon or the game at the ball field or the work coming tomorrow or the vacation they would take when vacation time rolled around.

No sound of Cheryl; not a hint of Dory.

He blew out a breath and leapt from the porch to the lawn, strode around the corner of the large house and scanned the woods while he headed for the back yard, the swing set, the flagstone patio, the tool shed at the back where the land suddenly rose, nearly steep as a wall.

Nothing there. Not even a bird.

Oh boy, he thought, a hand floating over his stomach while he told himself to stay calm. No problem. Dory's friends had come early, that's all. They were playing ball right now, even as he charged through the kitchen door, shouting his sisters' names.

Playing ball.

That's all.

The cellar door opened suddenly. Cheryl poked her head out and said, "What?"

Bern sagged against the counter. "You're supposed to be on the dock."

Cheryl climbed into the kitchen and shook her head as she rubbed the back of a hand across her forehead. "I'm not supposed to go anywhere without Dory. She's down-stairs."

The cellar was mostly unfinished, the only concrete flooring down in an area that held the furnace, the washing machine and dryer, and his father's worktable. The rest was hard-packed dirt and spiders. Bern hated it.

"What's she doing, for god's sake?"

Cheryl grinned, creating dimples. "Checking the furnace."

He blinked. "What? Dory?"

She glanced warily at the open door, then hurried across to him, crooked a finger to make him lean down so she could whisper.

"There's this . . . boy . . . she likes. She wants to make him think she knows stuff."

He turned his head to look her straight in the eye, and thought she was, without a doubt, the most beautiful munchkin he'd ever seen in his life. In a really odd way, he was glad he was going away because then he wouldn't have to see her exchange her love for baseball for the love of some dork who would only break her heart. On the other hand, he wished he could stay, to break that dork's neck.

"Stuff, huh?" he said, keeping his voice low.

She nodded.

"Heavy stuff, I guess."

She frowned.

"Can Dory lift the furnace?"

She shook her head.

"Heavy stuff."

And he waited until she got the joke, scowled, reared

back, and nailed his arm with a fist that better belonged to a lightweight. He yowled and straightened, grabbed her around the waist with one arm, lifted her giggling off the floor, and marched to the cellar entrance.

"Dory!"

"What?" The tone was obvious—she definitely had no time for a big brother.

"Up!"

"I'm busy!"

"Up!" he repeated sternly, using his free hand to reach around and whack Cheryl's rump as she wriggled, giggled, tried to bite his stomach. "Now!"

In less than half a minute, Dory tromped up the stairs, kicking each riser angrily, slapping her left hand against the wall. He backed away and groaned aloud. She was a mess—cobwebs in her hair, shorts and skinny legs mottled with dust.

"What," he said, "were you doing—digging out a new cellar?"

"Stuff," Dory told him haughtily.

"Heavy stuff," Cheryl said, and began to laugh, couldn't stop, and Bern put her down so she could crumple to the floor, hiccoughing, blushing, shaking her head vigorously when her sister demanded an explanation.

"Shower," he told them both, pulling Cheryl to her feet by one arm.

"Bern!" In unison, meaning *you're not my father*.

"No shower, no play." He waggled his eyebrows. "No shower, you get to spend the whole day with me."

He grinned.

They ran.

He dropped into a kitchen chair, propped his elbows on the table, and slammed his cheeks into his palms.

A week ago he had graduated from high school. He was supposed to be a college freshman now. A man. Just about. A man on his way to the beach bunnies in California, who wouldn't make fun of him because his father was a cop, wouldn't be friends just because his father was a cop, wouldn't try to get him into bed in some dumpy place that reeked of dead animals and dead sweat and dead spiders and dead air.

Bev.

Shit, he thought; what the hell did I do wrong?

Whenever you do it, his father had said last winter, as they walked through the woods along the ridge of the basin, *make sure it's right, son. I'd like to tell you to wait until you were married, or living with someone, but as old-fashioned as I am, I'm not entirely stupid.* The snow was shin deep, and there were deer tracks around the smaller trees, bark missing, signs of rooting around the underbrush. *Just make sure it's right.*

How will I know?

His father had taken a long time to answer. *I don't know. You will. Or you think you will. You'll have to trust yourself on this one, pal. This is one time I can't help you.*

So, he thought, staring out the kitchen door, it wasn't right. It was like a cheap motel or something. So what the hell did I do wrong?

Whatever it was, it had sure made a mess of the Spit party last night. First of the season, and a total disaster. He had gone only because he couldn't think of anything

67

else to do, had already seen the movies at the Globe
Twin in town, and didn't want his buddies to think he
was playing it big just because he was leaving the state in
September.

It was the usual thing: a fire in the concrete-rimmed
pit for late night warmth and cooking, tended by whoever was dumb enough to come last. A few parents drifting around and mostly keeping the three log huts that
had no walls, just a roof and rough support beams, a
raised floor with picnic tables and chairs, no screens—
protection from the elements and the bugs was no fun at
all. Most of the kids dancing and hanging out and checking the territory for the summer. Nearly thirty of them.
Under the trees, in the shadows, looking like Indians in
the early westerns he'd seen on television. A tribe, he'd
thought after about an hour; they were a tribe, everybody knowing everybody else, all the dirt, most of the
secrets, the stronger ones over here and the weaker ones
over there, all the women scattered and flirting like mad.

Except Bev.

She'd been with Thorny the whole time, and once the
parents had gone, leaving the older kids ostensibly in
charge, she had teased and wheedled a number of them
into taking a swim even though the lake water was still
spring-cold, and the spotlights Mr. Pitt had put in the
trees by the water still hadn't been turned on. Then
she'd returned from the changing hut in a bathing suit
that had taken the voice from the party—a few seconds
of dumbfounded silence before the whispers, the cat-
calls, the whistles, the charge for the narrow strip of sand
they preferred to call the beach.

She was practically naked.

A string bikini. Black. So black the shadows seemed to erase it.

Thorny had grabbed her around the waist, hugged her, threw her in, but not before she'd looked over the guy's shoulder, right at him, and her eyes said *this was yours, you sonofabitch, I hope you choke.*

"Bern?"

That's when he had left, walking through the trees to the path that led to the bridge. He'd looked down, then, at the creek the lake fed, seeing nothing, hearing nothing, getting angry enough almost to return, changing his mind when Nancy and two of her friends passed him. She didn't say anything, but her look said enough, and he was grateful to her for going on, and for not laughing.

A hand rapped his shoulder. "Bern!"

He looked around at Cheryl. "What?"

"Dory's ready to leave."

He nodded. "They here?"

"Yep."

"You gonna be careful?"

She nodded.

"You gonna hit a home run?"

"Three."

"Don't be greedy, Pint. Two."

"Okay. Two."

She skipped to the door and stopped. "Whatcha gonna do?"

He shrugged. "I don't know. Go to town, I guess."

She hesitated, then walked back and pulled a braid over her shoulder. She took his hand and put the braid in it. "Walk me to the door."

He almost refused. But there was a look about her

eyes, a tired look, wary, so he grinned and stood, and they hurried through the house to the front. He didn't ask her if anything was the matter; he had heard it last night while he'd been trying to sleep—a nightmare that had her whimpering. No one else was awake. His parents had slept on, Nance hadn't stirred, and Dory couldn't be wakened by a full-blown war in the back yard.

She'd stopped the moment he'd decided to get up to see if there was anything he could do.

Five minutes later, he'd gotten up himself.

"Are you sick?" she asked as he released the braid and opened the screen door.

"Who? Me? No."

"Dory says you are."

Once outside, he dropped onto the top step and stared at the station wagon filled with chattering kids, waiting at the foot of the lawn. Dory gabbed with someone through the back window.

"Well, I'm not," he said absently.

She said something he didn't hear as he propped his elbows on his thighs, cupped his cheeks, stared at the lawn.

"Lovesick," she said.

"Huh?" He turned his head without moving his hands. "What'd you say?"

"Dory said you were lovesick. Is that bad?"

I will kill her, he decided; Dad can arrest me, but I'll kill her.

Someone called her name then, and she grinned at him, leapt to the ground and raced across the grass. There were cheers, shrieks, a honk of a horn as the station wagon pulled away. He watched it take the curve and vanish, watched the sky and decided there would be rain tonight.

Perfect.

Absolutely perfect.

Just what he needed.

From where Marj stood, she could see the eastern side of the black rock, lurking in the trees like some poorly hidden, clumsy demon, and for no reason at all remembered the day Glenn had tried to show off for her and had fallen on the trail. She hadn't screamed, hadn't been able to move; all she could do was watch him roll, bounce off a tree, roll again, yelling and laughing all the way, ending up flat on his back and staring at the sun.

"Don't say it," he had told her breathlessly as she knelt beside him. "If you love me, don't say it."

She hadn't, but she'd thought it: *you goddamn jackass, you trying to kill yourself, you jerk?*

A door slammed.

Slowly she turned and watched Kim huff out of the house Marj was supposed to be showing to a Pennsylvania couple. A ranch-style home, sitting on a natural ledge six feet above the road. The ledge was several hundred yards long and supported nine houses, each separated from the next by a dense wooded lot. This was the last in line, and it was called, by all who knew it, the Lincoln Log place. It was, in fact, made of logs complete with the original bark especially sealed to keep the insects and weather out, and it looked so perfect, so unreal, right to the green-painted squat peaked roof, it seemed to have been pulled right out of a Lincoln Log can.

None of the kids recognized the reference.

All the adults did, and it pleased them to be able to know something their children didn't.

The front yard had been leveled and seeded, black-stained railroad ties forming a retaining wall broken in the center by uneven steps the previous owner had put in himself.

"I can't believe it," Kim said angrily, flicking something off the lapel of her maroon suit jacket. "Jesus, I can't believe it."

"Which," Marj muttered, one hand wrapped protectively across her stomach.

Kim flipped a disgusted hand.

The prospective clients hadn't shown yet. They were over an hour late. All in all, a good thing, she thought, because she'd just returned from the next house up the road, using their telephone to call Glenn's office—someone had smashed in the sliding glass doors in back and had ransacked the place. She had no idea what was missing, but there was no possible way it could be shown now.

Her husband had already left; the dispatcher had promised to get him on the radio.

And as she wondered for the fifth time in as many minutes where he could be, she heard the engine.

"When are you going to get that boy a new car?" Kim demanded as it sped up the road and skidded to a halt by the steps.

Glenn was out before the dust had settled, his jacket and hat off. He took the steps two at a time and strode across the lawn toward them, his left hand already out to take Marj's elbow, his right arm slightly crooked and close to his side—for his right hand to grab his gun in case it was needed.

And she almost wept when the first thing he said was, "Are you all right?"

Despite a resolve not to seem weak, she began to tremble, and he hugged her quickly around the waist, winked when she assured him she wasn't hurt, only unnerved, and walked with her behind Kim toward the back of the house.

"This is getting ridiculous," Kim said over her shoulder. "Are we going to have to start putting guards out here now? My god." She was angry. "Christ, am I going to have to start locking my own doors?"

Marj said nothing. She knew better. Instead, she dropped a little behind and watched as Glenn stopped at the corner and looked at the smashed doors, the overgrown yard, scanned the trees and forest floor. He nodded once. His right arm relaxed. And Marj leaned against the house, declining his invitation to go inside again.

"Kim knows more about what was in there than I do."

His smile was quick, understanding, and she folded her arms as she waited, lightly rubbing her biceps, thinking about coming on the burglar in the middle of his act. What do burglars do when that happens? Do they run? Shoot you? Hit you? Take you hostage? She'd heard enough stories to know that nothing could be taken for granted anymore. If the guy was an addict, she could have been dead; if the guy was an amateur, she could have been seriously hurt, or dead; if the guy was a pro, she never would have seen him.

She thought about what she had seen scrawled on the bedroom wall. In red. At first she'd thought it blood. She hadn't stayed long enough to find out.

After not more than a minute that seemed more a day, she pushed away from the house and walked toward Lake Road, toward the sun in the treeless front yard.

It wasn't as warm as she'd hoped.

The front door opened. "Marj?"

A half turn. "What, Kim?"

"One of us has to make a statement. You want to go?"

"Do I have to?"

"Hell no. I'll do it. I'll be more than glad to do it."

Kim's tone was hard, almost defiant; she was going to use this incident to make the same point she always did—at town meetings, in the newspaper, every opportunity she could make if there wasn't one ready-made: Hunter wasn't a small town anymore, and it needed more than a small town police force. That Glenn agreed with her in principle made no difference—they hadn't gotten along from the first day they'd met. Marj had decided it was a chemistry thing. Glenn told her the woman was out of her effing mind.

A few minutes later, he came out, scribbling in a small notepad, squinting, looking blindly at her and scribbling again. When he was finished and the pad in his pocket, he walked over and jerked a thumb over his shoulder.

"She wants to clean up in case those people come."

Marj stared at the house. "She can't do that."

"That's what I told her."

"And?"

"And she told me I didn't understand the politics of the situation."

Kim came out then, cheeks slightly flushed. If she'd been walking on a floor, her heels would have sounded like gunfire. "I'll meet you at your office. Sheriff." And she stamped down the steps, swung into her car, smiled encouragement, and somehow pity, at Marj and sped off—deliberately fast.

"So," Marj said, "what did you say?"

"So I told her that the politics of the situation was, if she touched just one piece of broken glass before Hacker Neilson got here for pictures and stuff, I was going to haul her ass to jail for obstructing justice."

Marj stared at him. "You didn't."

He nodded.

She didn't want to ask, but: "Would you?"

"Damn right. The woman's a basket case. Big frog in little pond, only she doesn't know the pond is a lake and there are wide-mouthed bass out here that'll eat her up before that tongue . . . uh, before . . ." He looked at her helplessly. "I think I screwed that up."

She smiled. "Yeah, I think so."

"But you get the idea."

She did. And it was going to be hell at work for the next week or so while Kim ranted about law and order and justice and enforcement, not once mentioning his name, not daring to since Marj now owned most of the firm. But it would be hell.

He took her arm as they started down the steps. "Besides, she's screwing Nate Pigeon."

"So?" She avoided his look. "It's her life."

"Hey, you knew that already?"

"Sure. He comes to the office sometimes, takes her to dinner."

"Right," he said sourly. "And I'll bet I know who pays."

She wondered then if he'd seen it.

"The guy's no good," he said, boots crunching on the gravel shoulder. "They suit each other."

His arm was steady, but there was something in his voice.

They stopped at her car, and he opened the door for her, glanced up at the house as she slid in. The steering wheel was cold. She rubbed her palms along it briskly.

"Glenn?"

"Yeah, I saw it," he said quietly as he closed the door and pushed the lock down with his palm. Then he leaned over, one arm across the window well. "What do you make of it?"

I am on the Way

"God, I don't know." Her hands were cold now and she rubbed them on her thighs. "Some religious thing?"

"You mean like, 'I am the Way and the Truth,' something like that?"

Her shrug was his answer. Then she grabbed her keys from her purse and jammed one into the ignition.

"Maybe," he said, and shook his head slowly. "Maybe not."

She didn't care. The engine turned over. "Is it the same guy?"

"As the others? I don't know that either." A finger rubbed under his nose. "Could be. But there weren't messages at the other places."

She listened to the engine, stared over the hood. "Was it . . . ?"

"No. Paint, I think."

It didn't reassure her.

TWO

THE hospital was a one-story H-shaped structure on the far south side of town, built on a low knoll above the creek that rushed out of the lake. In a setting deliberately park-like, the red-brick building could have been mistaken for an office complex had it not been for the red-lettered signs directing visitors to the emergency room, the administration block, the mental health wing. It almost seemed unfair, Loretta thought, to have such a pretty place be in such a pretty area. It ought to be more sterile. It ought to be more grim.

She sat on a bench beneath an oak tree that looked as old as she suddenly felt, smoking, the hospital behind her, a short space of lawn between her and the pine trees that blocked her view of the road. Hugh was in intensive care. Machines. Quiet nurses. The window to his room from the hall blinded with a curtain. The only thing the doctor would tell her was that they were running tests, her husband wasn't about to die as far as they could determine, and she was wasting her time here because the medication they were using would keep him out of it until the next morning. If anything changed, they'd let her know at once.

"Why?" she'd asked him. "He was only walking, for god's sake. He always walks. He's a fanatic about walking."

The doctor—Donald Milrosse and too damned young to know what he was doing—only smiled patiently and falsely and gave her words, not answers, until she'd had a belly full and left, the wood heels of her sandals smacking the checkerboard tiled floor. A cigarette out of her purse and into her hand before she was out of the building. A pudgy hennaed woman in a puffy pink smock had cautioned her about smoking. Loretta had stopped at the entrance, lit it, blew smoke as far as she could into the lobby, and walked outside.

And now that this one, the tenth, was finished, tasteless and burning her throat, she ground it beneath her foot and stood. Glared at the building—Hunter General, my sweet ass, it sounds like a goddamn soap opera for crying out loud. Glared at the sky daring to cover itself with clouds, strode to her car and got in. Her blouse, white enough to accent the onset of her tan, stuck coldly to her back; her tennis shorts clung to her legs damply.

She felt like a dog caught in the rain.

She felt like a middle-aged woman about to become a widow without having been asked permission.

"Oh Christ, don't start," she told herself, and drove

off, seeing and hearing nothing until she turned onto Springwood Avenue and decided she could use a cup of coffee.

Vorssen's was open, but there was plenty of room at the curb. The street was empty. Sunday afternoon, all the stores closed in spite of the June weekend, a bit of a breeze that somehow made her think the town the way she saw it was nothing more than an over-cute movie set.

A window table was free. She took it, ordered coffee from the cop's kid and, as an afterthought, a sandwich, and lit a cigarette. When the coffee came, she sipped and stared out the window. Briefly seeing Hugh in his bed, still strong-looking, still solid, as if he were playing a game, a trick, testing her for all those infidelities he had never, in words, ever accused her of. Wondering then if Nate was horny today. A quick smile not at all shocked by the thought, and she glanced with disinterest around the room, paying no attention to the well-dressed couples, the chattering quartets, at the tables who knew nothing about her, knew nothing about her husband, and so didn't give a damn.

The Erskine kid brought the sandwich.

Loretta thanked her, stubbed out the cigarette, and reached again for her cup.

"I am sorry," a softly deep voice said above her, "to hear of your trouble."

She almost dropped the cup as she turned sharply, and swallowed. It was a priest. He was lean and tall, complexion somewhat swarthy, eyes and short hair black, his youth still marked by a slight pudginess at his cheeks.

When he smiled, she placed a hand against her stomach.

"I'm sorry," he said. "Did I startle you?"

She shook her head dumbly.

He held out a hand she took limply. "Reverend Zachiah. Tom Zachiah. I'm the new minister over at Christ Church. On Bridge Street? The one whose bells don't work?"

"Oh," was all she could say. "Uh, thank you."

The smile quickened to a grin and vanished into concern. "I know I'm new in town, and I frankly don't know if you're one of my parishioners, but if you need anything, just give me a call." He touched her arm, smiled again, and she watched as he returned to a table near the back.

Jesus, she thought, returning reluctantly to her lunch; god, what a waste.

And ten minutes later, when a hand touched her shoulder, lightly, she turned with a smile that brightened just a bit when she looked up at Robbie Sandera, hat in hand, sunglasses dangling from his breast pocket.

"How's your husband, Mrs. Frennel?" he asked quietly.

Christ, she thought, why is everybody whispering?

"Okay, all things considered," she told him, glad he wasn't the priest, and disappointed. "It'll take a while, but he'll come around."

He nodded. "Good. Glad to hear it."

He winked support at her, slipped on his hat and left, stood on the sidewalk and put on his sunglasses while he squinted up and down the street and adjusted his belt. And nearly laughed aloud. She was right behind him in the window. He was posing for her and he knew it. Big strong cop surveying the home territory, looking for the bad guys, wondering if he was misinterpreting the signals he thought she was sending.

Like hell; and he strode up the pavement toward the office. He knew exactly what she wanted, and it amused him to tease her once in a while. But there was no way he was going to get involved with someone like that. She was a barracuda. Get him between her legs and she'd chew his throat out.

Besides, he liked Hugh too much.

And he wanted to keep his job.

Another check of the street, and he couldn't help a shiver at the emptiness he saw. On a pleasantly cool June Sunday, with all the people living here and the summer people already arriving, it should have been more crowded. Folks strolling, sitting on the benches in the park, sitting on the bank of the creek that split the town in half, window-shopping, going out for Sunday dinner. Just hanging around. Just . . . doing nothing.

But there was no one around and he couldn't get over it, never had been able to since the day he'd arrived from Philly. He'd thought then the place was a ghost town and that he'd made a mistake. Months later he still hadn't been able to figure out small towns. Years later he'd decided to stop trying.

At the corner a backfiring turned his head, and he saw a pickup more rust than wheels pull jerkily away from the curb. He frowned. It was Trace. And before he realized what he was doing, he hurried to his patrol car and got in, started it, crept around the corner and followed the old man.

He had been surprised that Erskine hadn't followed up on what was an obvious beating the old guy had taken, but he figured Glenn knew what he was doing. He just couldn't get that face out of his mind, the bruises, the bandage, the look in Trace's eyes.

The radio crackled.

Absently he grabbed the mike and checked in, cocked his head, and said, "Holy shit," to the air when the dispatcher was done.

He slowed as Trace turned left at the next intersection; he pulled over to the curb in the shade of a willow and rested an elbow on the window well. He supposed that Erskine already knew, that Gorder would have called him right away, as soon as the state cops had contacted the office. He also supposed that he himself would be expected to start patrolling the outer roads and lanes immediately, checking the hitchhikers more carefully, the abandoned farm buildings, the culverts and drains; maybe he ought to take a ride around the farms themselves, just to show the flag.

But he didn't want to.

Not until he was ordered.

In Philly he didn't really mind chasing the hardcore types because he wanted them the hell off his streets, permanently, one way or the other, with, and sometimes without, the courts and all their damned lawyers. But this thing was different. This wasn't Philadelphia. There were no alleys, no dark doorways, no slums, no river holes—there were only miles of open fields and miles of woods and trails and paths and caves and hills. Too many places for a man to hide that a city boy couldn't even begin to imagine.

"Three guesses," he whispered as he drove off.

"Three guesses where the bastard's gonna end up, and the first two don't count."

He reached Trace's house just as the old man pulled the dying truck into the driveway. Trace glared at him, hands jammed in his pockets, and stalked over to the curb.

"What?" he demanded.

Robbie glanced at the house and decided that straight out was the best way to handle it. "Just got some news about Jimmy," he said. "Thought you ought to know."

The old man's eyes showed him nothing. "Already heard," he said. "I got a telephone, y'know."

Robbie nodded. "Yeah. Well, I just wanted you to know we'll be—"

"Shit," the old man said flatly. "You think you can what? Help?"

Robbie nodded, already regretting his decision to stop.

Trace spat air. "The fucker's a ghost. There ain't nothing you can do." And he walked away, straight to the door he opened with two keys as the dog inside grew hysterical in its barking.

Well, screw you, old man, Robbie thought as he left, temper suddenly high, hands hard on the wheel. I hope the kid chokes you to death.

He braked too hard when he reached his slot in the parking lot behind the sheriff's office building, jumped out too fast, hurried too stiltedly around the corner to the front. Hell, let the sonofabitch's grandson come waltzing back home, waltz into that damned stinking house, waltz all over the old man's stinking face. Screw him.

At the door he paused, seeing the new preacher step

out of Vorssen's and put his hands in his pockets. Robbie wondered if maybe he ought to tell him about Jimmy Hale, convicted of matricide, patricide, locked away in a loony bin since he was fourteen. Out. Free. Walking the world as if he'd done nothing more than rob a candy store.

Welcome to Hunter, Reverend Zachiah, he thought, and put his hand on the knob, looked over his shoulder when a car honked at him, and couldn't help a grin when Loretta swept past, staring at him, almost daring him to leap back in his cruiser and catch her for speeding.

And when the deputy only waved, Loretta swore her frustration and pushed the car to sixty, ignoring the center line, once sweeping onto the rocky shoulder as if daring the trees to leap out and smash her. The brakes screamed when she pulled into the driveway, and screamed again when she parked in the garage.

Then she slammed the door and stomped out to the lawn.

She was angry. Hell, she was furious. At Hugh for trying to pretend he was twenty again, at the cop for looking down her blouse and doing nothing about it, at the new minister for being so damned handsome and so obviously not interested.

Shit on them, she thought, and looked up at the house—at the fake Tudor timbering, the overhanging second floor, the shrubs just so and carefully trimmed beneath the front windows, the canted brick trim along the brick walk and around the circular garden areas Hugh had assured her would grow flowers April to October.

There were no flowers in any of them now. The ground was brown and bare.

"Shit," she said. "God damn."

She took one step to the front door, snapped her fingers and turned around, to march across the road to the opposite shoulder without looking out for traffic. Then she headed down for Nate's house, rounding the corner to the back. There was no yard, just trees that needed pruning, and underbrush that needed clearing, and a flagstone patio whose seams were split with weeds.

She knocked on the back door, one foot tapping impatiently, sunlight slipping away as the clouds formed their cover.

Pigeon answered a minute later, and her mood shifted to crafty delight when his expression snapped from pleasure to sympathy and back, and his mouth didn't know what the right words were.

"Yes," she said bitterly, roughly pushing inside before could invite her, "he's all right. No, they don't know what's wrong. Yes, I would love a drink. No, I don't know how long he'll be there."

She didn't look around as she veered into the tiny living room and dropped onto the couch. She didn't chide him, as she usually did, for the books and newspapers piled on the other chairs, piled on the hearth, propped against the walls because he hadn't gotten around to putting up shelves. Nor did she tease him about the plates on the floor by the couch, or the glasses, or the forks and knives.

"Loretta," he said, standing behind her, "are you sure this is wise?"

"Jesus," she said angrily. "I'm with a friend, right?

Christ, my old man's in the hospital, I need a friendly voice. What the hell's the matter with you?"

She leaned her head back until she could see him, upside down. And she smiled as her left hand parted her blouse and one finger rubbed the flat above her breasts. "Oh," she said, "I get it. You're expecting someone, right?"

His glance to the door told her the answer.

"That Ollworth shit, am I right again?"

"He's got money," Nate told her defensively. "I can't turn him away."

Her hand left her chest and poked him awkwardly in the stomach. "You know, you've got to be the most inept dealer in the western world, no kidding."

He shrugged. "It's not my living. I don't care."

"Good for you." The finger moved, traced his zipper, returned to her blouse to open another button and run its nail along her skin. "Just remember who your friends are, writer. Your real friends."

"Okay," he said nervously.

"Okay," she mimicked. "Okay. I'm still thirsty."

He nodded quickly and hurried into the kitchen, and she curled her fingers up to look at her nails, pushed at her hair, finally slid onto on the floor, on her back, hands cupped behind her head, to stare at the ceiling.

She heard him pause at the couch when he returned.

God, she thought; Hugh, you're a bastard.

"He's only fifty-three, you know," she said, taking the offered glass as he knelt beside her. "Son of a bitch." She lifted her head, drank, sneered at herself when some of the liquor spilled onto her chest. "I hate this place. I fucking hate this goddamn place."

She drank without tasting.

Nate nodded as if he knew what the hell she was talking about.

"The fool is going to die and leave me alone out here," she said after her second swallow. "He'd do that. He would, you know. He'd die and leave me the house and expect me to stay here because I love him so much."

Nate sipped. He said nothing.

"And you know what?" she said, reaching for his belt buckle, "I probably will."

She grinned without humor when she reached in and grabbed him and he gasped. "The new preacher man is here," she said. "Let's pretend you're the pope and I'm a nun."

"Jesus, Loretta," he said, hands shaking as he scrabbled at her blouse.

"Whatever," she said. "As long as you fuck me."

THREE

FOR the first time in five years, Marj wished she hadn't picked such heavy furniture for the dining room. Sideboard, china closet, serving cart, table and chairs all seemed to belong in some stylish English manor house, not in a rambling home on a lake in New Jersey. Usually she enjoyed it, and the genteel elegance it signified; tonight, however, it was oppressive. The dark walls were inexplicably darker, the small chandelier didn't cast nearly enough light, and the wind outside shook the windows, casting mocking shadows, threatening rain that probably wouldn't come until midnight.

Even then it wouldn't have been quite so bad if she were the only one in a grey mood. But Bern only picked at his food, Dory and Cheryl had fought sometime during the afternoon and weren't speaking to each other, Nancy—increasingly impatient over a summer without a car—was put out because her father wouldn't lend her the last few hundred dollars she needed, and Glenn hadn't said two words to her since walking in five minutes before eating.

She sat at her end, facing her husband, watching the trees through the living room window. When a particularly strong gust made them all jump, she said, "You know, we could all take turns at the oven."

Glenn looked up from his plate, puzzled.

Her hands spread. "Well, if we're all going to kill ourselves over something or other, don't you think we ought to have some kind of plan?"

"Dory goes first," Cheryl grumbled.

Glenn blinked slowly before his lips finally found their way to a brief apologetic smile. "We could lock Bern in the basement," he suggested. "Let the spiders nibble him to death."

Nancy applauded. Once.

Bern said nothing.

"My god," Marj said, "whatever this is all about, it can't be the end of world."

"You already have a car," Nancy said, pouting.

"You will too, in a few weeks," her father reminded her without scolding.

Nancy rolled her eyes and said glumly, "The summer'll be almost over."

Then Cheryl accused Dory of deliberately spiking her while sliding into second base, which Dory countered by lifting a foot to show the sneaker she wore. Cheryl protested it was the thought, not the equipment.

And Marj relaxed. This, while not Disney sweet, was more like it, more like home. At least they were talking, the arguments finally subsiding into half-baked jokes, as she knew they would, under the weight of curiosity about what they called her adventure at the Lincoln Log house. She told them, again, what she had seen—though not the words on the wall—and Glenn answered their dozen questions as best he could. By the time dessert had been cleared away, the usual Sunday night fights had begun—who would watch what on TV, who would listen to the stereo, who could play outside for how long even though the next day was a school day.

"Mother," Dory said patiently, "school is over, for heaven's sake."

"School is over on Wednesday."

"We only have a half-day tomorrow."

"So enjoy it after a good night's sleep."

Dory squeaked. "Sleep? Bed at nine?"

Marj kept a straight face. "But of course. It's a new rule your father and I decided on this afternoon."

Glenn hastily pushed his chair back, coffee cup in hand. "Gotta do the dishes," he said, grinning as Dory followed him loudly into the kitchen.

Bern had already left for his hammock on the porch, and Marj was left with Nancy when Cheryl raced for the dock, bread and fishing line in hand, declaring open season on Dory's record, set last year.

"It isn't fair, Mom," Nancy said glumly.

"You had a deal."

"Yeah, but six weeks? What's six weeks?"

"Six weeks wasn't part of the deal."

"God," Nancy said. "You guys ought to be in the unions, you know that? God!" The hall telephone rang. She ran out of the room, ran back and said, "I'll take it upstairs, okay? Okay." And was gone again before Marj could find the breath to answer.

The back door slammed—Dory gone to mope in the yard.

She sighed, leaned back, closed her eyes when she felt Glenn's hand rest on her shoulders and begin a massage.

"Jimmy Hale got out yesterday," he said.

She stiffened. "Impossible."

His hands kept working. "That's what *I* said. Seems his lawyers found a few irregularities, and his time served and their appeal convinced the judge he could be trusted on bail."

"Where is he?"

"I don't know. No one does. That's why they called us."

In the dark of her closed eyes she tried to remember what the boy looked like, and failed. Only a vague sense of youth, and an image of the crowbar he'd used to bludgeon his parents to death. Although she didn't want to, she shivered, and Glenn's arms encircled her, holding her against the chair while his cheek rested against hers.

"It's a bitch," he said.

"Are you worried?"

"No." Simple. Truthful, as far as she could tell. "I just wish we had more men."

She made no comment. He'd been yelling, literally in some cases, for a larger force for three years. Hunter's population explosion had left them all astounded, and the opposing factions had, to date, been too involved with stabbing each other in front and back to do anything but make token improvements they could use against their political enemies. She knew that the four rookies he expected weren't going to be enough.

"What about me?" she asked then, letting him lift her from the chair and guide her into the front room, where she stayed at the arch while he crossed the carpet.

"What about you?"

"The house, Glenn."

He shrugged as he dropped into his chair. "Nothing there. Just like the others. Far as Kim can tell, nothing was taken, just busted up."

She rubbed her arms, held her elbows in her palms. "I don't like it."

"I know, sweetheart, but we're limited here, you know that."

the Way

She leaned a shoulder against the wall.

"A dozen men," he said, his face turned toward the window. "I could use a dozen more men to do things right."

"Would that catch the man who wrecked that house?"

"You never know."

Jimmy Hale.

"Jesus," she said, dropping onto the couch. "Would a hundred men do it?"

He looked at her then, without expression. "No. But it would help if you didn't sell so much property." His smile was quick; she barely saw it.

"I have a living to make," she answered sharply.

"And a town to kill," he said, turning away to the window.

She looked down at her hands; they were fists. Unex-

93

pected lightning washed the room of color; she stood and marched to the front door, slammed it open and screamed at Cheryl to get away from the water, though she knew the warning was superfluous; Cheryl was already racing for the house. She glared at Bern in the hammock, daring him to say anything smart. Then she marched back to the living room and said, "How dare you."

Glenn only stared.

Thunder echoed distantly.

She could feel it, tried to hold it back, but the words *i am on the Way* and the cabin *the Way* and the clients who never showed *i am on* overwhelmed her and underscored Glenn's apparent indifference.

She could feel herself breathing as if she'd just sprinted around the lake.

The wind creaked open the screen door, and slammed it shut again.

"How dare you, Glenn Erskine."

His face was impassive, and that snapped the chain.

"I don't have to remind you," she said tightly, "whose idea this selling business was. I don't have to remind you that it's my career whether you like it or not! I don't have to remind you that the reason our children can go to college sure as hell isn't your sheriff's salary." Her voice rose. Her cheeks flushed and warmed.

Stop, she warned; for god's sake, stop.

She couldn't.

"I'm as good at what I do as you are at what you do, goddamnit, and don't you *dare* blame me for this goddamn town's shortsighted, fatheaded politicians!"

"One house at a time, maybe," he said evenly.

"Hawkwood, on the other hand, is going to drop one hundred families minimum in my lap in less than a year. You want me to work double shifts and Christmas too?"

She felt her left hand grope blindly at her side for something to throw; she felt a burning in her eyes; she felt a burning in her stomach, and she knew that if she didn't leave soon she was going to throw up.

"You already do," she said. "Half the time you already do and you don't even know it."

"Then tell the damned council that I need more than four men," he said, still evenly, still staring. "You have more influence on them than I do. Obviously."

Bern came in with Cheryl on his back. They puffed and laughed into the living room, and swung right out again when Bern said, "Oops, sorry." He carried his sister upstairs.

Glenn didn't move.

Marj waited for an inhalation that didn't stab her. "If you want me to quit, just say so."

"Do you want to?"

"No."

"Would you?"

She shook her head, and felt dizzy.

"Then why should I? Just so you can tell me no?"

"You really are a bastard, aren't you?"

He turned away, to the window again.

The telephone rang. She looked at it, not six feet away on a small table in the hall.

"It's probably for you, Wyatt Earp," she said bitterly, and walked into the kitchen, out the back door to the porch, and picked up a lawn chair that she threw into the yard. Dory, sitting on a swing and watching the wind whip the trees, gaped until Marj snapped at her to get inside before the storm broke.

"But Mom!"

"Damnit, Doreen, do as you're told!"

And when she was alone, feeling not at all guilty at the look she was given as her daughter passed by fearfully, she wondered what else she could throw. But there was nothing left on the back porch but two more chairs, and they weren't heavy enough to be satisfying.

How dare he!

How *dare* he!

The door opened.

Glenn stood on the threshold.

"I'm sorry," he said.

She nodded.

"Really. I'm sorry."

She nodded again.

The door closed.

And on the wind that charged down the hill and slapped her face damply, she heard the sound of a baby crying. Crying in an empty crib.

III

The dream when it comes . . .

. . . is the sound of a large bell pealing only once, and once again, in the four-spired tower of a church made of stone, huge greystone blocks slowly turning age-green and huge paneled doors and the pervasion of incense that clings to the rows of empty polished pews and the arches of stained glass and the granite baptismal font and the clothes of the people who file silently down the center aisle, not looking at their neighbors, not looking at their children, looking only at the tall man standing and waiting on the other side of the altar rail, the tall man in white with the chalice in his hand . . .

. . . is the sound of a church bell that peals in its tower and causes the rafters to tremble and the walls to shift and loosen pale dust that falls in a slow shower to the shoulders of the people who kneel at the railing and wait for the Word while Communion candles spark and the flames cast their shadows and someone's shadow at the entrance stands in shadow, in the dark the candles and the sun cannot reach, the dark that crawls in waves beneath the doors and slips down the aisle and slips into the pews and into the pages of red-bound books of prayers and hymns . . .

. . . *I am* . . .

. . . is the sound of the voice of the tall man in white who glances up at the tower as he holds up the chalice, and looks down the aisle to the shadow standing in back, to the dark in the aisle, to the dark on the heels of the people kneeling before him, to the pulpit where the shadow moves as he watches the dark, to the book the shadow opens, the soft rustling of thin pages, to the words the shadow mouths that cling to the dark air as the bell peals again and the tower tips to one side and the people leap slowly, too slowly, to their feet and begin to run . . .

. . . *I am on the Way* . . .

. . . is the sound of the calling bell in the tower in the church, and in the hallway by the kitchen, and on the night table by the bed, and in the corridor outside the room where the sick lie and are dying; one strike, and there are echoes that cause the lake to rise, that send the deer fleeing, that cause a bear to bellow, that knock a sparrow from its night perch to the road where it bleeds . . .

. . . one strike . . .

. . . and silence . . .

. . . the sound of a church bell the church no longer has . . .

ONE

T HE water had been cold, then cool, now warm, except when he kicked his feet and it splashed high to his shins.

The sun had been warm, then warmer, now hot, except when one of the small drifting clouds blocked it for a moment and let the breeze do its work.

Across the cove, on the beach at the tip of the Spit, he could see pale blotches that were a handful of bathers, splashing, yelling, swimming out to the floating red platform anchored thirty yards from shore. Diving contests, pushing and shoving, the occasional halfhearted whistle from a lifeguard. And around the lake at various points, other swimmers, cries floating on the air; a small sailboat dead in the water; a canoe with an electric motor carrying a man and woman beneath a big umbrella.

He sat on the edge of the dock, boots and socks behind him, grey trousers rolled up to his knees. His shirt was open to the middle of his chest. His hat was beside him. And he wondered, if he took off the rest of his clothes, he might just slip under the surface and live the rest of his life as a fish. Then all he'd have to worry about was one of the kids catching him, giggling, and throwing him back.

"Daddy!"

Immediately, his shoulders hunched as he braced himself for the body that slammed into his back and the arms that locked tightly around his neck. He gasped loudly, comically, and made a great show of not tumbling head first into the water as Cheryl plopped down beside him, breathless and grinning. Her hair was unbraided, her jeans clean, her pullover blouse touched with ruffles and pink, uncharacteristic and a concession to her mother, just this once.

The school bus chugged away, and for a moment the air was stained by the stench of exhaust.

"Well," Glenn said, squinting at the sparks of sun on the water, "if this is Wednesday, it's done at last."

She nodded vigorously and applauded. "No more teachers, no more books."

"No more homework."

She applauded.

"No more boys."

"Da-ad!"

"Nothing to do all summer but help your poor little sister clean the house and cook the meals and all kinds of good stuff like that."

She punched his arm.

"Rough life," he said. His hands braced on the dock

and he lifted himself up, kicked the water, felt his arms begin to tremble before he settled again.

She copied him, swung back and forth between her arms, and said, "I'm going to practice all summer, you know. Every day. By the time I get to high school, they won't be able to stop me from getting on the team."

"No kidding? Then what?"

"Then I try out for the Braves."

He stared at her. "What? The Atlanta Braves? Why not the Yankees, or the Dodgers, or the Mets?"

"Because," she said, matter-of-factly, "the Braves need all the help they can get."

"I see." He rubbed his chin, scratched a cheek. "Then I guess you'll be in training. Jogging around the lake and things like that."

"Daddy, I'm not jogging all the way around the lake. That's too far."

"Too far?" He looked at her, shocked and dismayed. "Don't be silly, child. That's barely a stroll in the park, for god's sake. Why, when I was a boy, I used to walk three miles to school every day and not even work up a decent sweat."

Her expression doubted him.

"No kidding." He crossed his heart.

"I thought it was two miles," she said.

"I moved when I was a junior."

She hit him again before lifting her face to the sun and sighing. He looked down at her, holding his smile though he saw the dark skin under her eyes, the way her skin had begun to grow taut over her cheeks. She was aware of his attention; he could see the shifting under her eyelids.

"Why aren't you at work?" she wanted to know, turning like a sunflower blindly following the bright light.

"It got a little crazy. I decided to have lunch at home."

"Is Mommy home?"

He shook his head. "No."

Her face returned to him, eyes still closed. She stuck out her tongue, and he laughed, shoved her gently, and wished the child could help him find a way to apologize, to tell Marj how sorry he was, truly sorry, for speaking his mind without thinking how much he would hurt her. Since Sunday, life at home had been the electric minute before a thunderstorm, without the wind, just the tension. Their bed had been cold, their meals filled with chatter and laughs which would have died, he knew, had they dined alone.

He had been an idiot while being truthful, and there was no way that he could see to ease the injury without scarring.

And at night there was Cheryl.

One eye opened. "You were waiting for me," she said, not quite accusing, not quite asking.

He nodded, then reached for his hat and dropped it on her head. The shadow beneath the brim only made her eyes darker.

"I didn't mean to wake you last night."

"It's all right," he said.

"Mommy was mad."

"She wasn't mad," he contradicted gently. "She's just having a bad time at work. There's a lot to do and not enough hours in the day to do it. It makes her crazy sometimes."

"Like you." She grinned.

"Yep. Like me."

A family of ducks floated out of the cove right to left, silhouettes in the sun's reflection. Male, female, four ducklings. They didn't make a sound. And Cheryl didn't call them as she usually did.

He saw it then, was ready for it—a feverish red slowly spreading across her cheeks, the tears filling her eyes, the catch in her breathing, and when he lifted an arm, she cuddled against his side, silently, not moving when he lifted his hat and lay it on the dock behind them.

"Tell me," he whispered.

She squirmed as if trying to burrow inside his shirt.

"Pint," he said quietly.

"I'm a pretty big girl," was all she would say.

"I know that, sweetheart. But even big girls sometimes have a bad night now and then."

He felt the dampness on his side.

She squirmed again and put her arm as far as it could go around his back.

"Pint. C'mon. It's all right. What?"

"Something bad, Daddy," she said at last, voice muffled in his shirt.

"I know. I could tell."

And he watched the water, the swimmers, the sailboat finally moving, as she told him in gulps and sobs about a bell she had heard and a church she had seen and what she thought had been a man standing by the doors and what she thought the man had said.

He held her tightly, free hand pulling a handkerchief from his hip pocket so she could blot her eyes, blow her nose. It was no surprise that sooner or later her nightmares would touch on a church, on a preacher. For reasons he'd never been able to understand, clerics in black unnerved her. Spooked her. When she'd been much younger, she'd called them black ghosts.

"Pint," he said quietly, "did your mother tell you about the Lincoln Log house?"

She shook her head.

"Are you sure? About what happened on Sunday?"

"Daddy." A plea.

He stared at the water and decided the girl had heard it—*I am on the Way*—from one of her friends.

A yawn that made her jaw pop, and he asked her when the dreams had started. She only said, "A long time ago," and almost cried again.

"Hush," he whispered into the warmth of her hair. "Hush, the sun's out now." He explained that it was only a dream, dreams aren't like sticks and stones, and she told him that she knew that, she wasn't a baby, but it was scary, Daddy, and she was afraid.

"I think you watch too many movies," he told her, giving her a quick hug.

"Daddy, they're only movies. I'm not silly like Dory. She thinks they're real."

"I believe you, Pint, but sometimes they can get to you anyway." He hesitated. "I know they get to me."

It didn't work. She didn't say, *really, Daddy, you get scared too?* Instead she shaded her eyes, pulled away, and gave him wordless rebuke.

"Dreams," he said.

Her shoulders hunched; she kicked at the water.

He took a slow breath, not sure if she would really understand. "Dreams," he said again. "There's this thing in your brain," he tapped her head lightly, "that's called the subconscious. When you sleep, and if you have problems—boys, baseball, teachers, I don't know, problems—your subconscious tries to work things out for you. You get dreams." He blew out softly. "It's like working out arithmetic on the blackboard. Your brain's looking for an answer."

Her head turned, and she squinted at him. "I don't have any problems," she said. "I'm happy. So why don't I have happy dreams?"

Without an immediate answer, knowing he was lost, he whispered, "He can't get you, you know," and gathered her back to him, rocking her, blinded by the sun.

"I know."

A long moment.

"Then why are you so scared?"

"Something bad."

"Yes."

She shook her head. "No, Daddy, something bad's coming."

"The man? You think he's coming to get you?"

Jimmy Hale.

"No."

"Me?"

"Daddy, no!"

He took a long breath. Threatening guys in dreams, guys under the bed, guys hiding in the closet, those he could deal with. This was something different.

"Something bad coming," she repeated. "Just . . . something bad."

Hale. Damnit, it had to be. He'd said nothing about the man at home, but he imagined the kids had heard stories anyway from their friends. Hunter was big enough for plenty of secrets, yet still small enough for some of them to be common knowledge. On the other hand, unlike many of the other cases he'd worked on and told his family about, there had been no pressing for specifics, no theories volunteered, no punishments described in giggling detail.

Curious.

Unless, truly, they didn't know.

"Pint," he said when she said nothing more, "something bad's always coming around here when summer comes, you know that." You sound like a jerk, he thought. "People drink too much, someone gets in trouble in the water—it always happens when the summer people come. C'mon, sweetheart, you know that."

She mopped her face with the handkerchief and handed it back. "No."

"It's just a dream, silly."

"I *know* that," she snapped, and got to her feet, forced him to look up. The tears were gone; she looked too old. "You just ask Dory. She knows it too."

She was gone before he could stop her, running up to the road, across the lawn and around the corner of the house. He stared after her, frowning, trying to remember if he'd heard Dory moaning in her sleep as well, knowing full well he hadn't. And that bothered him. His children were having night-troubles, and he hadn't been aware. He should have been. He was their father. He was supposed to know these things and provide protection, and answers.

But no matter what Cheryl said, he also knew that the nightmares had to have been sparked by something, and most likely one of the movies she'd seen on TV. Sometimes, though he knew the films had been sliced to near incomprehensibility by the censors, something passed through—a scene, a character, a stray shot of a lonesome meadow—that for no logical reason bothered her. She thought monsters were silly, and she knew many of the tricks used to create them.

It was the fog.

It was the full moon.

It was the sound of footsteps on the road that most often trapped her imagination in the dark of the night.

But Dory too?

He swung around on his buttocks and wrapped his arms around his knees, letting the sun dry his feet while he stared at the house. This, he thought glumly, is just what I need. The first thing that morning, even before he'd sat down, he'd been told that the number of part-time summer cops he'd asked for had been cut by one-third. An hour later, Gorder had told him that one of the night shift patrolmen had nearly shot the new minister, who'd been out walking in the moonlight, the air conditioning in the rectory making the house too warm for sleep. Then, as he was preparing to leave for home for lunch, Kim Raddock had come in, hauling a clipboard and a petition that demanded better protection from the police force for a community that was being ravaged by a maniac. She didn't mention that she had been the one who had found the bodies Hale had left behind.

"Maniacs kill people, Kim," he'd said as neutrally as he could. "They don't break windows and steal twenty bucks and cheap rings."

"The principle," she'd answered primly, "is the same."

Gorder had snickered.

He had held his tongue, determined not to get into another argument.

As he pulled on socks and boots, he realized he had to deal with both the younger children, not just one. Cheryl's restless nights were no doubt feeding Dory's, whose room was next to hers. If this keeps up, he thought as he headed for the house, buttoning his shirt, we're all going to be zombies, for crying out loud.

On the porch he looked right, to Bern sprawled in t-shirt and cutoffs on the rope hammock strung from wall to corner post. "You," he said, "are going to turn into a waffle iron if you stay there all summer."

"Just waiting for the guys," his son answered, not opening his eyes.

Glenn nodded, paused in opening the door, and said, "Are you having trouble sleeping these days?"

Bern lifted his head. "Nope."

"Any weird dreams?"

"Only that I get stuck here for the rest of my life, that's all," the boy answered sourly.

Glenn propped the screen door open with his boot. "Y'know, when I was your age—"

"Aw, Dad, please."

"—I wouldn't waste a minute getting to the beach."

"I hate swimming."

"Who said anything about swimming? There were girls there, my boy. Girls. You remember them, don't you? Girls. In bathing suits. Trying to get a tan. Just dying for my big strong hands to put that cool lotion on their backs."

Bern raised an eyebrow. "They had suntan lotion then?"

"No," he said. "We would come down out of the trees and crush grass with rocks and make mush out of it." He let the door go, walked over, tipped his son from the hammock. "Go," he ordered as Bern laughed himself to his feet. "Find a girl. Find a rock. Find some grass. Just get the hell off this porch before I give you a job."

Bern screamed and vaulted the railing, looked back, screamed again, and ducked into the garage that was under his bedroom.

Glenn shook his head slowly, remembering his own father's reluctance to say anything to him about women, about sex; there certainly wasn't any of the kidding he and Bern got themselves into. That would have been . . . he let the door slam behind him . . . hell, there was no 'would have been' about it. It was just out of the question.

The telephone rang.

As he picked up the receiver, Dory raced down the stairs two at a time.

"Dad!" she cried. "Dad, she's here! Aunt Susan's here!"

And Robbie Sandera said in his ear, "Boss, you'd better get down here. Someone saw Jimmy Hale."

"Shit," he said. "Be right there."

He left the house at a trot, ignored the low white car pulling up on the shoulder, and swerved left toward the driveway just as Bern came out of the garage, wiping his hands on his shorts. "Bern," he said without stopping, "stick around until I call from the office."

"Why?"

A stern look brought him a quick obedient wave, and he nodded back brusquely as he slid into his car and backed out onto the road the instant the engine stopped coughing and caught. Dory called him. Cheryl shrieked around the far side of the house. But he didn't stop, didn't slow down, managed only a glimpse of the woman half in and half out of the white car—curly dark hair, bare midriff, short legs. He didn't need to see any more—the large dark eyes, the round cheeks, the round bosom, hips to match and made to hold while dancing. He didn't want to see any more. Not now. Not until she talked to him and he tried to sense what she wanted.

The road swung left and he slowed, swearing as he neared the high arch of the narrow stone bridge. It had been built before the Civil War, was now being repaired by a crew of roadmen who seemed to spend most of their time standing around shaking their heads. One of them waved as he passed; the others only watched, cigarettes in their mouths, shirts off, skin tanned and dirty. He acknowledged them with a spare nod, sped up again, and took the next right turn behind a spiraling plume of dust. Muttering to the wheel. Scowling. Hoping to hell the sighting hadn't been in town, praying that Bern would stick around until he was sure there was nothing *something bad* to worry about.

As the car straightened, fishtailed, straightened again, he saw a blur on his left, a girl in pink on a bicycle, and a check of the rear view mirror showed him Nancy, pedaling up Lake Road. He almost stopped, had a foot on the brake, then changed his mind and went on.

He was worrying about nothing.

There were thousands of people in Hunter, especially now.

What he needed to do was keep his mind on his driving before he ran up a tree and ended up with Hugh, in Intensive Care, sucking air through a tube while Marj stood by and wept and watched the machines do his breathing.

Please, he prayed as he ran the first stop sign; please, let it be Gorder and one of his damned UFOs.

Nancy straddled the bike and looked anxiously over her shoulder, saw the brake lights on her father's car wink on, wink off, and she let out a slow shuddering breath in relief. At the same time, she wondered why he was in such a hurry that he didn't even wave. An accident, probably; that was about the only excitement Hunter ever had, probably some dumb tourist who'd stopped in the middle of the road just because he'd seen a deer or a woodchuck.

Whatever it was, she was grateful. At least she wouldn't have to explain why she wasn't at work.

Because, she'd have to tell him, *that asshole Vorssen pinched my ass in the kitchen and I slapped him and he fired me, that's why, okay?*

And if she told him that, Emanuel Vorssen would be in one of the basement cells, battered and half dead, before he could even think the word "lawyer."

But I am not going to cry, she told herself as she pedaled on toward the ball field; I am not going to cry.

Why should she? After all, she'd just lost every chance she'd ever get to have her own car, and she'd slapped the fat face of a town council member, and she'd screamed enough obscenities as she'd stormed out of the restaurant to provide dessert for every town in the county. Why should she cry? Just because that sonofabitch had come up behind her, asking her about something or other, she couldn't tell, his voice was too low, and the next thing she knew she felt his palm on her buttock. She'd been too surprised to say anything until, evidently convinced she didn't mind, he'd pinched her. No thought was required—she'd whirled around and slapped him. When his fat-lipped mouth dropped open, she slapped him again and shoved him away, tore off her apron and walked out.

He came to the kitchen door just as she rounded the counter; he called her a whore. No. He yelled it. And fifty heads turned in astonishment. That's when she'd lost it. When every gutter word she'd ever heard whipped at him over her shoulder, at the top of her voice.

And when he yelled, "Slut!" she was at the door. Frozen in rage. Turning so slowly she could see herself turn, reach over the head of a kid sitting at the near table, and grab a salt shaker she threw without bothering to take aim.

She thought the man had ducked. She didn't know. She was outside and running, vision smeared, cursing her street clothes still back in her locker. Looking like a total idiot, grabbing her bike and racing off in a short pink dress that was too damned tight anyway, and too damned revealing, and too damned bad because now she'd blown it. Everything. The car. Her life. Never again able to show her face in town without having people look at her, point at her, whisper about her behind her back.

"Shit," she whispered.

And cried anyway.

Until she reached the field, heard the voices, and stopped, swiping at her face with the backs of her hands, wishing she had a tissue, sniffing and tossing her head until she felt she'd be able to pass and not have anyone see her so upset and ask a bunch of stupid questions which she'd have to lie to answer. Of course, it would be easier to take the short route home, but her sisters would be there, probably Bern too, and the one thing she didn't want was a family investigation. What she needed was a little time to herself, to figure out what she was going to say to her father when he found out what happened.

And he would.

Oh Jesus, he would.

She walked the bike, keeping it between her and the field as it opened to her on the right. There was a game on the closest diamond, maybe a dozen guys all together, and a handful sitting on the bench behind a three-sided cage that framed home plate.

She stopped.

In spite of her resolve to keep moving, she stopped, and she stared.

Thorny and four others were on the bench, nudging each other, watching the game. But behind them stood a slender young man in a white t-shirt and jeans who, she knew, was a shade shorter than she, with tight black hair, a perpetually pale face, and the darkest blue eyes she had ever seen in her life. Right now he wore sunglasses, and from the angle of his head she knew he was looking at her.

Oh my god, she thought; oh my god, he's home.

Brady Jones was home, and he was looking right at her.

Her left hand fluttered over her chest, looking for something to smooth down, straighten, put back into place, while her right hand almost lost its grip on the bicycle's seat. She fumbled for it, lost it, recovered it with a curse, and when she looked up again, he waved.

She waved back, and the bike fell.

"Damn," she said, and instead of picking the bike up, she kicked at it, swore again, and wanted nothing more than to be able to raise it over her head and toss it into the lake.

Of course. Why not? Brady Jones comes home all the way from UCLA, sees her, and not only is she a horror from crying, she's making an ass of herself by playing games with a stupid bike. Of course. Why not?

Then Thorny saw her and waved, and at the same time Brady picked a bat up from the ground and mimed bashing Ollworth's head with it, once, twice, three times, and four, making her cover her mouth to stop the laugh. When Thorny suddenly looked up, the bat was on Brady's shoulder. He stood and said something Nancy couldn't hear, Brady shrugged, Thorny stepped over the bench and said something else.

Jeez, she thought, and couldn't turn away when Brady

dropped the bat and dusted his hands against his jeans, spread his arms innocently when Thorny said something else and shoved his shoulder. Shoved it a second time. Had his hand out to do it again when Brady took one step forward, placed a palm against Thorny's chest, and pushed him backward until the bench caught the back of his knees. He went over, flailing, and landed on his rump. Brady stepped over the bench, looked down, lifted his sunglasses, dropped them, and shook one of the other kid's hands before walking away.

Toward her.

Standing like a complete total jerk in a waitress outfit in the dust.

"Hi!" he said.

She smiled. "Hi!"

"You goddamn shithead!" Thorny shouted.

Without asking, Brady picked up the bike and started walking, forcing her to walk with him. "You know," he said, "I don't want to sound like I'm a snob or anything, but that guy's too stupid to live, you know what I mean?" He flipped up his sunglasses, stared at her, flipped them down. "I think I've sort of come at the wrong time, huh?"

She almost said yes.

"No," she told him. "I just got fired, that's all."

"No kidding?"

"I wish I were," she said miserably. "Now I'm never gonna get my car."

"No sweat," he said. "You just call me, I'll be your chauffeur, okay?" He laughed. "Good old Thornton will kill me." Then, suddenly, he stopped. "Oh. Hey. God,

Nance, hey, you two aren't . . . I mean, Jesus, I haven't . . ." He started walking again. "Oh hell."

At first she didn't know what he was talking about. And when she figured it out, she couldn't believe it: he thought she and the jerk were going together, and it actually seemed to matter. Oh god, she thought; oh god. And it was all she could do not to clamp a hand to her chest to keep her heart from pounding its way free. It was stupid. She was stupid. Things like this just didn't happen to her. It was crazy. She was going on a senior, Brady was going on a sophomore, and he was studying biology or something like that. What the hell is he doing, walking along like this, talking like they were old friends when they barely knew each other even before he went off to college, and if she didn't stop thinking and say something quick, he was going to think she'd gone retarded or something.

"No," she said, and caught a sob when her voice squeaked.

"I'm sorry. I didn't mean—"

"No," she repeated quickly, a quick shake of her head. "I mean, we're not together or anything. I mean, he thinks we are, but we're not. No." She shook her head. "No. We're not, I mean. Going together. Ever."

Please God, she prayed then, strike me dead, now.

A full minute passed before he said, "Good."

He stopped, examined the bike, and said, "Do you think two people can fit on this thing? I mean, if we keep walking this way, it'll be tomorrow before we get to your house, and your father will kill me."

Nancy didn't know what to say, and heard herself saying that she thought it might be possible, barely, if they were careful; and before she could take a breath, before she could caution herself about letting some vague bubble inside her breast explode her into disaster, she was seated behind him, arms around his stomach, cheek against his back. Wobbling and veering side to side until he was able to pump enough speed to at least keep them from toppling.

Into shade.

Into sunlight.

Not saying a word until, seconds later, it could only have been seconds later, they were in her driveway and her sisters leapt from the porch, shouting something about Aunt Susan who was making something in the kitchen that was going to make them all weigh a ton. When they saw Brady, they stopped as if striking a glass wall.

Nancy took the bike reluctantly; the handlebars were hot. "Thanks," she said softly.

"No problem. You feeling better?"

Don't blush, jerk.

"Yes. Thanks."

She heard Cheryl and Dory whispering from the middle of the lawn.

Brady turned to them, lifted his sunglasses, dropped them, and said, "Uh, could I call you?"

"Sure. I guess."

"Friday?"

She grinned. "You can try. After my dad finds out what happened today, I may be in for life."

"No sweat," he said. "I'll be your lawyer and spring you."

"Okay."

He nodded, waved to her sisters, and started back up Lake Road in the direction they'd just taken. He didn't look back. Nancy waited, but he didn't look back. And she didn't realize the girls were flanking her until Cheryl touched her hip and said, "Gee, Nancy, he's *old*."

And Dory said, "Dry up. Do you see those arms? Oh god, I'm gonna faint."

Nancy looked down at her, not quite frowning.

"Did he kiss you? Wow, did he kiss you?"

"Don't be gross," Cheryl scolded.

"Did he?"

"Don't be gross," Nancy told her, and wheeled the bike into the garage, propped it against the side wall, and walked back into the sun, one hand pressed against her stomach. She was behaving like a kid. She could feel it. She could hear it in her voice. And she had to get hold, now, before anyone realized what a real jerk she was.

"Hey, Nance?"

She looked to the porch. Bern came toward her, car keys in one hand. "What?"

"Let's go," he said, waving the keys toward the white car she'd just noticed on the shoulder. "Dad just called. He wants to see you." He nudged her when she didn't move. "I think you don't have a choice, Sis. I do believe the man is royally pissed."

The car was long, a brilliant white inside and out, and low enough to force him nearly double as he slid awkwardly into the driver's seat and waited for Nancy to get in the other side. It smelled new. It felt new. And as his sister, hands trembling, snapped on the seatbelt after two attempts, he noted with a silent groan that Aunt Susan had spoiled it by getting automatic transmission.

It rumbled when he turned on the ignition.

It threw him back against the leather seat when he pulled away from the house.

"Take my car, it's okay," she'd said, leaning in the kitchen doorway, keys already in the air. "If you wreck it, I'll just cut your head off." Then she'd smiled. And he'd grinned. And he'd thanked what luck he had left that he didn't have to stay in the house any longer. He liked his aunt. He liked her a lot. She never seemed to worry about money, or what people thought, or what his parents thought about her. She was as unlike his mother as any human being could be.

And she was beautiful.

And she was his aunt.

And he squirmed even now when he felt like the hand of a ghost the hand she had slapped lightly on his rump when she'd first walked through the door.

It *was* a slap.

It had to be.

After all, even though she wasn't all that old for an aunt, she was his aunt.

It couldn't have been, couldn't have meant, anything else.

"What did he say?"

He cut the turn to the bridge too sharply. "He said I was to get you down to the office right away."

Nancy looked at him. "I mean, what were his exact words?"

Puzzled, hc starcd back. "His exact words were, 'When your sister gets home, I want her in my office before she gets a chance to breathe.'" The road crew scrambled out of the way as the car jounced over the bridge, nearly left the ground on the other side. "What happened? You steal a car or something?"

"Nothing," she said glumly, attention on the road ahead.

He didn't push it. But she'd been crying, her eyes were puffed, and he had a bad feeling she'd done something to blow her deal with Dad.

"Need some help?" he asked.

"Not from you," she answered, turning her head away slowly.

She was pale, too, he realized, slowing as the first cross-street swept toward him too fast. Not enough sleep, probably. That's what you got from having a sister who had the world's champion nightmares. If Cheryl had one tonight, he figured he could smother her with a pillow and be the hero of the family.

A rusty pickup slowed them to walking speed before they reached Springwood Avenue, and his left hand drummed the dashboard until he saw Nancy's hands twisted in her lap. The knuckles were bloodless.

"Hey, Nance?"

She grunted.

"If you need some cover or something . . ."

"Lawyer," she muttered.

"What?"

"Lawyer. What I need is a lawyer."

A silent whistle and a silence, but she volunteered nothing, and he drifted out of his lane to try to see around the truck, veered sharply back when a speeding station wagon blared at him. The pickup barely moved.

He saw Trace through the truck's back window and tried to will him into moving over. The light at the corner turned red, and the truck slowed even more, brakes sounding like metal rubbing against metal.

"Christ," he said, slapping the wheel.

Nancy reached for the dashboard radio, pulled her hand back, dropped it back into her lap.

A car passed them in the opposite direction, pulling a trailer on which two rowboats were lashed.

"Hey," he said, suddenly leaning back and grinning, "remember the time when Aunt Susan was here and we told her about the monster that lived in the lake?" He bobbed his head. "We had the raft then, remember? And you got that stuff from Thorny, the diving kit, and we made a fin like we'd seen in *Jaws,* that kid that scared the shit out of the whole beach? I got Aunt Susan out in the middle of the lake and you came over from the Spit. She was supposed to scream and all that, remember?" He started to laugh as the light changed, the pickup backfired and moved. "She nearly broke your back with the oar. God, I thought you were dead."

His laugh faltered when he looked at her, stopped when the car behind him honked its horn.

"It was funny."

"Not then," Nancy said, sliding down in her seat.

"Yeah, well."

"You didn't stop her."

"I tried. You know I did. God, she's strong! She almost broke my damn arm."

"She . . ." Nancy finally looked at him. "She should've killed me. God." Her hand wiped her face.

"Maybe you could just take me to the bus stop. Maybe I have enough money to get me to Canada."

Around the corner, the sheriff's office across the street, the flagpole in front sounding hollow metal gongs as its ropes snapped in the breeze. There were no parking spaces on this side, so he drove to the next intersection, turned right, and used the first driveway he came to to make a U-turn.

"C'mon, Nance, what happened?" His voice hardened. His left foot tapped the floor. "Somebody try something with you? At work? Is that what happened?"

She shook her head.

He stopped at the corner, checked the traffic, looked behind him and saw nothing but empty street. He turned and poked her arm. "Nance, come on, what happened? I'm not moving until you tell me."

When at last she spoke, fast and flat and clipped and not shifting her gaze from the street, he couldn't believe it. It was crazy. But he didn't tell her that because of her hands—the squirming, the white, the rigidly clawed fingers that tried so hard to strangle each other. And when she dared him with a look to call her a liar, he jammed the accelerator home and shot the car onto the avenue, not caring about the horns and curses, slamming on the brakes when he darted into a space just below his father's office.

Nancy barely moved.

"I'll go talk to him," he said tightly.

"No!" The seat belt snapped back; she grabbed his arm. "Don't say anything, okay? Just . . ." She opened the door. "Just don't say anything. Besides," she added when he joined her on the sidewalk, "what the hell could you do?"

He wanted to tell her that he could shove Vorssen's piggy face into the meat grinder, tear off his legs, serve his gut for lunch, throw him through his precious goddamn plate glass window. But she wouldn't believe him. She would probably laugh. And when he held the door open, shivering at the cold air that jumped over the threshold, she suggested in a quiet voice that he might as well stay here while she went in to face the music.

No way his look told her.

She shrugged.

He followed her inside, closed the door behind him, stood for a moment to let his vision adjust.

The outer office was fairly large, split by the waist-high counter that ran the room's width. To the right of the door, in front of the large window, were a half dozen padded chairs with metal armrests; to the left was a wall on which had been nailed a bulletin board. Behind the counter were four desks, all of them wood, none of them occupied. Along the right-hand wall was the radio, and Pete Gorder was there, leaning into a microphone, chewing a cigar, flicking a switch as he looked up, saw them, nodded, and ignored them.

The room was pale green.

The lights hung in fluorescent banks from the acoustical ceiling.

A door in the back left corner opened and Audrey Cray stepped out of the stairwell that led down to the cells. She had a folder in one hand, a pen in the other, a pencil stuck through her tightly curled red hair over one ear. She looked at him, at Nancy, and cocked her head in silent question.

And in the doorway on the right, just past the counter flap that provided access to the back, stood his father.

Oh shit, Bern thought; oh shit, we're gonna die.

But he followed his sister into the office, considered one of the chairs and decided to stand against the wall, hands loose in his pockets, one ankle crossed over the other. Nancy stayed in the middle of the floor, her head down, hands still wrestling, and he saw a muscle on the back of her neck suddenly bulge and subside.

"I have," Glenn said as he took his seat behind the desk, "a paper here." He held up a yellow sheet. "Mr. Vorssen, it seems, has signed a complaint against you." His free hand snapped up as Nancy opened her mouth. "Let me finish."

"Dad," Bern said.

"You either keep quiet," his father ordered, one finger pointing, "or you leave."

Bern stiffened, and scowled.

"Now," Glenn said to Nancy, "it says here that you assaulted him, used foul language in his place of business, and upset his customers." The paper slapped to the desk top. "Personally, I think it's a crock of shit."

It took Bern a moment to realize what his father had said, another moment before he grabbed the nearest chair and hurriedly scraped it across the floor behind his sister, whose legs had begun to sag. She sat heavily, and he stood behind her, not knowing what to do next until his left hand floated up and landed on her shoulder. She started. The hand lifted. She grabbed it and pulled it back down.

"It is, Dad," she said, words splitting over a sob.

"It is what, honey?" Glenn asked.

"A crock. Of shit."

I'll kill him, Bern swore while she repeated the story she'd told him, only this time in more detail, rage and humiliation instantly taking over; I'll kill the bastard, I'll kill him, so help me I'll tear the shithead's throat—

And he blinked at the vehemence, astonished, a little bewildered, and took a deep breath, held it, let it go as slowly as he could.

When she was finished, Glenn picked up a ballpoint pen and asked her a series of questions Bern paid no attention to, because it had just occurred to him, looking down at the top of her head, that this summer was thoroughly jinxed. Jesus, it was jinxed. Fogged out of its goddamn mind. Fever dreams for crackpots. Bev leaves him, Nancy gets hit on by her boss, Dad and Mom are fighting worse than he'd ever seen them, and Cheryl was keeping half the town awake with her stupid nightmares. The only one who seemed in control was Dory, who was too busy trying to impress some boy to see what was going on.

"Bern."

He looked up. His father was not quite smiling.

"I have all I need." The pen tapped the paper. "Do me one more favor and take your sister home."

Bern nodded, frowned, suddenly stepped around the chair and demanded to know why Nancy had to be put through all this when it was obvious, wasn't it, that she hadn't done anything wrong? "Jesus, you treated her like—"

"—like everyone else," Glenn said calmly. "That's

right. And probably more so because she is my daughter, and if I did nothing, it wouldn't look right."

"Who the hell cares what it looks like?" he yelled.

Nancy nudged him. "Hey, Bern, c'mon."

"No," he said to her. "No." He looked back at his father. "It's like . . . it's like you didn't believe her until she told you to your face. That isn't right."

Glenn rose from the chair, and Bern stepped back before he knew he had moved.

"Son," he said, pointing at the complaint sheet, "when someone comes in here and makes a formal accusation, I don't care who does it and who it's against, the law says I have to do things a certain way. So I do. But I never believed Nancy was the guilty one for a minute. Never." He glared and dropped the paper. "And I never forget that the law doesn't give a damn who's my relative and who isn't."

Bern felt like a jerk.

He stammered something he hoped to hell was an apology so he wouldn't get clobbered, and let Nancy lead him from the office. The silence behind him was unnerving, so he stopped at the threshold and said, "Dad, I didn't mean—"

"No. And you didn't think either." And suddenly his father smiled. "But it's nice to know you care."

His answering smile was feeble, and when he turned to leave, he collided with Nancy, who fluttered her eyelids at him and said in quivering falsetto, "Oh Bern, dear brother, do you really and truly care?"

"Aw, beat it, you creep," he told her sourly, and headed for the door.

"But dear brother, you have to take me home," she

said so sweetly he wanted to turn around and bash her. "After all, you care, right?"

Christ. If it wasn't for the fact that she wasn't crying anymore, that her smile was real this time, he would have gladly made sure that all those perfect white teeth were a little crooked from now on. What a hell of a thing for his father to say! Now he was going to be in for absolutely the worst summer of his life. Jesus. Christ. She was going to make his goddamn life miserable, and there was nothing he could do about it but take it and pray that September change places with July. Immediately. If not sooner.

She was already in the car when he took the wheel and pulled away from the curb. Too fast. And suddenly remembered the reason he'd come in the first place.

"I'll kill him," he promised her. "I swear I'll—"

"Bern."

He shut up.

But he wasn't going to forget.

TWO

THE smells had been in the house so long, Iroquois Trace knew them only by their absence when he went outside: mildew, burnt food, sour milk, dust, cigarette smoke, the stench of dried urine that came from the cellar. He didn't care. Not any longer. It was only one more cross strapped to his shoulders, one more blow of the bat God used to keep him in line. For it to be any other way would have been a shock, would have made him suspicious, would have had him cringing in a corner, waiting for the next blow. But he never thought about whether he was happy or not; it all just was. Neither did he think about what people would say if they ever came inside and saw the drapes on all the windows, not heavy enough to keep all the light out but sufficient to keep him drifting through dusk; he didn't give a damn if they saw the newspapers scattered on the floors, saw the dishes that lay cracked and crusted in the sink, the bare mattress on the bed upstairs, the empty boxes and bags of dog food that cluttered the kitchen until he rousted himself to trash them. All he cared about, now, was making the house safe. Safer. And when he looked into the refrigerator and saw that he needed meat, he swore, punched the door, and stalked into the living room.

Mars was sprawled on the couch.

Trace glared at him, the lazy sonofabitch, snapped his fingers, and the black Great Dane lumbered to its feet, ears up, eyes wide, head slightly cocked as it searched the air for something that didn't belong.

The old man smiled.

Some people had boxers, pinschers, bulldogs, shepherds, even them sonbitching pit bulls that could tear a leg off and come back for the other. He couldn't take the chance. He couldn't dare hope someone else could do the job for him. He had brought Mars home as a puppy, raised him in the cellar, fed him raw meat and small animals he'd caught in the back yard and the woods behind, and trained him to hate anything that wasn't Trace. Anything. It was the only way. To believe otherwise would leave him vulnerable. And he would be damned if he was going to die without giving a good fight.

"I'm out," he told the beast.

Mars snorted, and trotted into the hallway where he would wait patiently until Trace returned. Sitting in the dark spot between the kitchen and the foyer. Listening. Always listening. Hind legs taut, teeth ready to bare. It was why Trace, four years ago, had had the entire house carpeted, wall to wall—he didn't want the animal slipping on bare flooring. Purchase was important; speed vital.

Trace fumbled in his pockets, searching for the pickup's keys and the small leather change purse in which he kept all his money. He had no checking account. He had no savings account. When his social security and pension checks arrived in the mail—at the box in the post office, to keep the postman from the door—he cashed them. If he didn't have the cash, he didn't buy it. If he didn't buy it, he didn't miss it.

When he was ready, he looked at the dog again.

"Be back," he said.

The dog growled, more like a lion signaling its presence.

Then he was outside and in the cab, ignoring the fresh air, backing the truck into the street and heading for the butcher's. He would have gone out to the supermarket on the highway had he had the time, but there was no time left. Jimmy was out. Jimmy could be in town. Trace didn't dare leave his house for more than a few minutes.

The truck backfired.

Trace drove slowly, checking all the mirrors, the road ahead, all the yards, the shrubs, cursed the high hedges. A patrol car passed him, and he grunted disgust as he watched it. One cruised his street at least once an hour, ever since that stupid spic with the stupid mustache had told him about Jimmy. Like the cop really cared. Like he really gave a damn. Trouble was, goddamn cops around here weren't even white anymore. Used to be, Hunter was a good town. Feared God, feared the Devil, doors unlocked all night, and no damn kids smartass enough to give an old man sass. Now the cops that weren't even white anymore took to watching him night and day, as if they'd be able to do anything once Jimmy returned.

Of course, if they got lucky . . .

He snorted, spat through the window. There wasn't enough luck in the world to stop Jimmy from coming home. He knew that. Just as he knew Jimmy would be here soon. He could feel it. He could smell it in the night air.

It was why he had bought Mars.

He'd known it even then, almost ten years ago.

Jimmy would be back to finish what he'd started.

The pickup lurched over a pothole. Trace turned it into a small parking lot behind a row of five shops. There were back entrances for those who didn't want to take to the avenue, and he chose the middle one, inhaling deeply as he passed the huge refrigerators, the chopping tables, the lidded barrels filled with trimmed fat and meat on the verge of spoiling, soup bones and entrails.

Mars would die and go to heaven in a place like this.

He wandered into the front, grateful he was the only customer, eyes tearing slightly at the glare that bleached the street outside a flat white. When the butcher saw who it was, he only nodded and told him to take whatever he wanted from the back. It was a deal they had. Trace opened the purse carefully, took out a roll of bills with two fingers, and looked up without raising his head. A figure was named. Trace sneered, as close to a laugh as he could get. Another figure, somewhat lower, made him nod just as the door opened and a woman in loose black t-shirt and jeans came in. She hesitated when she saw him, but Trace only looked at her in disgust, wondering how the hell poor old Hugh could stand being married to someone like that.

Still . . .

"How's the man?" he asked.

Loretta answered with a smile more a shrug. "Off the tubes and machines, thank god. They're still running tests. He'll be all right. Home by next week, I hope."

Trace handed over his money, leaned over the counter to watch the butcher count out the change. As he did, his gaze drifted to the window, to a break in the glare where someone had stopped to look in.

He gasped and dropped the purse.

"Oh, Jesus!" he said.

Jimmy.

Loretta took a step toward him. "Trace, are you all right?"

Jimmy was out there.

"Oh Jesus!"

Loretta looked to the butcher. "Maybe we should call . . . Trace, is something wrong?"

Trace looked at her, didn't know her, grabbed the purse and ran to the back. Frantically he grabbed a paper bag from a tottering pile on a table and shoveled in as much meat and bone as he could before slamming open the door and running outside, not paying any attention to the woman who had followed him to the threshold, asking him again if he needed any help.

Loretta watched him open-mouthed, clamped an anxious hand to her chest when the pickup nearly sideswiped a car turning in. A horn. A flurry of curses. And she returned to the counter where she picked up the package of chopped meat she'd called in for an hour ago.

"He ought to be locked up, you know," she said as she left, not bothering to wait for the butcher's answer. Then, standing in the shade of a fat-crowned maple, she looked both ways slowly, trying to make up her mind whether to visit Hugh now or wait until tonight. The sun was hot. The package was heavy under her arm. A chilled drop of perspiration made its way down her spine.

What the hell, she decided wearily, and walked down to her car, threw the meat on the passenger side, and drove toward the hospital; what the goddamn hell. It wouldn't make any difference when she saw him, now or at midnight; he'd only lie there, eyes closed, eyes open, acknowledging her presence with a sigh now and then but otherwise acting as if he were a vegetable just waiting to be tossed into the pot. It infuriated her. It was like he was giving up, even though he'd been told time and time again that he hadn't had a heart attack, that his lungs were just fine, that there was nothing anyone could find wrong with him, so what was his problem?

Milrosse, a world-class wimp if she ever saw one, suggested she give permission for the shrink to have a talk with Hugh. In his mind, the jerk had ventured; it seems to be all in his mind. Loretta had refused, angrily. Hugh wasn't crazy. She didn't know what was wrong, but she knew he wasn't crazy.

Her throat clogged, and she coughed to clear it, pulled over suddenly, just before Midrow Bridge, and turned off the ignition, hand trembling so violently the keys rattled in their case.

She couldn't go.

She couldn't stand to see him like that.

Damn, she thought, and glanced around blindly before getting out, standing on the empty sidewalk, feeling as if there was someplace she ought to be and was late. An appointment. A meeting. A look to her right, at The Willows restaurant with no window in front, only a tall wood door with the day's menu framed to one side, and she stepped under the building's brown beam overhang, out of the sun.

A little peace was what she wanted, and after a moment's indecision, she moved to the steep flight of stone steps beside the bridge and climbed down to the creek, here thirty feet or more wide, five deep in its center. Two decades ago a walkway had been put in along the bank on either side. Benches had been installed. One globed streetlamp in the center. The land above the walk was high and steep, coated in ivy, marked by a few shrubs. At the end of the walk the willows began—dozens of them that brushed the stream's surface and hid the houses up there from view spring and summer. The area wasn't much used—there were no signs—and she was alone when she sat on a bench halfway along and stared at the water.

It was shallow, swift, taking her gaze and drawing it toward the shadows under the bridge. Back again. And back. While she wondered what the hell had gone wrong with everything, with her and Hugh, that made her make an ass of herself with asses like Nate Pigeon.

She reached down between her feet and pried a stone from the ground, threw it into the water and saw the ripples vanish before they'd gotten started.

A tear found her cheek, and she let it touch her jaw

before wiping it away. Self-pity or remorse; it frightened her because she didn't know which.

And Hugh lying on that damned bed, sighing, only once talking and that about a hand he said had touched his neck as he'd fallen. He said he'd been marked. Then he'd stared at her and told her it was only an hallucination. He'd smiled. And sighed again, and was silent.

"Damn you," she whispered, and tossed another stone. "Damn."

And looked up and saw a tall man in black standing at the foot of the steps on the other side. Because the sun was almost directly in her eyes, she thought at first he was nothing more than a shadow, until he took a step toward the water and sunlight caught the white collar around his neck. He lowered himself until he was in a crouch, balanced on his toes, hands draped over his knees.

Zachiah, she remembered; his name was Zachiah, and she was startled when she wondered if maybe he could help her. He was supposed to do things like that, wasn't he? That was his job. She almost laughed. Neither she nor Hugh had been to church in years, and the idea that some stranger might give her advice was ludicrous.

She looked away, to the willows, and watched them trap the sunlight and cast it in fragments to the stream.

She looked back, and he was gone.

She frowned as she scanned the walk and couldn't find him, checked the steps and the bridge and couldn't find a sign. With right hand rubbing left arm thoughtfully, she rose from the bench and stepped off the walk to the narrow verge between stone and creek. It was dark under the bridge, the oval light on the other side too bright for her to make out the water, much less anyone making his way along the bank.

Something splashed behind her.

She started, stepped back, and looked around wildly when someone called her name.

"Here, over here!"

Swearing at the way her heart and lungs were working, she shaded her eyes and spotted Kim Raddock's daughter across the water, wearing a bright lemon shirt and bright lime shorts, making herself comfortable on a bench with someone else she didn't immediately recognize. They exchanged waves, and Bev asked how her husband was doing.

I should get cards printed up, she thought glumly. But she managed to give the girl the news without shouting, nothing new, everything old, and with another frown toward the spot where the minister had been, she waved a goodbye, deciding there was no sense going home right away. What the hell. Maybe he'll talk today. Maybe he'll . . .

"Bye!" Bev called.

Loretta waved again without turning around.

"Weird, Bev," said Thorny Ollworth, stretching his legs out toward the stream and yawning. His left hand kneaded his stomach, his right wrapped around the back of his head. "That woman has serious mental problems."

"Her husband's in the hospital, knock it off," she said, pushing herself into the corner, drawing her legs up so she could curl a hand over her shins.

"Still weird."

God, she thought, glared at him, and considered yanking off his sunglasses and shoving them down his throat. The trouble was, he'd only think it was foreplay and try to take her, here, in the open. A quick glance up to The Willows, to the wall-long window that overlooked the creek. There were no diners. She could only see a bit of white on the tables. A flare of gold from brass candlesticks. Then she looked at him again and shook her head without moving. This was stupid. This was terminal. What she ought to do, if she had any brains, was call Bern and find out if he was willing to talk or something. But if she did that, she'd be admitting that maybe, just maybe, he'd been right and she'd been wrong.

"Y'know," Thorny said, drumming a thumb on his stomach, "this is not the most thrilling day I've ever had in my life." His head tilted toward her, eyes hidden, no smile. "No offense."

She ignored him. The water was smooth, muttering to itself, and she wanted to listen. She did not want to go back to his place, high on the lake's eastern ridge, and wait for him to prove what a man he was. Which he wasn't, much of the time. Hard body, hard brain. When he saw her naked the first time, he'd fallen to his knees and prayed she'd never leave him, and she'd laughed, believing herself flattered. The two times after that, he'd only stripped and taken her, rolled over and lit a cigarette.

Somehow, for no reason at all, she knew that Bern wouldn't do something like that.

God knew there had to be something more to sex than that. There had to be. If only because of the sounds she'd heard her mother make from behind the closed bedroom door. Wild sounds. Jungle sounds. A hell of a party.

Fun.

Maybe it was her.

He reached over awkwardly and put a hand on her bare knee.

She brushed it off.

"What's the matter?"

"Nothing."

The hand returned, and was knocked off again.

"Jesus." He sat up, scowling. Then he leaned over and looked left toward the trees, looked back at her without straightening. "Hey, it sure looks cool under there." His smile was soft now. Friendly. "Bet no one could see us from up above, y'know?"

"Fuck you," she said wearily.

He grinned. "That's the idea."

She groaned and stared at the water again. That was the exact problem. All he wanted to do, since the first time, was get his hands under her shirt, or her halter top, or whatever she wore; down her pants to her rump; out of her clothes altogether and onto the nearest flat surface. In and out before she even had a chance to work up a sweat.

Jungle sounds.

Party.

Christ; and she shoved herself off the bench just as he reached for her again, and walked to the water's edge, knelt down and plucked a blade of grass she blew off her palm into the creek. It spun crazily for several seconds, then took the surface as if rolling over rapids. She watched it until the sun's glare erased it. And didn't turn when she sensed Thorny move to stand behind her.

"I want to see Nance," she said.

"What?"

"That sonofabitch attacked her, remember! Maybe we can cheer her up."

He snorted. "That asshole couldn't attack his own wife, for Christ's sake. Erskine's all right." He hunkered down beside her. "Look, let's—"

Bev swiveled to face him. "No." Her hand went to his shoulder. "C'mon, Thorny, please?"

"I am hot," he said. "I want to get cool. I do not want to sit around with some freaked out bitch, y'know?" He smiled when her other hand took his other shoulder. "Bev, this is supposed to be a vacation, remember? We are not babysitters. Way I hear it, she probably winked at the old goat or something anyway. You know how she is, right?"

"Right," she said, and pushed him into the water.

He shouted and flailed, tried to stand, fell, tried again and with sunglasses dangling from one ear staggered blindly to the middle of the creek.

"You bitch!" he screamed, and fell again.

Bev's smile was stiff. So was the finger she showed him before marching to the steps and grabbing the wood railing. A look back over her shoulder—he was stumbling toward the bank, the water to mid-thigh. Then she climbed, hauling herself up with one hand until she reached the sidewalk. Her car was at the curb, and she got into it quickly, made sure she locked the passenger door and drove west, past the older buildings, the more used-looking shops. The two gas stations. A body shop. A two-story brick building whose windows were boarded up, but she remembered that years ago it used to be what her mother called a five-and-dime. Broke now. Gone.

Like Bern, she thought, and slapped the steering wheel hard enough to make her palm sting.

"Shit."

The tears were there and she shook her head to banish them, shook her head when they fell, and kept on falling until Hunter was behind her—one mile, and a disdainful look at the spot where that new development was going with some stupid name that made it sound like only zillionaires could live there; three miles as the forest closed in, the road narrowed and began to climb, and she saw a man walking toward her along the shoulder on the other side. She gave him no more than a glance before the road crested and she headed down again. There was an intersection another mile along that would, if she turned left, take her straight into Pennsylvania.

Instead, she stopped, dried her eyes, lit a cigarette, turned around.

The man was still walking, dressed in one of those silly pink shirts with a white collar and cuffs, good grey trousers, the black of his shoes long since paled by dust. At the sound of her approach he turned and held out a thumb. A tie, dark red, was pulled away from his neck.

She passed him a second time, tapped the steering wheel, reconsidered, and slowed. Stopped.

Jesus, Bev, she thought, and checked the rear view mirror to watch him hurry toward her, favoring his left leg. At the limp she felt better. Besides, the town wasn't all that far away. And he was well-dressed. And, she decided as he leaned over and smiled at her through the window, not half bad-looking either.

She reached over to unlock the door. "Where you headed?" she asked.

"Hunter?"

"Hop in."

He nodded his thanks and sat heavily. "God, it's hot."

The engine sputtered before catching. "It's only June. You should be here in July, August. You think this is bad, you'll fry then, believe me." A glance showed her the sweat on his cheek, the way his light brown hair was dark against his skull. He was puffing quietly. "You been to Hunter before?"

"Nope."

"Car break down?"

He nodded. "Hope to hell there's a decent mechanic and tow truck up there."

"At the station," she told him, the speedometer telling her she was going too damned fast, but she couldn't slow down. "They'll probably rob you."

His smile, from this side, was gentle and pleasant. "No doubt. But I'm not all that dumb, I think." His eyes closed. "Thanks again."

"No problem."

A small house back in the trees. A larger one, closer to the road, its yard overgrown, a car without wheels up on blocks outside the garage. A shack that sold bait beside a new showroom that sold power boats and canoes. A bar with a graveled parking lot, a house beside it wanting paint, needing shutters. An empty lot. The "Welcome to Hunter" sign, the size of a billboard, a woman water skiing, the man in the boat behind her standing up and waving.

"That's new," the man said.

Bev blinked as the sign passed. "I thought you'd never been here. You know this place?"

"Oh yes," he said, slowly turning to face her. "Oh yes, I sure do."

THREE

AFTER discarding a notion to delay his return by making a complete swing around the lake, Glenn pulled into the driveway behind Susan's white car and sat there while the engine coughed to silence. A glance at the house, and he asked himself if he ought to go in right away. Maybe the kids and their aunt were having a conference or something. Or maybe Susan and Marj were trading marriage horror stories in the kitchen. Or maybe no one was home, the kids with friends, Susan out for a walk, Marj still at her office.

A shriek from the back. Another one. Laughter.

Nuts, he thought, and climbed out and stretched and looked at the house again.

Nuts.

Once, it had been a simple place, when he and Marj were first married. Two stories and no frills, white clapboard and black window trim, a long two-car garage attached to the right, no discernible style save it wasn't cut from a mold, wasn't advertised in Sunday papers and given a fancy name. Then he and Grover Pitt had added a porch front and back when Marj got tired of the concrete stoop. Bern came. And Nancy. Dory made him realize that sooner or later privacy was going to be in short supply. So he and Grover got to work again, this time with friends and favors, and an addition had been raised over the garage.

The birch grew high alongside it, the evergreen shrubs high in front. Flowers neither one of them seemed able to maintain. New coats of paint, the color never changing.

A long time. A lifetime.

And in September Bern would leave, one room empty; next year it would be Nancy.

He had never noticed how large the house was until now.

He felt then the tug of a depression coming on, and he scowled at it, growled at it, walked heavy-footed across the lawn and around the side. This is no time for a funk, he ordered; no time for misery you bring on yourself.

At the corner he stuck his hands in his pockets and leaned against the house. Cheryl kicked in the swings, pushed by Susan. Dory sat on the ground crosslegged, screaming, "higher, higher," clapping her hands and laughing because she knew that Cheryl was scared to death of heights. Except on the swing.

Susan hadn't changed much.

She was still shorter than he by a head, dark hair still curly and long, slender except for the size of her bust, her face round and her eyes dark and darkly lined and her chin surprisingly blunt and outthrust. He could see the glint of a gold chain around her neck, spotted the rings on her fingers. Even in tennis clothes she insisted on jewelry, unlike her sister, who virtually had to be bribed to wear anything but her wedding band whenever they went out.

Why, he asked her silently, did you bother to come back?

Dory saw him first and scrambled to her feet, yelling to the others as she ran over and hugged him. He looked down at her, seeing himself there as he saw her mother in Cheryl, and kissed her forehead wetly. And almost frowned. Ordinarily, such affection outside of a good-night kiss would make her lips twist in disgust; this time, however, she only hugged him, and held on.

Susan waved.

Cheryl called out, "Daddy!" but didn't leave the swing.

He lowered himself to the grass where he stood and pulled his daughter down beside him. "Having a good time?"

"Sure," she said, moving to her left to leave no room between them.

"Your Aunt Susan all right?"

"Sure." An examination of his face made him exaggerate a frown. "You had one of those days, huh, Dad."

"It shows?"

"Yeah. You look old."

Cheryl began to slow down.

"It is not a good thing," he suggested, picking at the

grass between his knees, "for a child to be smarter than her father. If you know what I mean."

"Sorry."

"No need. I probably look a hundred years older than when I left this morning."

Dory picked at the grass too.

But she was right, and "bad" was the kindest way to classify the day.

The sighting of Jimmy Hale that had driven him from the house had been thankfully false, a farmer's wife hysterical when a bum made himself at home in a dilapidated barn. Then Vorssen demanding that Nancy be thrown in jail for life. Nancy telling her story, and Gorder, after the kids had left, talking to him for an hour to calm him down. He had to dress down the cop who'd nearly shot Reverend Zachiah, stop a fight at Duke Massi's between two summer people arguing about whether there really were bear in New Jersey, talk to the figurehead mayor about the cutback in summer cops, and listen while Kim Raddock read him her petition.

Four times he'd called Marj's office to apologize.

She hadn't been in all day.

"Dad, am I fat?"

He looked at his daughter, pretended extensive examination. When she didn't smile, he said, "No, don't be silly." Not fat. Not overweight. Heavier, however, than most of her friends and not carrying it well. "Why?"

She didn't answer, only shrugged.

Oh lord, he thought; oh lord, it's a boy.

"You losing sleep over it?" he said.

She glanced at him, looked away, and made a slow shrug that told him that her weight wasn't the problem.

Susan laughed merrily; Cheryl shrieked without fear.

"Dad," Dory said, plucking at the grass, "how do you get happy dreams?"

He watched Cheryl demand one last push, watched Susan reach out to oblige. "You know when you're just falling asleep, you sort of daydream?"

Dubiously: "Yeah."

"Well, it doesn't always work, but sometimes I just pick out all the good stuff I can think of and tell myself that's what I'm going to dream about tonight." He smiled and poked her, rocked her to one side. "I tell myself I can fly and save the world, things like that."

"You can fly?"

"Sometimes. In the good dreams."

Another question was thwarted when Cheryl threw herself on the ground in front of him, grabbed his ankles and slithered toward his stomach. "I am a conda," she said. "I'm going to crush you to death."

"Anaconda," Dory corrected scornfully. "God, you don't know anything."

He looked up then, squinting, as Susan joined them. "Hi, stranger."

She winked at him. "Hi yourself, Wyatt. You get the bad guys today?"

"No," Dory answered for him. "They robbed the bank and escaped."

She nodded. "That kind of day."

"Damn right."

Cheryl reached his waist and burrowed her head into his stomach.

Susan crouched at his feet, her expression telling him

he should get back in the car and drive as fast as he could to someplace where they didn't know him.

Wonderful, he thought sourly, and let his gaze sweep from the yard to the house to his daughters to the sky.

"Nancy's in her room," Susan said quietly.

"She told you, I guess?"

"We oughta get a lawyer, Dad," Dory insisted. "Sue that guy for every dime he's got. That's sexual harassment, you know. He could be arrested."

"Yep, I guess he could."

But Vorssen wouldn't be; he'd made sure of that. On the way home, with no compunctions at all, he had stopped at the restaurant. The moment he walked in the door every customer had looked away, and had stopped talking. Not even a fork scraped across a plate. To the sound of the overhead fans slowly *throp*ing he'd walked straight into the kitchen and, with a look, cleared everyone out.

Only one word made it out of Vorssen's mouth before the man realized that the sheriff wasn't there on official business. Instinct had him grab for a ladle, but Glenn had his wrist before he could swing it.

"She told me," he said quietly, forcing the man back one step at a time. "Now you tell me she's a liar."

The man had sputtered, saliva gathering at the corners of his mouth.

"I can talk to the other girls, the waitresses. I can talk to the ones who've quit."

When the words finally came they made no sense. A defense, a plea, Glenn had no idea. Vorssen was against the wall between an oven and a freezer. Glenn still had his wrist and he pulled the arm up slowly, twisting until the ladle fell to the floor.

"But I'm not going to," Glenn told him, his voice remarkably calm. "At the end of the week you will send Nancy two weeks' severance pay. You will also send an apology. And you will remember," he added, leaning suddenly close, "that I will talk to every girl you hire from now until the day you get the hell out of my town."

Vorssen's face reddened. "You can't do that!"

"And I can't do this either," he'd said, and put a knee into the man's groin as hard as he could, and stepped back to let him fall into a curl on the floor.

He'd walked out and told the nearest waitress to take a break, that Vorssen was thinking about the future of his business. One of the other waitresses giggled. One of the customers at the counter winked at him.

And when he returned to his car, he laid his head against the wheel and cursed himself for five minutes, and was thankful he'd left his gun back in the office safe.

He'd made one more stop, at the bank's drive-up window, before heading home.

Now he disengaged Cheryl's arms from his waist and took Dory's hand to help him to his feet.

"Maybe you could just shoot him, Dad," she said.

He was shocked to see she wasn't smiling. But he only said, "You mind watching them a minute more?" to Susan before going inside, hesitating at the foot of the stairs, then taking them two at a time to the second floor. Nancy's room was to the right, across from Bern's. His son's door was open; he wasn't inside. Nancy's was closed, and he knocked, heard a muffled voice, and went in.

Marj was there, sitting on the bed with all its ruffles and stuffed animals, Nancy beside her, holding her hand.

"I had a talk with Vorssen," he said before either of them could speak.

"What did you say?" Marj said sarcastically. "Give him till sundown to get out of town?"

He looked at her, his eyes slightly narrowed. She was daring him to say that the law doesn't allow him to play favorites, that not even his daughter can be granted special favors. He didn't smile, didn't feel a thing as her mouth opened when he told her, "Something like that, yes."

Then he sat beside Nancy and reached into his hip pocket to pull out an envelope. He placed it in her lap.

"What is it?" she asked.

"Open it."

Marj questioned him silently; he only watched his daughter's face as her fingers, trembling, fumbled with the flap before reaching in and pulling out a handful of bills she almost dropped in her astonishment.

"Oh my god," she whispered.

"Glenn," Marj said, astonished.

"Tomorrow, you and I will go down to Wortan's and let him talk you into something you don't want." He used a finger to turn Nancy's face toward his. "Then I'll pick out the sensible one which you won't want either." He smiled for the first time. "Then your mother will remind me about the green convertible I had when I was in college and how I used to ruin her hair and scare her to death because I didn't think an automobile like that was built to do less than ninety. Then and only then will you pick what you want."

The girl said nothing. She wept. She embraced him and let the money spill onto the bed. And he looked over her shoulder at Marj, who met his silent apology with one of her own, and the three of them shifted and hugged and shifted until Nancy finally said, "I think I'm being smothered," and started crying again.

It was another fifteen minutes before he stood and slipped a hand into her hair, combed it away from her face. "Rest a while, okay? I'll be up later, to see if you want to eat."

Marj was behind him when he left, and he slipped a hand around her waist as they moved toward the stairs and down.

"You know," he said, "this is turning into a madhouse."

Marj hushed him with an anxious look over her shoulder, and guided him into the living room where she sat him on the couch, sat beside him, took his hand. "I'm sorry."

"Me too."

"I overreacted."

"You had a right."

"I know."

He looked at their hands; they seemed older somehow. "I feel like I ought to explain, but . . ." He leaned back. "It's a bitch, ain't it?"

She joined him, and stared at the ceiling. "You said it." Her grip tightened. "Glenn, I have to tell you that Grover called me today. He said that the Hawkwood people have approved all the designs. They're going to start building next spring, maybe sooner, if they get all the permits and the land can be cleared quickly."

His eyes closed, his chest sagged.

"Are we going to fight?" she asked.

"I can't," he said. Not yet, he thought, and wearily told her about his day, and about his talk with Cheryl and what she'd hinted about Dory's companion dreams. "If I only knew," he said, "what's brought all this on, I'd take care of it. Or at least I'd try."

The room shifted to twilight, the sun ducked behind the house.

"Why is it, Marj, that every goddamn problem in this town and every goddamn problem in this house has blown up all at once? What the hell did we do to deserve this?"

She had no answer for him and he knew that there was none. It just happened, that's all. Some days were perfect and some days weren't and there was no sense at all beating your head against the wall.

"Shit," he said loudly.

"Damn right," she agreed.

"And I'm hungry, too."

"Susan's cooking tonight. She insisted."

"Oh Jesus," he groaned. He sniffed the air and groaned again. "God, please don't tell me. She's going to make some of her famous—"

"Spaghetti's done!" Cheryl yelled happily from the foyer. "C'mon, guys, before we eat it all up!"

"Is that a promise?" he asked, and Marj hushed him with an elbow. Yanked him to his feet and kissed him.

"About Hawkwood," she said.

"No," he said sharply. Then, more softly, "No, not now. Okay? Let's just wait."

There was no chance for a reply. Dory came in and huffed at them until they grinned and allowed her to herd them into the dining room where Cheryl and her aunt served dinner with flourishes and vaudeville Italian accents. By the time the plates were filled and steaming, Nancy joined them, kissed Susan on the cheek and took her place at the table. Glenn watched her carefully, assured himself she was fine, then stared at his meal. The others were eating as if they hadn't been fed in a month; he was having a time just lifting his fork.

Susan believed fervently in the kitchen without chaining herself to it. She ate constantly and to Marj's dismay appeared not to gain a single pound. She also believed that she was a superior chef, and her variations on simple meals were legendary in the family.

"Daddy," Cheryl scolded.

He grinned painfully at her.

Susan, seated opposite him, only winked and sucked a strand of pasta slowly into her mouth. "Great stuff," she declared, and the rest of them agreed.

He tasted it. An eyebrow lifted. He tasted more. He looked up and saw her smug grin.

"I didn't have time to do it right," she said. "I just opened a jar and the box. You can relax."

And feel like a complete jackass in the process, he thought as he ate, and drank the red wine Marj poured for him, and listened as Susan told them all how she'd been traveling alone along Highway 1 on the West Coast when, suddenly, she decided that she'd been traveling enough, that Wesley was gone and there was nothing more she could do. It was time to settle down. She'd seen enough of the country to last her for a while, spent enough of her money to realize that it wasn't going to last forever. So, she announced, she had taken an apartment in the city, had found a job in an advertising firm, and was going to get on with her life, all mourning done.

"It was the sign, of course," she said. "I knew it right away."

Of course, Glenn thought.

"What sign?" asked Dory, wide-eyed, entranced, giving him every indication that Aunt Susan was what she wanted to be when she grew up.

"The sea gull, Dory." The woman nodded emphatically. "I was just going along, minding my own business and looking for seals when it landed on my car *while I was driving,* and I knew it was telling me that I was pushing my luck."

"Oh wow," the girl said breathily.

"I went right back to my motel, packed, and—" she threw out her arms—"here I am!"

Marjory applauded. Dory leapt from her chair and kissed her hard on the cheek.

After exchanging tolerant glances with Nancy, Glenn decided it would be wise to keep his mouth shut, and only smiled his pleasure as the meal grew more raucous, the wine poured more frequently, and Cheryl's complaint that she ought to be at least allowed to taste some for crying out loud, was just shy of being demanding before he ended it by lurching to his feet and declaring a moment's peace. Out of pity for the old man who wasn't used to all this noise.

Dory gave him the raspberry; Cheryl looked to the ceiling in mock disgust; Marj shook her head in amusement and offered to help clean the table. Susan, however, wouldn't hear of it. She enlisted the girls to help her and told Glenn and Marj she'd meet them on the porch.

Glenn agreed and headed directly for Bern's hammock, had just lain down with a theatrical groan when an automobile braked sharply in the drive.

"Oh Christ," he muttered.

Marj, who had decided to bring all the summer chairs over so they wouldn't have to shout their conversation, leaned against the railing and said, "Hi, Loretta, what brings you here?"

"Oh Jesus," he said, and swung his legs to the floor. His head felt ringed with helium, his mouth coated with wet wool. And he had to blink twice before he was able to bring Hugh's wife into focus.

"Glenn, I'm sorry," the woman said, standing at the foot of the steps. "I don't mean to bother you."

"No problem," he assured her. And rubbed his cheeks hard when he saw the concern in her eyes, the way she kept shifting her weight from one foot to another. "God," he said, "is it Hugh?" And braced himself for the bad news.

But Loretta shook her head quickly. "No. No, he's all right, thank god. But I was at the hospital today. Seeing him." Her left hand raked through her hair. "When I left, I got in my car." The hand gestured, flopped to her side. "My meat was gone."

He waited.

"My meat," she repeated, obviously expecting him to understand without question.

He took a step down, sat down, and inhaled. "Loretta, someone broke into your car and stole some meat?"

She sagged in visible relief. "The car was locked, Glenn. I know it was. But it wasn't until I was in it that I realized I hadn't unlocked it. You know?"

"Okay. And the meat?"

Thinking: why the hell didn't she go to the office instead?

She told him she'd had a package of meat on the front seat, and when she looked over, just before leaving the hospital grounds, it was gone.

Then she held out a piece of paper. "There was this thing instead."

He took it, frowning, and saw that someone had left her a note, smudged, barely legible.

"Glenn, Hugh spoke to me this afternoon. For the first time in days, he spoke to me."

He read what was left of the note.

"He said, 'I ain't going home, Loretta. I'm staying here 'cause he's coming.'"

"Who?" Marj asked.

Loretta said, "I don't know. He just closed his eyes and wouldn't say anything else."

"The door was locked," Glenn said.

"I swear it." And the woman crossed her heart.

The note said: *I am   the Way.*

And Glenn thought, oh Christ, Jimmy Hale.

IV

The dream when it comes . . .

Cheryl sat on a bench in Central Park, her hands folded loosely in her lap, her beret slightly canted and pinned to her fair hair. Her coat was made for spring, her skirt a summer shade, and the party shoes her mother bought her were patent leather, with silver buckles, and gleaming black.

Behind her was a tall and spreading tree whose name she didn't know, whose leaves were turning colors and dropping from their branches, sashaying to her shoulders, balancing there and falling, to her lap, to the ground, to the path where pedestrians crushed them and didn't hear their screams.

In front of her, on the other side of the path that wound out of sight left and right, on another bench as faded as her own, was a man in a tattered tweed overcoat, fingerless woolen gloves, and heelless western boots whose tips had been stained too many colors from too much walking through garbage and through rain. His face was a dark mask beneath a wide-brimmed straw hat, and though she tried not to look at him, tried to ignore him while she waited as she was told she must, she couldn't help seeing him from the corner of her eye—watching her, sometimes smiling at her, sometimes sucking his lips between his teeth and making a wet smacking sound.

When he shifted, crossing one leg over the other, she held her breath.

When he leaned back and spread his arms over the warped back of the bench, she held her breath again.

When an elderly woman in a long fur coat swept past behind a tiny poodle on a leash, and the man was gone, the bench empty, she closed her eyes tightly and wished herself home.

She didn't like the city.

She had been here only once—and this time didn't count—and had been awed by the mountain buildings, the herds of people, and the rush of traffic. They all frightened her, made her cringe, made her slap her hands to her ears to muffle the constant noise that didn't die when the sun set, that seeped and crept and oozed through the hotel window and danced around her bed, giving voice to the room's corners and keeping the lights outside alive. The moment she had stepped off the train, she told her father and mother she wanted to go home.

And lovingly they smiled at her, and tenderly they comforted her, and they didn't understand about the monsters below the rusted gratings that chuffed and roared and breathed hot steam at her legs, about the monsters with siren voices that hunted her all day and signaled to each other all night and wailed when they found her, huddled beneath the blankets though the room was much too warm.

They didn't understand, and they smiled at each other when she tried to warn them, hugging her with gentle laughter and telling her how much fun they were having, how much more fun they would have, and how many stories she would have to tell her sisters and brother and all her little friends when they took the train home. In one week. Seven days. Seven sunrises too late.

The woman in the fur coat came back the other way, the poodle now behind her and yapping at the ground, snapping at an acorn, snapping at the leash.

Cheryl watched it, watched the woman, until they turned a bend in the path, and when she looked around, the man was there again, on the bench, straw hat low, legs crossed, hands deep in his pockets, a dark red tie pulled away from his throat.

Sit still, she told herself; sit still, sit still.

A squirrel chattered at her from the tree she couldn't name.

A white-bibbed brown cat with a stubbed tail raced from behind a litter bin and chased a low-flying leaf that caught the breeze and spiraled upward, leaving the cat behind to look at her with one milky blind eye and show her its teeth. She smiled at it. It arched its back. She whistled to it softly, and it dropped on its side, rolled onto its back and batted at nothings while the remnant of its tail whipped the path until a dust devil was born, spinning in place for several seconds, growing tall as a man and cleaning the path of its leaves and fallen twigs and finally, the cat.

The man on the bench kicked out a raw scuffed boot and the devil fell in upon itself, scattered itself, and died, and the cat yowled in fear and anger as it ran across the grass, into the trees, with the squirrel chasing after it, chattering and scolding with its tail and fur puffed.

A boy on a bicycle sped by her without looking.

Two men with briefcases and umbrellas strolled by her and didn't smile.

Then the man on the bench stood up and stretched, and Cheryl told herself to sit still, sit still, it was only a dream, she ought to know that.

But the man kept on stretching, leaning back, leaning back until the hat fell from his head and bounced off the benchseat and rolled to the ground where it spun slower and slower and slower and slower still until it stopped, its straw crown stained with grime, its frayed band holding a frayed white feather that didn't move when the breeze blew again and stirred the hat, stirred the leaves, and stirred the man to pushing back his light brown hair with one hand while the other reached into his pocket and pulled out a long knife.

He smiled.

His eyes were wide and crossed; his lips were wide and moist; his chin trembled and his cheeks pulsed and his forehead shone with perspiration as he took a step toward her.

Sit still.

And another, wiping the knife against his coat.

Sit.

Stepping on his hat and crushing the crown until it bled.

Still.

Smiling and nodding and licking at the saliva that bubbled at the corner of his quivering wide mouth.

Don't

move.

Cheryl blinked, looked to her left for the boy on the bicycle, looked to her right for the woman and her noisy poodle, looked directly ahead just as the man raised the knife to the level of his chest and opened his eyes even wider to show her the empty sockets.

She screamed.

The man laughed.

She pushed off the bench and ran down the path, one hand on her beret, the other at her side, screaming for help, screaming for her mother, rounding the bend and skidding to a halt at the edge of a cliff.

The park was gone.

The city was gone.

There was nothing but sky and wind as far she could see, and no steps in the cliff's face to save her, no weapon on the ground, no boy, no woman, no cat or tiny dog.

She turned, breathing heavily, feeling her cheeks grow warm and flushed. Something must be done, but she didn't know what; someone had to be called, but she didn't know the name.

And when the man came around the bend, wiping the knife on his pink shirt, still smiling, still drooling, she reached up to her beret and pulled out the pin that held the hat to her fair hair, and when he leaned over to kiss her she jabbed it straight into his eye.

He laughed and plucked out the pin, studied it carefully, licked its point, then threw it over the cliff and threw a kiss swiftly after.

Then he threw the knife as well, and leaned down and touched her shoulder.

She backed away, nearly fell, and he gripped her and pulled her to him.

Her eyes closed, her lips trembled, and she wanted more than anything to be able to cry.

But she could feel him. There. Waiting. The smell of him like damp wool, the feel of him like wire, the sight of him when she finally looked like something that had died in the farthest corner of the deepest tunnel in the world.

When he saw her expression, he shook his head and winked and said with winter's voice, "Not yet, little girl. Not yet. Not yet."

Then he kissed her dryly. On the cheek. On the forehead. On the chin. On the hand.

And released her when she gagged, bent over, sat up and fumbled for the lamp at the side of her bed.

And said, "Mommy," when she saw the slow moving shadow of a straw hat on the bedroom door.

ONE

H E sat across the rumpled single bed with his back against the wall and slowly stroked Cheryl's hair with his palm. She was asleep, her cheek on his thigh, her bare feet on her pillow, and on the floor in a dark sleeping bag was Dory, lightly snoring, hands clasped across her stomach, twitching now and then. Through the greylight of first dawn he could see a half dozen posters of baseball players taped to the opposite wall, a stuffed penguin wearing a baseball cap on a small pinewood desk; the closet door was closed, the door to the hallway opened to a fading black he refused to look at—an hour ago, he thought he'd seen something moving out there.

He yawned.

He shivered and rolled his shoulders.

A few birds began a choral trilling, and hushed when something rolled or ran through the brush on the hill.

Tired; God, he was tired.

He had heard his daughter cry out not long after midnight, and he'd managed to get up without waking Marj. When Cheryl saw him in the doorway—"What's wrong, honey, you okay?"—she'd whimper-screamed and threw herself off the bed into his arms. Not five seconds later Dory ran in, sobbing, babbling, and between them he heard the stumbling story of a man in the park and a dog and a knife and a cat and a cliff, and he'd hushed them and kissed them and soothed them and swore not to leave the room again, not even after they slept.

Something bad, Daddy.

They hadn't slept right away.

"I want happy dreams, Daddy," Cheryl had pleaded, curled up in his lap.

Tired; so damned tired.

But he kept reassuring them he was still there, once stretching out his leg so Dory could touch his foot.

Lord, he thought; lord.

He knew, or at least had read of, dreams sometimes being claimed as premonitions; he knew, or at least had been told of, dreams that had come true if the teller was to be believed; but even if he were inclined to accept that this was the case and not a simple case of too much snacking, he refused to believe that such a thing could infect both daughters at once. And in the same way. That was impossible. Therefore there had to be a movie, a book, a scary story at the heart of it.

It couldn't be Jimmy Hale.

166

It couldn't be.

He yawned.

something bad

And his stroking hand stopped when he saw pale white hovering in the doorway. His heart raced and relaxed when Marj stepped into the room, hand at her throat, nightgown rippling in the breeze that came chilled through the bedroom window.

Nightmare? she mouthed.

He nodded, and saw her look perplexed at Dory on the floor, Cheryl in his lap, could see the question before her lips even formed it: *both of them?*

Exhausted, he nodded again and leaned his head back, half-closed his eyes. Gently she lowered herself to sit on the bed, on his right, where she took his free hand, squeezed it, kissed his cheek, lay her head on his shoulder. He considered signaling her to go on back to their room, but he decided he liked her here better. She was warm. The nightgown was soft and cool where the folds drifted over the back of his hand. And the smell of her, at dawn, was the smell of her when they were young and nightmares were confined to just trying to pay the bills.

It didn't take long for her to pull up her legs, curl herself, cuddle, and fall asleep.

He yawned.

Maybe it all had something to do with the child's menstrual cycle, the upheaval, the grim acceptance. Dory's had started only a year ago, but Cheryl, according to Marj, showed all the signs of starting early, as she had. And she would turn eleven before autumn ended.

Or maybe it was a boy. Dory was still trying to figure

out what the hell they were for, and with Bern losing his girlfriend and Nancy not having anyone steady, maybe Cheryl was confused—playing baseball as well as she did, with the future she had planned, didn't quite sit with a boy's image of a sweetheart, even in this day and age, at least in Hunter.

Or maybe it was him.

The summer people were flocking in like the Canada geese who lived in the cove. Seldom home now, and now arguing with Marjory about too many things—maybe it was him. Maybe he didn't give them enough time and they thought he'd deserted them, didn't love them anymore, didn't care.

His eyes opened to stare at the ceiling: bullshit, he thought.

And remembered the cloud.

And fell asleep and didn't awaken until someone adjusted a light blanket across his shoulders and he turned his head and opened one eye and realized he was lying down, on Cheryl's pillow, and sunlight had brightened the room to a glare.

He sat up and looked at his watch. "Jesus, it's after nine!"

"Relax," Marj ordered, sitting on the edge of the bed. "I've already called Pete. The bad guys can wait for another hour anyway." She shifted as he pushed himself up and rubbed his eyes, and yawned, and saw her already dressed for work. "Cheryl didn't say anything about her dream. Did she tell you?"

He nodded and eased his feet to the floor. Rubbed his head vigorously. Scratched his chest until it hurt. Stood and told her all he knew while he padded into the bathroom and grimaced at the reflection that blinked back at him, red-eyed. Then he explained all his theories before telling her he didn't know.

"But Christ, this is getting serious, Marj. Neither of them are getting any sleep anymore. We have to do something before they get sick."

He opened the medicine cabinet and reached for his razor, saw an unfamiliar amber plastic bottle in the corner, picked it up and read the label. Sleeping pills. He frowned a question at his wife, who only said, "I'm under a little pressure, okay? I took one. It didn't work."

Pressure, he thought. Right.

Ten minutes later, still not quite awake, he was dressed and in the kitchen, Marjory leaning against the counter with a cup of coffee in her hand.

"Glenn, you're not suggesting a psychiatrist, are you?" she asked carefully.

"What?" He looked at the slices of buttered toast, the orange juice, and his stomach burbled. "No. I don't think so anyway. I don't honestly know what I'm suggesting." He looked up. "But this can't go on, Marj. They really are going to get sick. I don't think there were any problems Wednesday night, but last night . . . it must have been a pip."

She reached back to place her cup in the sink. "I agree. When I get home, I'll have an old-fashioned woman-to-woman, see what I can find out."

He bit the toast; it was cold.

"Where are the kids?"

"Gone."

He was surprised. "Already? All of them?" A look at the ceiling. "My god, how the hell do they do it? They hardly slept at all."

"Youth," Marj told him. "Remember? Besides, would Cheryl miss the change at a game?"

He grunted, coveting the energy, wishing he could shake off his bad times as easily. "Bern and Nancy too?"

She nodded. "I think Susan took them over to Wortan's." She smiled. "Just a preliminary look around. She called it 'scouting the territory.'"

A laugh that felt good. "I take it that's supposed to be a hint."

Her response was a one-shoulder shrug. "I think they did say something about meeting you for lunch."

He cocked his head warily.

"At Duke's," she said. "One o'clock. I don't believe they said anything about going Dutch."

"I'm surprised she can wait that long." He pinched his neck lightly, forcing the last of the sleep away. "How about you? You going to be there?"

She reached back into the sink, adjusted the cup, ran water in it and poured it out. "I don't know." A hesitation. "Grover and I are going to the site. Surveyors are supposed to mark it off starting today."

"Oh." Take it easy, Glenn, it's too damn early for this. "You going to be late then?"

"I doubt it."

He nodded, gave her the smile she expected, and listened for the front door to close. Then he yelled, "Shit!" and threw the toast into the trash, drank the juice at a gulp, and glared at the refrigerator until his vision began

170

to blur. He stood and went to the porch, breathed deeply several times, and tried to decide whether to go first to the office or drive out to Loretta's and talk to her again. That note. The car door couldn't have been locked, but he wondered if there was a true connection to the Lincoln Log house or if it was just someone, a kid, playing a stupid joke.

No; not a joke.

Though he had no tangible proof, just an acid sensation in his stomach and an itch at the back of his neck, he *knew* the warning had to have been left by Jimmy Hale. The kid—if he ever had been a kid—was back. Hiding somewhere. Taunting him, daring him . . . laughing at him.

So strong had been the feeling that yesterday he'd had every available man out on the road, checking and double-checking the surrounding farms, abandoned buildings, all the obvious places. Then they had taken to as many of the woodland trails and paths they could before nightfall.

And had found nothing, not a sign.

He hadn't expected them to.

Hale wasn't going to be so stupid as to be caught sleeping under a damned bridge.

But if he wasn't wrong, if his instincts were still working, Hale hadn't returned for wholescale vengeance, either. He had a target, a simple one—Iroquois Trace.

Which was why, last evening after supper, he'd driven over to the old man's house.

"Now what the hell do you want, Erskine?" the old

man had yelled above the barking of his dog. The door had opened only a crack.

"Mr. Trace, Jimmy—"

"I know, goddamnit! You think I'm senile?"

Glenn had resisted kicking in the door, had taken a deep breath instead. "I just want you to come with me. Until we find him."

Trace had laughed caustically. "You crazy?"

"Protective custody, Mr. Trace. You'll be safe in one of the cells."

"The fuck I will," Trace had answered, and had slammed the door, thrown the bolts, while Glenn knocked again, then pounded, then stomped off in such a quaking rage that he'd driven around for an hour before he could think clearly again. Then he ordered a patrol to sit directly in front of the old man's house all night, don't bother to hide their purpose, and shoot the sonofabitch if he tried to make them move.

Their relief would come in the morning, this time with surveillance more circumspect.

He didn't need to bother Loretta then; he chose the office.

After he had parked in the lot behind, he looked down at the barred windows beneath his office marking the string of eight cells in the basement, usually empty save when the weekend drunks and rowdies came out to play. He'd have to have one of the guys clean up. Today was Friday. Party time in old Hunter. Son of a bitch.

He sat for another minute in the shade, but the world didn't accommodate him by going away, so he stepped out into the sunlight and was once again struck, as he was every summer, by the difference in temperature between here and the lake. A good five degrees warmer here no matter how it was measured. Hotter, he amended as he walked toward the front; hotter, because obviously June had forgotten how pleasant it was supposed to be. By noon, easily, it was going to be ninety.

As he reached out to push in the door, a longbed pickup backfired to a halt at the curb, making him jump, turning him around. A burly man in short sleeves and baseball cap leaned out of the truck.

"Hey, Glenn, you got a minute?"

He nodded and stepped into the street. "What's up, John?"

John Wortan opened his door and swung easily down, hitched up his ill-fitting spot-worn jeans and walked back to the truck's bed. "I think we got a problem."

Wortan, whose brother owned Hunter's first and largest car dealership, worked one of the few remaining farms in the area, a dairy operation that used to supply a good portion of Sussex County and some small places in New York. Now he was barely hanging on despite the selling of some of his land. Larger companies were undercutting him, and his family was too large. They had known each other since childhood, and Glenn didn't want to see him go.

A convertible squealed around the corner, radio blasting, until Glenn turned to face him, and the driver saw the silver badge on his chest. A nod, then, a friendly wave, and the vehicle slowed to a crawl.

"Sic 'em, copper," John said. "Sumbitch could be a killer."

Glenn stared until he realized that he'd been glaring at the driver. "Nah. I'll let Robbie take care him."

John grunted mock disgust.

"So what's the problem?" Glenn asked, looking into the bed and seeing nothing but a tarp.

John yanked the canvas aside. "I don't know. You tell me."

Glenn felt his meager breakfast stir and turn to acid, and he turned away quickly and leaned back against the truck. "Jesus."

"Right."

A young buck lay inside, blood spattered and dried across its flanks, hind legs splayed stiff, tail upright.

It may have been shot out of season.

Glenn didn't know.

Because its head had been torn off.

"Do me a favor, John," he said, taking his time getting back to the sidewalk.

"Way ahead of you, pal," Wortan said. "I'm heading for the vet's right now. Just thought I'd let you know."

Glenn's smile was sour, and Wortan laughed as he swung back into the cab and pulled into the traffic without bothering to signal. Glenn watched for a moment, then went inside and closed his eyes briefly at the air conditioning that was usually too cold for his taste. Audrey was filing, Gorder was at the radio, Sandera was at his desk on the telephone; Glenn checked the log book, saw nothing had happened the night before, nothing this morning, and almost made it to his office before his stomach roiled again. He thought he was going to throw up. He grabbed the jamb and breathed urgently through his mouth, smelling and tasting bile and telling himself he wasn't going to do it, not here, not now, it was only a damned deer, for god's sake, and he'd seen worse in hunting season so what the hell was the matter?

He straightened. Dropped his hand. Walked to his desk and fell into his chair.

"Jesus."

Normal. By god, this was going to be a normal day if it killed him. Nothing was going to upset him. Nothing out of the ordinary was going to happen. He was going to read through the night's reports, shoot the shit with Gorder, take an hour or so on the road and then meet his kids at Duke's. Where they would tell him about every car on Wortan's lot, and he would have to guess by her eyes which was the one Nancy wanted the most and which was the one she thought he'd let her have. A grin. This might even spark Bern into wanting one. He gave the boy two weeks in California before he got the call, wondering what the possibility was of raiding his savings account.

Normal. Mangled deer aside—and it was probably a bear—this was going to be a normal summer day.

A knock on the wall, and he looked up, saw Robbie on the threshold, a pad in one hand. "Got a minute?"

He nodded, not at all liking the expression on the man's face.

Normal, damnit!

Sandera dragged one of the chairs close to the desk, and grinned. "We—"

Gorder rapped on the frame. "Sheriff?"

With a melodramatic groan, Glenn threw up his

hands, leaned back, and pointed to another chair, which the dispatcher immediately pulled up alongside Sandera. The two looked at each other, waiting for permission to go first, finally laughing quickly as Robbie deferred to the older man.

"Okay," Gorder said briskly, "we got a thing here, just come in. That new guy, Plowright, he was stopped on Juniper a couple of minutes ago."

Glenn frowned in quick thought. "Juniper. Juniper. That's where . . . oh shit."

Gorder nodded. "Yep. Got it in one. Old man Vorssen, he runs out to the street and flags Plowright down, nearly gets his ass creamed, Plowright can't drive for shit. Seems Vorssen and his old lady were at their son's overnight, down in Morristown, some kind of birthday or something. Got back this morning, kitchen door jimmied, kitchen trashed, some crap written all over the wall." He looked down at a sheet of crumpled paper in his left hand. "Some Biblical stuff, I think."

" 'I am the Way,' " Glenn quoted.

"Right. Something like that." Gorder glanced up without raising his head, cigar pointing like a dead finger. "Just like the Lincoln Log place."

"Swell." He pinched the bridge of his nose between thumb and forefinger. "Is—"

"The kid's taking care of it. Got whatshisname, Neilson, already on his way with the camera and shit."

"Thanks."

Gorder answered with a lazy salute.

"God, if Kim Raddock hears about this, there'll be vigilantes in the streets by noon."

"I doubt it," Sandera told him. "She's got problems of her own."

Glenn almost smiled. "Y'know, there's a penalty in football for piling on, guys. Give me a break." He sniffed. "I have an idea—why doesn't one of you tell me Jimmy Hale's been found floating in the Hudson."

Nothing.

"Damn," he said. "All right, Robbie, what is it?"

"It's Beverly," the younger man said. "She went out yesterday afternoon, hasn't come back. That was Mrs. Raddock on the phone. She's upset."

"It's not forty-eight hours," Glenn reminded him, even though it didn't matter. Officially, Beverly wasn't a missing person; as far as Hunter was concerned, if she wasn't home within an hour of whatever curfew she had, she was. "Okay, Pete, get the patrols on it. Ask around. Nothing official, nothing hysterical. Robbie, you want to—"

Sandera nodded. "Yeah. She was driving that red thing of hers. I already checked the county cops and the hospitals—nothing. No accidents at all in the county last night."

"Shacked up," said Gorder.

Glenn lifted an eyebrow.

"Shit yeah, it happens all the time. She's shacked up with some punk, no question, case closed. Can't get away from it this day and age." He turned to Robbie for confirmation. "Them Commie teachers, long hair and shit, they let 'em loose for the summer, they're ripe for it, you know what I mean?" He took out his cigar, stared at it, threw it in the trash can. "Ain't got the values anymore, all they want to do is destroy society from within. Let the boys have their way with them, handing out diseases left and right, wearing those skimpy . . ." He stopped. "I mean . . ."

Glenn nodded sagely, trying not to laugh as Gorder obviously remembered that Bev until recently had been Bern's steady girl. "I'll keep it in mind, Pete."

"Nothing personal, Sheriff."

He waved a hand and said to Sandera, "Get going. I'll be on the road in a minute myself." Then he stopped the deputy with a raised finger. "I'll be seeing Bern and Nancy for lunch. Maybe I'll find something out."

"Right," Sandera said, and left in a hurry.

Gorder sat for a moment longer, staring at the floor.

"Something else, Pete?"

"Pigeon," he said quietly.

"Who?"

"Nate Pigeon." He scowled. "I know you think I'm off the end half the time, Sheriff, but that Pigeon's dealing, we both know it. Maybe he knows about Beverly."

Cautiously, Glenn nodded. "Yeah, okay. So why didn't you tell Robbie?"

Gorder cleared his throat. "I . . ." He folded the paper and slipped it into his breast pocket. Then he stood and hooked his thumbs into his hip pockets. "Sheriff, I want to talk to him myself."

Glenn blinked, once, slowly. "You're kidding."

"I am a cop, y'know."

"But the radio—"

"I've been training a couple of guys. Hell, even Audrey can do it if she'd stop combing her hair once in a while. I do get sick once now and then, y'know. You think I have wires to my house or something?"

In all honesty, Glenn had never thought about it because the number of days a year Pete had called in sick couldn't even be counted on one hand. Yet he didn't know anyone in Hunter, including himself, who was so adamantly, fiercely opposed to drugs and drug dealers. It had been, for both of them, exceedingly frustrating that none of their covert investigations had turned up any solid evidence against the so-called writer; that he in fact dealt was simply something they "knew" without proof. It was instinct.

"Let me think about it, Pete."

"I'm not going to hurt him," the dispatcher insisted, and followed it with a smile that would have frozen a geyser. "No kidding, Sheriff."

"Just let me think, okay?"

"Sure." The man saluted, pulled a cigar from his pocket and chomped on it as he strode from the room. The radio crackled. Pete's voice was harsh.

Finesse is the way, Glenn cautioned himself as he stood and opened the bottom drawer; finesse, and no way in hell Pete's going to have at Nate alone—that would be tantamount to condoning legal murder.

He strapped on his gunbelt, adjusted it, and walked to the door where he watched Gorder snapping orders to one of the patrols, watched Audrey attacking her typewriter as if it were a man bent on her virtue, and widened his eyes when Sweet Aster elbowed the front door open and dragged in Thorny Oilworth. Thorny's hands were cuffed behind his back, and he fell against the counter stomach first without the deputy's help.

"Drunk," Aster said in disgust. "He was baptizing himself in the creek under Midrow Bridge."

"Gotta have the light, Mr. Erskine," Thorny said, grinning stupidly, his cheek on the counter. "Gotta have the Light if I'm gonna find the Way." He hiccoughed and began to sing, softly, a country song about love and loneliness and his baby leaving him for a traveling man.

"Call his damn father," Glenn said as he lifted the flap and walked toward the door. "And put him in a cell 'til the old man gets here."

"Can I shoot him first?" Aster wanted to know.

"Only if he throws up all over my office."

He opened the door and sighed at the heat, immediately hurried away when the singing abruptly stopped and Audrey yelled, "For god's sake, not there, get a trash can!"

Please, he prayed as he jumped into his car, let this be only a warning, not the real thing. I don't think I can stand it.

He had left his sunglasses folded on the dashboard shelf, and he hissed and swore when he put them on and felt as if he'd been branded; the air conditioning took two eternal minutes to work, and he swiveled the nearest vent to blow the cool air directly into his face; he used the radio to tell Pete he was on the road—and consequently warn the rest of the day shift he was out and prowling—and Gorder responded quite solemnly that Hunter and the world will now rest much easier and be thankful. He smiled and shook his head. The automobile wheezed as it jerked out into traffic.

And when he saw Sandera's cruiser parked in the middle of Midrow Bridge, its lights flashing, Sandera gone and a few curious pedestrians gathering at the head of both flights down to the creek, he was tempted to speed up and look the other way. Gripped the wheel and watched himself pull in behind the patrol car, turn on his warning lights, and grab his hat and slap it on as he stepped onto the road.

He looked over the wall and saw Robbie a hundred feet up, at the end of the sidewalk. When he whistled, Sandera turned, shaded his eyes, then beckoned once, abruptly. Please, God, not Hale, not Bev, he thought as he hurried to his left and took the stairs as calmly as he could. A deputy, he couldn't see who it was, had stationed himself at the head of the staircase on the other side of the creek by The Willows to keep the inquisitive from coming down. By the time he reached the bottom another deputy had taken this side as well. They must have seen the lights too; Sandera hadn't called in.

"What?" he asked flatly as he approached.

Sandera, one finger working at his mustache, cleared his throat and pointed upstream. "Something up there. I thought I spotted it before."

He hesitated. "Bev?"

"No. I don't think so."

He nodded a *let's move then* and they left the pavement for the high grass, the low branches, pushing their way north along the bank that slowly began to flatten out. A dragonfly hovered over the creek. A puff of gnats flew into his face, and he snorted to clear them from his nostrils. There was shade, but the heat still found its way in; there was a breeze, but it only served to make the heat worse.

Sandera said nothing.

Glenn inspected the ground where they walked, seeing only an occasional tossed candy wrapper, beer can, looked up and saw the high wooden fences that marked the houses bordering this part of the water. No one looked back at him. The dragonfly followed, as did the gnats and a mosquito he bloodied on his wrist and wiped off on his rump.

The ground softened. In addition to the lake, Marda Creek was fed by dozens of tiny underground springs that transformed the area into near swampland before it ever reached the stone bridge that linked Lake Road's two halves. No kids ever played down here. No lovers made their temporary beds. It was too much like a tiny marsh, and there were, as always, the rumors of copperheads and water moccasins.

Several times willows detoured them, and he wondered how Sandera had been able to see this far in. He checked over his shoulder—the pocket park was gone, willow branches moving languidly like tendrils.

"I was already down here," the younger man said, coming back to join him. "I was looking for her. Under the bridge. I started to walk, got a little ways, and . . . come on."

They pushed through a screen of willow and he saw it, snagged on a dead branch lying partway in the creek—a bright yellow top torn from neck to midchest. It wasn't a man's. He knelt in the mud and stared at it, squinting, massaging one cheek as he scanned the creek in both directions. Sound became muted. Focus concentrated. There was nothing on the ground that showed him anyone had been here, nothing on any of the nearby shrubs that showed him anyone had passed through. The shirt had either been thrown here, or had floated down. There was no struggle. There was no blood.

Without moving he said, "Have you gone up toward the lake at all?"

"I haven't even been this close. As soon as I saw it I started back to get you."

The creek began to narrow here, and several slick brown rocks could have served as stepping stones from the other bank. Glenn looked back toward Midrow Bridge, leaned forward, blinking away sweat, pushing back his hat—a minister dressed in black stood just beyond the closest willow, not clearly seen, fragments of dark and light as the thin branches and dangling leaves shifted in the breeze.

"Robbie," he said quietly, and looked back at the torn shirt, at his dark reflection in the water.

"Yes?"

"Do me a favor and go back and talk with—" He turned his head again and jerked his thumb.

Sandera looked. "With who?"

The minister was gone.

"No one," he muttered and pushed himself to standing. "Did you see the Ollworth kid?"

"I saw Sweet trying to get him out of the car, that's all. Half out of his gourd, he looked."

"He was down here. Messing around under the bridge. Go talk to him, see if he saw anything, heard anything." He took off his hat and wiped his brow with a sleeve. "The bastard's drunk, but he knew the girl. I think they were going together." He gestured. "Check it out."

Sandera nodded. "I'll send Hacker when he's done taking pictures at Vorssen's."

"Come with him," Glenn said. "I'd like you here just in case." It was his way of saying Robbie would captain the case. The man smiled his thanks, and a promise, and wasted no time leaving.

As soon as he was out of sight, Glenn picked his way past the shirt, cautiously, peering into the brush, up the steep bank through the trees, trying not to speculate on what he had thought he had seen. He only wanted to find something else besides the top—a sneaker, a pair of shorts or jeans. Christ, even a used condom. He did not want to find Beverly. And by the time he'd gone another hundred yards, he knew he wouldn't. There was too much undergrowth, the land too slippery to walk on, reeds and weeds and high grass too dense to plow through without signs. Nothing had passed here in at least a week, and he turned around with more relief than he thought he could feel for someone not his own.

One more look at the shirt still snagged on the branch, and he hurried back to the bridge, told the deputy at the stairs what had been found and to go back there, now, and watch it until the photographer and Sandera returned. Then he hurried to his car and got in, sighed at the cool air that touched the sweat on his face, and decided he wouldn't wait until lunchtime—he'd try to catch

Bern and Nancy at the car dealer's lot. Maybe they had seen Bev, and knew where she'd run to.

He snorted.

Run to. Right. If that was Bev's shirt, she hadn't run anywhere, and isn't that going to be a hell of a thing to have to tell her mother.

TWO

DICKIE Wortan's Auto Carnival, three-quarters of a mile west of Midrow Bridge, was three uneven acres of scarred blacktop centered by a brand-new hexagon glass showroom whose roof was tinted dark green and sported a flagpole that had never been used. Behind it was a rain-stained concrete block that housed the service area. Beyond that was a leg of ragged woodland a hundred yards deep. Lampposts spaced around the perimeter and throughout the lot itself were barber-pole striped, and between them sagged wires along which had been fastened multicolored plastic pennants. When the wind blew, the pennants snapped, like tinder in a fire; when the wind paused, the pennants hung limp and reflected the sun.

It was, Bern thought as he mopped his face with a sleeve, like walking through an oven.

The dark glasses weren't doing him much good at all, but taking them off would be worse. The sun had set miniature bonfires across the windshields of every car on the lot, and looking down each row was like staring down a tunnel ablaze with white flame. He squinted. He felt a headache stirring between his eyes. He followed his sister as she checked out every vehicle, new and used, and did it again. And again. Each time, however, whatever system she was using to keep track of what she liked knocked off another one.

She hadn't spoken to him in almost fifteen minutes, not since he'd tapped her on the shoulder and said, "Where the hell'd you learn about carburetors?" as if, he realized too late, he thought her too stupid to even know how to spell it. But he tagged along anyway, grunting knowingly now and then, nodding when she did, tsking when she passed by something he wouldn't have minded himself.

It was driving her crazy.

He knew it.

He didn't stop.

As long as he had to be here, there was no reason why he shouldn't enjoy himself. Aunt Susan had given up after ten minutes, claiming shopping to be done and promising to return in time to take them to the diner. He had already read all the brochures in the air-conditioned showroom, sat in all the cars, checked under all the hoods. Dickie Wortan and his two salesmen left him alone. They knew what was going on; he could see it in the way they ignored him and watched Nancy. Then he read the brochures again and returned to the heat.

Tsking.

Nodding.

Until Nancy halted hip-cocked in front of something that looked to him like a pregnant blue roller skate and said, "Yeah," very quietly.

Bern couldn't help himself: "What, that?"

She nodded without looking at him. "I think so. It'll get me around."

"So will your bike. Probably faster."

She turned then and slapped her hands to her waist. "I am not a millionaire, you know, for god's sake. We're talking economy here. This thing's a fuel-injected four, overhead cam, front wheel, four radials, and it'll get me where I want to go when I want to go and won't get me broke in the process."

He gaped.

"It also has only eight thousand miles. If that creep tells me a teacher owned it, I'll puke."

He almost smiled.

"So," she said, pushing him aside with a palm, "out of my way, toad. I'm going to wait inside until Aunt Susan gets back. It's hot out here."

He watched her, looked down at the monstrosity she wanted to call her own, and sighed. Corvettes all over the damned place, a Ferrari, an old Jag that with some work could make serious noise on the back roads, and she has to be sensible. He wasn't surprised. Their father would never approve the sport cars, she knew it, and went right for what she knew he couldn't argue against. It'll save hassles, no question, but it sure as hell wasn't any fun.

He headed for the showroom, and swerved abruptly

before he had gone a dozen yards. A blotch of shadow from the arced sign over the entrance wasn't cooler but at least out of the direct sunlight, and he leaned a shoulder against the white wood post, hands in his jeans pockets, watching the cars shoot past as if they were driving through enemy territory. A dark van marked with surveyors' symbols headed west, and right behind it was his mother's car. He fumbled a hand free and waved, but she hadn't seen him, and he stepped onto the shoulder to watch her drift around the next bend. She's going to do it, he thought; she's really going to do it. Millionaires and executives crawling all over the place. Trees bulldozed. People sneaking out in the middle of the night to get some free firewood. She really was going to do it.

From now on, life was going to be hell at home.

He glanced over his shoulder. Dickie Wortan himself—fat, bearded, and more hair than Bern had ever seen on a grownup—had Nancy in a chair, smiling at her, holding out a glass of clear liquid. He was smiling. His head bobbed once. Another second, and the blimp will probably drop down and kiss her feet.

His lips curled in revulsion. He looked back to the road. Houses on the other side, old, one virtually tilting, divided by wooded or rock-pocked lots slowly filling with garbage and rusted abandoned appliances. Once a year Hunter sent trucks out to clean them up; less than half a year later they were filled again. A puff-chested rooster with an iridescent green hood and violently red wings strutted through the dust. Bern could see a dozen hens in the weeds behind it, keeping their distance but following just the same.

A hawk rode the currents.

A crow squawked at him from a telephone pole.

Sweat tickled down his nape, and he reached behind him to trap it on his spine.

C'mon, Aunt Susan, he begged silently; please, get me out of here.

Then he saw the brown car and straightened, turned slowly as his father drove onto the lot and pointed at him to follow.

Oh shit, now what, he wondered.

Nancy had already seen Glenn. She was on her feet, pointing for Wortan's benefit as she dropped the papers she'd been holding, then hurried toward one of the exits. Bern was in no rush—the excitement and fun were ruined now that Nance had made her choice, and his father would probably praise her forty ways from Easter for being so levelheaded.

Dull, he thought; Christ, how goddamn dull.

Nancy reached the car first, hands clasped at her chest, waiting for her father to get out. When he did, hat still on, she reached out to take his arm and turn him around. Bern rolled his eyes. Nancy dropped her hand. Glenn beckoned without looking around and Bern didn't like the feeling that wormed into his stomach.

He had no sooner reached the trunk than Nancy said, "What do you mean, she's gone?"

"Who?" Bern asked, thinking suddenly of Pint and Dory, playing at the ball field.

Hat low over his eyes, Glenn leaned back against the

car and squinted at the showroom, squinted at the sky where the hawk still hung, black and silent, hardly moving. Then he stared at them both. "Bev. Raddock."

Bern swallowed. "She run away or what?"

"I don't know, son. Her mother saw her last, sometime yesterday afternoon. She's a bit worried. Either of you see her since?"

"No," Nancy said at once.

Bern shook his head.

"If she got mad at her mother, or was feeling bad, where would she go?"

To me, Bern thought, and checked himself before he spoke. No. Not anymore. That was yesterday, a long time ago.

Nancy glanced at him. "Maybe . . . Thorny," she said in almost a whisper.

Bern's nod was slow, grudging. "Maybe." He looked at his father. "You ask him yet?"

"Robbie's trying to right now."

"Trying?" Nancy paled. "God, is he hurt?"

"No, just drunk. He's in the tank."

"Shit," Bern said, and didn't apologize when Glenn glared at him.

Silence, then, until the wind snapped the pennants.

And as his father explained what his deputy had found snagged on the branch, Susan pulled up behind them, frowning as she got out and looked at them all. "Trouble?"

Nancy explained, and Glenn asked them to keep an eye out, for Bev, for strangers, and told them he'd still meet them for lunch in an hour.

It was as if nothing was wrong. As if Bev was just off on a pout or something. As if nobody really cared because she'd show up sooner or later. And it made Bern so angry he couldn't help the fists that bulged in his pockets, the pulse of a vein at the side of his neck. They were going to have lunch while Bev was gone, and talk about a stupid goddamn blue car Nancy would probably wreck before she got it back to the house.

"Aunt Susan," he said, interrupting and not caring, "can I borrow your car for a while? I . . ." He looked at his father. "I'll bring it to Duke's. One hour." Iron across his chest; rust in his mouth. "Please?"

"Bern," said Glenn, "I don't think—"

"Please?"

"Dad," Nancy said quietly.

Susan bounced the keys in her palm, then tossed them over with a quick smile.

"Thanks," Bern said, leaned over and kissed her cheek, and almost took off his left hip in his haste to get the door open and himself behind the wheel. He didn't check to see what kind of looks they gave him as he U-turned and sped out to the road; he didn't check the rear view mirror as he swung west and spun the trees into a blur. He didn't care. There were only three places Bev could be if she wasn't with Thorny; if she wasn't there, she was probably out of the state, or—

The ridge that formed the lake's basin came to an abrupt end half a mile beyond the "Welcome to Hunter" sign. The slope to the top was gradual, and marked by a rutted dirt road liberally studded with rocks partially exposed by rain and wear. Halfway up, underbrush and saplings began to close in, and he stopped the car, not wanting to ruin his aunt's paint job. On foot, fifty yards farther up, he plunged off to the right, following a deer trail that led to the cabin Bev had brought him to the night of the prom.

It was empty.

But someone had cleaned it recently—the mattresses had been replaced by a pair of army cots, the cobwebs swept from the rafters, the dirt and droppings from the floor; cardboard had been tacked over the broken panes, a ragged sheet of plywood over the back window. The fireplace had new logs piled in it. An empty beer bottle sat on the hearth, a candle jammed into its mouth, wax dried down its sides.

"Jesus," he whispered.

But Bev wasn't here, and there was no time to wonder who had taken the place over. Some kids, maybe, though he hadn't heard anything about it; some guys from town, sick of the litter, wanting to use it for . . . whatever; the owner, whoever the hell that was.

It didn't matter.

Bev wasn't there.

Nor was she at the beach on the Spit, and no one had seen her, no one had heard her talking about taking off, which she generally threatened six times a summer.

And she wasn't at the old well, on the other side of town.

It was visible from the road if you knew where to look, though its roof-and-posts had long since rotted and fallen away. The story was that a small stone house, now moss-covered remains behind the well, had belonged to a witch who used to live there during the Civil War. The townspeople tolerated her because she kept the crops growing and the cattle alive and the lake and creek well-stocked with fish. They named the creek after her, to keep her happy. But there was a drought. There was anthrax. In the middle of a December night someone burned the place down, and the witch hid in her well. They sealed the well with stone, and later with concrete. Bev and he would come out here once in a while and lean on the chest-high well wall, trying to peer through the wide cracks that time had forced in the seal. Together they had decided there was nothing down there but water, and had planned, this year, to come out one night and break the seal free. Maybe even climb down to find the witch's bones.

She called it "our place," because everyone else thought they were crazy.

Bern called it "our place," because in the dappled sunlight spring and summer the red in her auburn hair seemed like sparks, and in the moonlight it seemed like silver. The harshness that too often marred her face was softened; the bitterness in her voice bled away into the dark. Here, more than anyplace else they went, she was the Bev he cared for, liked to be with, liked to love.

But she wasn't there, and there was no sign that she had been.

He returned to the car and sat sideways on the front seat, the door open, engine idling. He gazed across the road and didn't see a thing. He stared at the sky between the branches and saw a dark cloud sweep over the woods, shortly trailed by another. He wanted to believe, desperately to believe, that she was okay. Nothing had happened, this was Hunter, and she'd just taken off. A fight with her mother, or with Thorny, and she'd taken off, feeling sorry for herself. She'd be back. Any minute she'd be back.

She had to be.

She was Bev.

She had to be.

Jesus, he thought, what the hell have I done?

Viciously he threw a stone, threw another, and swung in behind the wheel. He drove as slowly as he could, waving traffic around him when it crept up behind, staring into the trees, through the shadows and the shade, almost stopping when he got to the Frennel house and saw Mrs. Frennel's car in the driveway. Maybe she had seen something—the red car, anything—and knew it wasn't so. She was too busy with her husband in the hospital. He drifted on, eyeing Nate Pigeon's house, not seeing Bev's car and knowing that didn't mean she hadn't been there. It was possible. But it wasn't very likely. Though he and every other kid in the county knew how Nate supplemented his writing income, he also knew that Bev liked her beer and not much else in her system. Thorny and his self-indulgent friends were the ones with enough money to bring Pigeon and his merchandise to the back door. Bev never did; she played her own game.

Before he knew it, he was back in town.

Before he realized it, he had parked in front of The Willows and had walked to the top of the stairs. No one was with him, no one down below but a bored-looking cop sitting on the far bench. But his father had already been there, and Sandera, and had found nothing.

A hand briefly touched the center of his back, making him jump and grab for the railing.

"I'm sorry," a gentle voice said. "I didn't mean to startle you."

He almost swore, and smothered it with a weak smile when he saw the black suit, the white collar, the dark-tanned face. "It's okay, Reverend. I was . . . it's okay."

As he backed away a step, the minister grasped the railing in both hands and leaned over and down, sighting along the creek. "It seems that I've come here at a bad time." His head turned; he smiled. "Maybe I'm a jinx."

Bern laughed nervously, not knowing what to say. He couldn't even remember the man's name.

"Did you know her?" The man nodded toward the water. "The missing girl. Did you know her?"

"A friend," he said.

The minister lifted his chin. "Ah. Well, friends sometimes do strange things, Bernard," he said. "They are, in many ways, mysteries."

"You can say that again," he muttered, surprised that the man had pronounced his name correctly, making it sound almost English, almost . . . not half bad. And suddenly he was shaking the minister's hand, repeating the man's name, and feeling as if this stranger was someone he didn't have to suspect was pushing his profession instead of himself. The old rector had been a local joke, as bad as the Baptist fire-and-brimstone preacher whose congregation could be heard on Sunday mornings all over town. They didn't sing well, but they sure sang loud. The only sound ever heard from the Episcopal church came from the bell that rang before each service, and every Sunday sunset, until it had cracked a few years ago and had never been fixed because the church had no funds.

"We used to go together," he heard himself saying, looking back at the creek, seeing Bev down there with him, holding hands, following the dragonflies Bev said were the witch's familiars hunting for her body. "I haven't seen her for a while."

Okay, Bev, he thought suddenly; goddamn knock it off, you've made your point, you can come home now, okay?

"My father thinks she's probably all right," he continued. "He's the sheriff. Sheriff Erskine? I guess you met him already, probably. He thinks she's all right." He shook his head. "I don't know."

Something splashed in the water.

The deputy was throwing stones.

"You know," Bern said, turning with a grin, "she used to—holy shit."

The sidewalk was empty.

He'd been talking to the wind.

Turning in a slow circle, he saw no one but a few pedestrians crossing the bridge, a handful more across the street heading for the shops. Back at the creek, the deputy had his hat off and was furiously scratching his head.

Okay, he thought, and was suddenly angry. Too many damned things were going on around here, making him look the fool, making him feel too damned helpless.

He walked briskly, long strides, arms swinging and almost rigid, ignoring the heat that slammed on his shoulders, the glare from shop windows, the glares from those who brushed against his shoulders because he wouldn't get out of the way. And by the time he'd gone a single block he felt his legs begin to harden, his breath come hard, and the sound of cars and chatter and radio music and footsteps became muffled as he struggled, seemingly swimming through the humid air, flecks of dim red at the periphery of his vision, spinning yellow stars that swooped in front of him and died. His mouth opened, throat dried. He blinked away stinging sweat. He stared at the sidewalk and watched his feet move and didn't feel a thing. Something was wrong, he knew it, and was too hot to think about it. No thought at all. Just a faint, distant humming that grew as the red grew and spread as his back and chest dampened and deepened as he slowed, and paused, then veered toward a striped blue awning and leaned heavily against a wall of brick between a window and a door to a shop he couldn't remember.

Someone came up to him, a woman, blurry face lined with concern, but though her mouth moved, he couldn't hear what she was saying and he waved her away, his arm heavy, his fingers limp. She shook her head and reached for his arm. He gestured again, tried to curse at her for interfering but his lips wouldn't move. She took his hand and tugged, and he followed because he had no choice, across the street and into a store where the cool air, the cold air slapped his knees to buckling.

"Oh god," he groaned, and dropped into a chair the woman had dragged behind him. He wanted to throw up. He bent over, forearms on his thighs, and let his head drop.

"Here." A hand with a plastic glass of water. "Sip it. Gulp it and you'll cramp."

Twice grabbing before he was able to hold the glass, and he had to lean back to drink. And nearly choked when Aunt Susan took a handkerchief from her pocket and dipped it in another glass she held.

"I . . ."

She hushed him by mopping his face with the cold water, and as he sighed, and sipped again, he realized he was in Kornell's Shoes, and several women with several children were staring at him from their seats.

"What did you do, walk from Philadelphia?" Susan demanded, kneeling beside him, fresh water on the handkerchief now cooling his wrists.

"I . . ." He emptied the glass and just barely didn't choke. "I was going to Duke's."

"From where?"

"The bridge."

Her expression was doubtful as she touched his forehead with the backs of her fingers, brushed the hair back from his brow. "C'mon, Bern, you know better. Nobody gets overheated walking one lousy block."

"In this town they do," he muttered, puffed his cheeks, blew a breath, and pushed himself to his feet. The ceiling lowered, the walls shifted, and he rubbed his face harshly with both hands. "I'm okay," he snapped when she moved to help him. "I guess it was—where's Nancy?"

"At the diner. With your father. Waiting for you."

She touched him again, a cool damp palm gently to his cheek. "I don't know what's the matter with you, kiddo, but you're not walking anymore. You stay here, I'll get the car. It *is* still in this state, isn't it?"

"Aunt Susan—"

Before he could stop her, she fished in his pocket for the keys, looked exasperation at him, and left. He ignored the women; the children were already checking out their new shoes. And he stood at the doorway, seeing nothing but the sun's glare until the white car backed into view, causing more than one driver to lean on his horn at her maneuver.

When he got in, she waited until she could make a U-turn, saying, "This is probably illegal, but what the hell, my brother-in-law's the law in this berg, right? You think he'll fix a ticket for me?"

He didn't laugh.

As they swung around he saw Reverend Zachiah standing on the bridge. He twisted around to watch him, and lost him when Susan completed the turn.

"I couldn't find her," he said, the car heading in the opposite direction, the minister gone. "I looked all over. I couldn't find her."

"She your girl?"

He slouched down and closed his eyes. "Was."

"Carrying the torch?"

Shut up, he thought.

"No, not really."

"Okay," she said agreeably, and they were stopped by the traffic light. "Damn. Honest to god, one lousy light on this stupid street and I have to get it. Story of my life." She drummed the wheel with her thumb. "Nancy's picking up her car tomorrow."

He grunted.

"Cute."

He grunted.

"She says she's going to show it off to some guy."

"Right," he said sourly. "Thorny, right? Jesus, what an ass."

The light changed.

"No. That wasn't the name, I don't think."

He opened one eye to look at her, saw a bead of perspiration jewel on her temple and sat up quickly. It was the sexiest thing he had ever seen in his life, and Jesus Christ, Erskine, she's your aunt!

Susan shook her head slowly, frowning. "No. Some guy named Jones." She laughed. "God, how original. Jones."

He was warm again and looked straight ahead. Your aunt, you jackass, your goddamn aunt!

"Jones?"

"Think so. Maybe. Hey, a sign! It's a parking space!" Without warning she turned sharply, throwing him against the door. "God, what luck!"

Lucky I'm still alive, he thought, and grinned at her when she smiled and asked if he was all right.

"Yeah. Thanks."

"No sweat." She giggled. "Sorry. No problem. But we'd better get inside before your father has a fit. He might think we've eloped." She touched his leg with a finger. "You going to pass out on me?"

"No." He opened the door. "Y'know, the only Jones we know is a guy named Brady."

"That may be him," she said, slamming her door, coming around the car to take his arm. "Escort me in. Your father will think you've got manners."

"Don't bet on it," he said.

She hugged the arm to his side and laughed.

"And besides, it can't be Brady Jones."

"Why not?"

Bern shrugged. "Can't be. He's dead."

THREE

DESPITE the tail end of the lunch hour, the diner had still been crowded when Glenn returned from the showroom, praying the clouds he spotted would bring some cooling rain later on. Duke was fast at the grill while Cornelia and the two other waitresses slipped between the customers like a breeze more effective than the huffing air conditioner could manage. The conversation level was high without being noisy, three ceiling fans brought the smoke up to form thin bands and drifting clouds, and when he stepped inside, a pair of teenagers lingering at the magazine rack suddenly decided they weren't interested in anything but finding a place to sit.

He arrived alone. Susan and Nancy had decided to do some quick, celebratory shopping before eating. The papers had been signed, the handshake done, and arrangements made to pick the car up the following noon. He'd been given no choice, but he didn't mind.

Luckily, there was an empty booth toward the back and he'd claimed it quickly, called an order of coffee to Cornelia, lit a cigarette, and leaned his head back, half closed his eyes. An image of himself flashed against the opposite seat, and he managed a quick smile. This wasn't the sort of place where he'd find people like Kim Raddock. Marj called its patrons "hardware store types" without insult. And she was right. Road crews came here when they were working in the area, clerks and tellers and those pinching pennies, the older folks who didn't much care for the frills of Vorssen's or The Willows or the Clearwater.

By the time Nancy had raced in he was close to being as relaxed as he could get, grinning as she perched opposite him with one leg curled under her and told him for five minutes without taking a breath how she was too excited to eat, and how Aunt Susan had spotted her car near the bridge and had gone to fetch Bern. She had chattered so rapidly he could barely catch every other word. She had laughed. She had almost wept. Twice she had leaned over and kissed him. And then, once again apologizing that she was far too excited to sit still, to eat, she'd told him she was walking home—to think about her car, what she would call it, how she would take care of it, taking out the manual and brandishing it as she explained how she'd memorize the whole thing front to back. When she was gone, he had sagged as if he'd been bucking a hurricane wind for the better part of an hour. But it was a good feeling. A reminder of how it had been with his own first car, too many years ago to bother to count.

The mood hadn't lasted. By the time the door had closed behind her, he had realized with a start what a mess he had made of things that morning. Two mistakes, horrendous ones, that not even the rawest rookie would have made if they'd had any common sense.

From the snaps and snatches of conversations he overheard, the story of Bev's disappearance had already ripened on the grapevine. The spirit was murder; the tone confusion. And it was all because he hadn't followed his own long-established procedures, all because he had jumped with both anxious feet to the conclusion that the woman's top found at the creek belonged to the teenager and not someone else. It was stupid, and unforgivable, no matter how likely the assumption was. And he'd compounded the error by the way he'd spoken with Bern and Nancy, not cautioning them but presenting her disappearance with all the implications of foul play. He hadn't realized it until Bern's expression, much too late, registered. By then the boy was gone, and Nancy and her aunt had herded him into the dealer's.

Christ, he thought, maybe I ought to retire.

Too old.

Jesus.

He yawned so hard his jaw popped.

Not old; just damned tired.

He lit another cigarette, looked up, and saw his son and Susan in the aisle, arm in arm, and he couldn't help noticing the sidelong looks she received from the men at the counter stools. Approving. At least one of them wistful lust. It came close to making him laugh, and as he half rose in greeting, he was able to give them a smile that wasn't strained with guilt. Bern he would talk to now; Nancy he would catch at home.

"Nothing," Bern said glumly as Susan slid into the booth to sit against the wall. "I didn't see her anywhere."

Perfect, Glenn thought, and blessed the boy for giving him the opening.

"Look, Bern, I should have made it more clear before that—"

"Hey, Sheriff!"

Sweet Aster stood in the aisle, beckoning.

"God," he said, and beckoned himself.

Aster pushed his way past a school of departing lunchers and gestured again. "Hey, Sheriff, Mrs. Raddock's back at the station. She—"

Bern was past the deputy before Glenn could even move. He looked an apology at Susan, who only shrugged ruefully and said, "Good luck," in a small voice.

He grabbed his hat, slapped it on, and followed Aster to the door, pausing when he passed John Wortan drinking coffee at the counter.

"John!"

"Hey, Glenn," the farmer said. "How you been?"

"Fine," he answered automatically. "So what did the vet say?"

Wortan frowned. "The vet?"

"Yeah, about the deer."

"Dad, c'mon!"

Wortan looked away, looked back, clearly puzzled. "What deer we talking about, Glenn?"

"Jesus, c'mon, John, the one you showed me in your truck this morning."

The man lifted a hand. "Glenn, I don't know what you're—"

Bern grabbed his arm and yanked him away. "Dad, for god's sake, c'mon!"

The boy pulled him for several steps before he shook the grip off to look back at the farmer, who was staring after him. Another summons, this one from the deputy, and he cursed that there was no time to ask another question. Besides, how the hell could the guy not remember? It took no effort at all to bring back the blood, the flies, the stench of the carcass. No effort at all.

Then there was the heat, and the rush up to the station. Bern was already at the counter, watching Kim Raddock intently—she stood in Glenn's office, her back to the door, and Aster whispered, "She came in about five minutes ago. I just found out where you—"

"Don't worry," he said, and told Bern to either sit down or take a walk.

"Dad—"

"This is not a negotiation, son."

Kim turned at the voices, and Glenn pointed to the chair, then the exit, before taking off his hat and hurrying in to join her. He closed the door and offered her a chair. She nodded, stiffly, but remained standing as he forced himself to calm while walking around his desk. On it was a pile of jewelry. Costume jewelry. Three small envelopes he knew bulged with money. Not very much, but more than Bev should have.

Kim's face was flushed, her eyes narrow and close to tears.

"Kim, please. Sit down."

She batted the words away brusquely, bit her lower lip. "I called everybody," she said, lifting her chin as if trying to see over his head. "Twice. Probably three times. When I couldn't find her, I . . ." She exhaled, closed her eyes. "I looked through her room. I don't know. A clue, I guess. Looking for a clue." Her eyes opened. She worked at a smile that snapped out when she pointed. "I found that stuff in her closet." She did sit then, heavily. "It's her, isn't it. She's . . ."

Glenn saw no purpose in lying. "Either that, Kim, or she's hiding it for someone."

The hope in her expression wasn't surprising. "You think so? You think maybe it wasn't her?"

"I don't know," he said truthfully. "The only way we're going to find out is to find her. And so far . . ." He shrugged. "No one, none of her friends—"

"Nobody," the woman confirmed bitterly. A glance over her shoulder. "Bern?"

"Sorry, no. He told me just a couple of minutes ago that he'd been to their favorite spots, all of them, and she wasn't there."

She began to cry. Not a sound, not a warning beyond a lift of her shoulders—just the tears that eventually streaked her makeup and gathered on her jaw before dropping onto her chest. He moved quickly to stand beside her, offering a tissue she took but didn't use. A few words, useless, a pat on her shoulder, and he opened the door and beckoned Audrey in. A nod in Kim's direction. Audrey nodded back and went inside.

Bern was in a chair by the door.

Aster was at his desk, waiting.

"What did the kid say?" Glenn asked the deputy.

"Nothing. He's passed out."

"Shit!" He glared helplessly around the room. "Get down there, wake the bastard up. Drown him in coffee, call a doc if you have to." He strode to the counter and said, as Bern got hastily to his feet, "I want you to go home. There's nothing more you can do."

"But Dad—"

Bern cut himself off when he saw the look on his father's face. Obviously nothing was going to change his mind, so he said, "Let me know, okay?" and went out into the heat without waiting for an answer, jammed his hands in his pockets and tried to figure out what to do next. Something; he had to do something, for god's sake, he couldn't just go home and sit around and wait and "*Jesus!*" when a dark shadow passed in front of him, stopped and returned.

Reverend Zachiah ducked his head in apology. "I seem to make a habit of startling you, young man."

"I'm . . . it's okay, don't worry about it."

The minister gestured in thanks. "I just wanted to tell you that I didn't mean to leave you back there." He looked down the street. "At the bridge. I sensed you wanted to be alone, so I just slipped into The Willows, where I was heading for my lunch when I saw you."

Right, Bern thought, and left me alone to talk to myself like some kind of nut. Thanks a hell of a lot.

"No problem," he said, and with a vague farewell

wave walked off, not knowing where he was going, snapping his fingers like a cat whips its tail, ducking off Springwood onto Lake Road, into the shadows of the old trees. Trailing a group of kids in bathing suits heading for the lake, hurrying around them when they decided to start a game of shoving and mock snarling; standing on a corner to wait for Iroquois Trace to make up his mind which way he was going to turn in his pickup; leaving the trees and shade and Hunter behind, kicking at stones, at pebbles, picking up a length of branch and flinging it into the weeds.

Pausing at the ball field and wondering how the hell they could play when Bev was missing.

No one noticed him.

No one waved.

He turned around and took the fork to the old stone bridge, veered away from it and crossed the footbridge to the Spit. The picnic ground was crowded, only a few recognizable faces as the summer people took over, proprietary and boisterous. He followed the path to the beach and leaned against a tree. Watching the swimming, the horseplay, unable to figure out why he was here when he knew Beverly wasn't.

Unable to understand why he should care so much when it was she who dumped him, not the other way around.

A sailboat hissed past the float.

Beyond it were several more, a pair of rowboats, a trio of canoes.

Across the lake, to his right and straight ahead, he could see blots of color on the other beaches.

Bev was gone; life goes on; son of a bitch.

When a small beachball landed at his feet, he picked it up without thinking, spun it in his hands, blinked against the sun and saw a little girl waiting patiently on the sand. She waved. He smiled. She pointed. He tossed her the ball and decided to go home, maybe Bev had called, maybe Nancy was there and could help him think, maybe . . .

"Damn," he whispered, and trudged back to the road, by the time he reached the house feeling as if he'd carried a boulder there on his shoulders.

The dock was deserted.

The house was empty.

He considered going to his room, changed his mind halfway up the stairs and strolled into the kitchen where hushed high voices brought him to the back door. Cheryl and Dory sat on the back steps, a backpack between them, heads close together; they seemed to be arguing.

"Hi," he said, pushing open the screen door.

Cheryl in her surprise bumped down one step, and Dory glared up at him. They both wore jeans and short-sleeved shirts, Dory with a red headband, Cheryl with her baseball cap and pigtails tied with rubber bands.

He crouched down at the backpack and poked at it with a finger. "You guys going somewhere?"

"Camping," Cheryl said quickly.

"Hiking," Dory said at the same time.

He squinted past them at the slope. "It's hot. You'll fry. I'll have to pick you up with a sponge."

"I've done it before," Dory reminded him stoutly.

Right, he thought; and the first woodchuck they see is going to send them screaming for the police.

"Does Mom know?"

"Sure," Cheryl answered, scrambling back to the top and dragging the pack into her lap. "We called her at the office. She said it was all right."

"Just the two of you?"

"Well, you can't go, dopey," Dory said, then looked at her sister, looked up at him. "We're supposed to get tired, see. You won't let us get tired."

He nodded, then shrugged.

"So we can sleep, silly," Cheryl told him.

"Oh. Okay."

"And then we won't have the bad dreams anymore."

He shifted to sit crosslegged. "Pretty bad, huh?" But they didn't have to answer—he could see it in the dark gathered under their eyes, the way their hands jerked when they spoke. "You figure tired will do it?"

They nodded quickly.

"Well," he said, untangling himself and standing, "good luck."

"Happy dreams," Cheryl said.

"Huh?"

"You should wish us happy dreams, not good luck."

God, he thought.

"Okay—happy dreams."

And when he returned inside, Cheryl leapt off the steps and shrugged the pack into position. "C'*mon*, Dory," she said. "We gotta go *now*."

Dory hesitated, the tip of her tongue pushing between her lips. "It's scary."

"But we agreed."

"Yeah, I guess."

Cheryl reached for her arm, changed her mind and started walking. It didn't matter if Dory came. The chicken. If she had to, she'd do it all by herself. Besides, it was her dream, and she was the one who was causing all Daddy's and Mommy's troubles. She was the one who made Beverly the Dope disappear into thin air. So she was the one who had to take care of it. She didn't really understand everything that Daddy told her; she didn't know what kind of problems she had that her brain was trying to tell her about. Unless it was joining the Braves instead of the Yankees. But that was silly. And anyway it didn't matter. She was going to have happy dreams no matter what and make everything right again, and if Dory didn't want to help her, she would do it all herself and be a hero. Maybe even get some ice cream. Maybe some cake. Maybe the boys would let her play without being such pains, so she wouldn't have to wrestle them just to get a turn at bat. It was easier in school, a lot easier, because the teachers let her play and the boys couldn't say no. In summer it was different. In summer they called her names and laughed at her, and when Mommy told her it was because she was better than most of them, it didn't make her feel any better, not at all. It wasn't fair.

At the back of the yard she looked back at the house. Dory stood on the porch, dancing from foot to foot.

"You coming or not?" Cheryl called.

Dory kind of threw up her arms in a way that made Cheryl want to giggle. She looked like a stork. A fat stork. But she came. Slowly. And when she was near enough she said, "Why don't we take the road?"

Cheryl sighed loudly. "Honest to god, Dory, use your head, okay? Suppose somebody sees us?" She pointed at the slope. "We have to go that way."

Dory adjusted her headband. "I guess."

Cheryl looked at the trees, looked back at her sister and took a step toward her. "We gotta get rid of him, Dory," she whispered. "We just gotta."

And Dory nodded, raised a shoulder, nodded again and plunged into the woods.

Cheryl stayed in back, knowing that Dory would poop out in a few minutes, and then she could take the lead. She knew the way better than her sister. She'd already walked it three times, just to be sure, spending most of yesterday dragging up the cots and candles she'd found in the junk her father piled in the garage and Bern never cleaned out like he was supposed to. And if they didn't stop a zillion times along the way, they'd get there long before the sun went down. There would be plenty of time to eat the cookies and cupcakes she'd smuggled in the pack, drink the soda, have the chocolate bars she'd taken from the refrigerator. Mommy would be pretty mad, but by then it would be all over and nobody would care.

"We're gonna get eaten by bears," Dory grumbled half an hour later.

"No, we're not," Cheryl said. "All you do is hit them on the nose and they'll run away."

"Who told you that?"

"I saw it on TV."

"That's dumb."

"I don't care. I saw it."

They followed a dry creek bed across the slope, left it when it headed downward, and climbed again, angling southwest toward the ridge. Birds yelled at them, a chipmunk darted into a hollow log, Dory with her arms spread wide steered them away from a large patch of poison ivy.

"I'm hungry," she complained.

"Not yet," Cheryl told her. "Not 'til we get there."

"Damn."

"And don't you swear at me, Doreen Erskine!"

Dory mumbled something she didn't understand, but she didn't ask her to repeat it. It didn't matter. Not now. They were on their way. They were really going to do it. And she was really secretly glad that Dory was with her, because she didn't think she could do it by herself. Not really. No. Maybe the walk she could do because that was the easy part. But not the other thing. She didn't want to have to do that alone. And that made her think how glad she was that Dory had had the dreams too. It was funny. She didn't think people could dream the same thing, but Dory did. And that meant she had a partner, though she wished it was Bern or Nancy because they were bigger and stronger, but she guessed that big kids didn't have bad dreams like she and Dory did, and so they wouldn't be any help at all. Nancy would only call her an airhead, and Bern would only try to tickle her out of it. But not Dory. Dory was just as scared as she was, and that was the best thing about it— Dory was scared, and she was scared, and so they wouldn't do anything stupid because they knew, better than anybody, what would happen if they did.

Dory stopped, stretched her neck, dropped onto a rock and wrapped her hands around her knees. "I can't see the house," she said when Cheryl came up beside her.

Cheryl looked down the slope—trees, and fallen

trunks, and piles of leaves from the winter before, and things moving they couldn't see, and the sun not quite bright because of all the branches that moved in the breeze.

"So?"

"So I can't see anything at all, that's so."

"So?"

Dory looked at her. "Are we lost?"

"God," Cheryl said, and moved on, no longer climbing, using the contour of the slope to take her south. The ridge, she knew, was only a little way above her, but there was a trail there, and people used it, and she didn't want anyone to see them and tell their parents. She didn't know if Bern believed the lie about the tired—

"Cheryl, wait up!"

—but it would have to do until it was too late for them to stop her.

"Cheryl, damnit!"

She whirled. "Don't swear! I told you, don't swear!"

"Why not?" Dory said angrily.

"Because *he* does."

Dory's mouth opened, closed, and she lowered her head and marched on, using a thin branch for a whip and not looking up until at last they reached the clearing.

"Oh boy," she said.

Cheryl hesitated.

The sun was out, but a small dark cloud took the nice from all the blue. Cheryl crossed her fingers; she didn't want rain. God, that would be terrible. Rain, this time of year, meant thunder and lightning most of the time. She didn't want rain. She didn't want thunder.

"I don't suppose you forgot the stuff," Dory said.

Cheryl swung the pack around to her chest, snapped open the flap, and pulled out a small bottle. She held it up for her sister to see.

They stared at it.

They stared at each other.

Then Cheryl said, "Happy dreams."

And Dory said, "Right."

And for a minute Cheryl thought she was going to cry.

Dory clapped her hands. "Okay. Let's get going. I want to eat. I want some chocolate." She grinned. "And then I want to knock that creep right on his ass."

Cheryl started to scold her before she grinned back and said, "Happy dreams."

"The best."

"Damn right."

And they laughed.

V

The dream when it comes . . .

"**R**ELIEF!" Marjory cried in mock joy at the change in the weather. "Thank you, God, thank you!" Then she turned away from the door and muttered, "If I really get lucky, it'll be a flood and I'll drown."

No one responded. She was alone in the office. For the second day in a row Kim hadn't come in, hadn't called, and the other two agents Marj had hired a year ago were out dealing with clients and not expected to return unless a sale was made. Which she knew wasn't likely considering the properties being offered. To remain here, then, was pointless. There was nobody to contact, no follow-ups to be made, no filing, no typing. Yet she didn't want to leave. Instead she stood by the window and looked out at Springwood, convinced she could almost see the temperature dropping as a gray-bottomed cloud drifted over town and buried the sun. When she craned her neck she could see several more behind it, and a bank of near black that crawled over the horizon.

The air conditioning was off.

The room was still cool.

Sunlight returned briefly before fading again.

A palm pressed across her hair, slipped over her cheek and covered her mouth. How was she going to do it? How was she going to tell Glenn that the Hawkwood project had suddenly developed a probable fatal disease. One of the surveyors had discovered it as he'd tramped with her and Grover Pitt through the wooded tract west of town—underground springs. The man wouldn't estimate how many there were or how deep they were, but as he and his partners had packed up their equipment, he told her that several days of good rain would make the center of the area sodden, without question. Foundations would soon weaken. Basements would flood. Lawns would grow moss. He couldn't understand why they hadn't noticed it before, couldn't believe they had thought it simply standing water from prior showers.

When they left, she exchanged the urge to cry for a jolt of temper. "You knew," she accused Grover Pitt. "Goddamnit, you knew, didn't you?"

Pitt, his eyebrows up and his left hand raking through his chest-long beard, said, "What if I did? What if I lied? Would it make any difference?"

In her rage, and growing humiliation, she'd almost slapped him, and he knew it and backed away with a cruel pitying smile. But he'd said nothing else, and she'd done her best not to run back to the car. When he finally called after her, asking her to wait, she ignored him. He could walk back for all she cared; what she needed was time alone to think, a way to approach the problem without panicking.

By the time she reached the office, she knew that Hawkwood was dying. Dead, once the news got out. And if Glenn smiled, or even twitched in that direction, she knew too that she would hit him. Or worse—she would walk out.

"Oh hell," she whispered, and rested her forehead against the glass, closed her eyes, felt the heat even as the sun disappeared again. "Oh hell."

She hadn't contacted Kim; the woman had enough problems of her own and didn't need to hear this. But Pitt had called shortly after she'd returned, speaking quickly to prevent her from hanging up, attempting to persuade her that too many potential local jobs were at stake, too many political favors were on the line, for her to tell the developers the truth and force abandonment of the project. Let them find out later, he'd said; let the builders handle it, they know about these things and the springs can be worked around, no problem, not really, it happens all the time, it's not the end of the world.

She'd hung up on him.

He hadn't called back.

"Oh hell."

For over an hour she'd sat at her desk, staring at nothing, hands drifting and settling and drifting again, running through scenarios that might, were they miracles, save all her plans; for another hour she'd scrambled frantically through the agency's files, searching for loopholes, choking back tears, feeding her temper again as she thought of all the dreams Pitt had laid in her lap and encouraged her to nourish; then she'd gotten up, took the telephone off the hook, and stood at the door, watching the shoppers, the traffic, the sky, the clouds, and prayed that she'd be able to find some way to salvage the business, protect it from scandal.

If she failed, she was finished. Word would be out, and it wouldn't be long before the listings dried up, commissions just smoke.

She didn't care how Glenn reacted. She needed to see him. She needed to hear his voice.

Quickly she snatched up her purse, switched off the lights, and locked the door behind her. The air had definitely cooled, and had darkened without quite growing dim. The few people on the sidewalk moved anxiously, with anxious glances at their watches and the sky. To her right, a block west, several teenagers climbed up from Marda Creek and boisterously piled into a car that bellowed across the bridge behind a corkscrew of exhaust. They made her think of Beverly, evidently not yet found or Kim would have called with the news.

Poor thing, she thought and turned left; poor me.

The wind picked up, rustling paper along the gutter, snapping the fringes of storefront awnings, kicking grit into her face and forcing her sideways for several steps. She could smell the rain now, a cool dampness and threat of thunder that reminded her to stop at the ball field on the way home and pick up the kids. Unless she called from Glenn's office to see if Bern was there to do it for her. Her own car was in the town lot, and once at the corner she almost decided to get it, in case the storm broke sooner than she thought.

An upward glance over her shoulder.

No. No need. There were still pale strips of blue between the clouds, and those above the horizon were still no larger than a wide belt.

Besides, she needed to walk.

At the second corner she shaded her eyes and peered through Vorssen's window in hopes of seeing Nancy to give her a wave—until she remembered. And glared. And had to order herself to cross over before she went in and tore the sonofabitch's eyes out of their sockets.

Another gust slapped her back.

Nate Pigeon stumbled out of Duke's and they nearly collided.

"Sorry," he mumbled.

"It's all right, my fault," she mumbled back, and hurried on.

Does he know? she wondered; does he know where Beverly is?

The torn front page of a supermarket tabloid tangled itself around her feet, lightly scratching, and she kicked out, swearing, until it fluttered into the street.

Hotshot tycoon beats newsprint to death, news at eleven.

She grinned without humor and paused at the third corner to take a deep breath. It would do her no good just to barge in and dump all her problems in Glenn's lap. She had to have a plan. She had to know what she was going to say before he made some snide remark about Hawkwood, and her job. But nothing either grand or poetic came to mind by the time she reached the office, and she stood there hesitantly, biting her lip, watching a portly deputy struggle with the flag as he tried to unhook it from its mooring.

Then his hat blew off, and she snared it before it rolled into the gutter.

"Hi, Mrs. Erskine," he said, grinning sheepishly.

"I thought you were supposed to have two people doing that, Sweet," she said, striding onto the grass, the hat pressed to her stomach.

He grunted as he clumsily folded the flag into a serviceable square. "I am. But . . ." He shrugged.

She returned the hat with a smile and followed him inside, shuddering at the cold air now so obviously artificial. Glenn's door was closed.

"Is he in?" she asked.

Audrey, at her desk, nearly fell over in her haste to get to her feet. "Hang on a minute, Mrs. Erskine. I'll tell him you're here."

She didn't protest. Ordinarily, she hated the way the deputies treated her, as if she were someone special, someone to be curried. It made her feel uneasy. Even after eleven years, she couldn't tell if they truly meant the courtesy or were smirking behind her back. She started when a high-pitched yowling drifted up the back stairs just as Audrey knocked on Glenn's door and disappeared inside.

Pete Gorder shook his head wearily. "Don't worry," he told her, taking his cigar from his mouth and spitting dryly. "That's only the Ollworth creep."

"My god, is he all right?"

"Drunker than any ten sailors I care to name," the dispatcher said with contempt. "Stupid bastard keeps throwing up, screaming about ghosts and goblins, you name it, he's yelling it." His laugh was disdainful. "Damn fool knows you can't see ghosts in the daytime."

"Oh." She dropped her purse on the counter and tried to make quick sense of her windblown hair. "Right."

"It's them Commies, y'know."

She knew better than to answer.

He leaned back in his swivel chair and stared at the wall over his equipment. "It's all your basic mind-fuckers—sorry, Mrs. Erskine. Drugs is what I meant. Commie drugs make you see things you ain't supposed to."

"I see."

He looked over his shoulder. "Like ghosts in the daytime."

She nodded.

And Glenn's door opened.

Audrey hurried out with a strained smile, Glenn appeared on the threshold, and Marj despite her vow couldn't help the single tear.

With a long silent sigh, Robbie sat on the trunk of his patrol car and took off his hat, held it between his knees, swung it back and forth. Not fifteen minutes ago, after talking with the sheriff about the discovery Mrs. Raddock had made in her daughter's closet, he had parked at the western end of Field Street, the last before Hunter gave way to the lake. He had stepped over the curb, walked ten feet through high weeds to the chain link fence that marked the drop to the creek below, and he had stared at the water until his eyes began to tear. He wanted to know if Beverly had been down there. He wanted to know what the hell he had missed, what was hidden in the weeds and thorn brush that would give him a hint. One goddamned hint that would lead him to the girl.

But there was nothing. He'd been this far, down there, four times since returning with the photographer, and he'd found nothing at all. None of the patrols had seen anything, none of her friends knew anything, no one in town it seemed had ever seen her car.

And now it was going to goddamn rain, which would no doubt wash away whatever footprints, signs of struggle, signs of . . . whatever, he hadn't caught.

His chest rose, and fell, and rose again as he straightened to stretch the stiffness from his back, and to remind himself that he wasn't Sherlock Holmes, deducing a man's weight, age, and occupation from tobacco ashes. Already there were five bands of volunteers, picked only two hours ago, searching the fields and the ridge. Twenty men in all. He himself had called the local farmers and had bullied promises from them to ride their own pastures, search their own streams and branches of Marda Creek. By tonight the state boys would be brought in. By tomorrow night someone would have to notify the Feds.

It didn't seem that Glenn's faith in him had been properly placed.

"Damn," he said tonelessly and set his hat back on, slapped a fist into a palm and hissed at the stinging that laced across the knuckles of his left hand. A shake of his head at his forgetfulness and he blew on the redness as he slid to the ground. There was no blood, and none had been spilled, but Thorny had screamed and thrown wild punches one too many times for Sandera's already exasperated temper, and he had shoved the kid hard against the cell's cinder block wall, tripping over the cot in the process and hitting the wall as well, making him look the damned fool. Then and now he was sorry it hadn't been the kid's chin. As it was, the son of a bitch had cackled hysterically, and told him to watch out, the ghost was gonna get him because the ghost was loose and pissed.

At least, he thought, as he made his way to the driver's door, there hadn't been a crack about police brutality. That would have gotten the kid a night in Hunter General. And him a week's suspension, if not outright canned.

He coughed.

He spat.

As he slid into his seat, he looked up the street and saw a man walking away from him, down the center line in the middle of the next block.

"Son of a *bitch*," he said, but couldn't move. He didn't believe it.

There was shifting shadow, and dimming light, the wide-crowned chestnuts lining the street waggling their lower branches as the wind gusted, and settled, and gusted again. The lawns were empty. No one sat on their porches. The windows were blind with curtains; a wind-chime rattled instead of sang.

The man was tall, slender, and blond; his stride was steady, his shoulders slightly swaying; he wore a pink shirt with a white collar, grey trousers, and he carried a gun in each hand.

When Robbie fired the ignition, the man turned around with no haste at all, and he recognized Jimmy Hale.

"Holy Jesus!"

Hale smiled and kept walking. Backward. Bobbing his head as if he were humming to himself.

Sandera unholstered his revolver, glanced down to be sure its chambers were loaded.

Oh my god.

Then he reached for the mike, taking care not to lean over, and brought it to his mouth as he switched on the loudspeaker bolted to the cruiser's roof.

"Hold it right there, Hale," he said, his voice magnified to thunder as the wind leapt from the trees and scattered leaves from the gutters.

The young man didn't stop.

"Put the guns down."

Hale raised his right arm, raised an eyebrow, and fired into the air.

"Put 'em down, Hale. Now!"

And the car jerked forward, settled and rolled slowly, as he felt the saliva freeze in his mouth, felt a chill shudder in waves through his chest. He switched to the radio and swallowed a yelp when Gorder loudly demanded to know who the hell had interrupted his transmission.

"Pete, it's Robbie."

"Good for you. What's the trouble?"

"You better get hold of the sheriff. You're not going to believe this but—"

Hale aimed carefully at the patrol car and fired once. Robbie ducked, and the right side of the windshield webbed around a sudden hole.

"Robbie!"

Without the luxury of thought, Sandera fired back, his left hand out the driver's window, his elbow propped on the door. "Put it *down!*" Fired again quickly, and Hale jerked sideways, staggered, came up with his right shoulder a sudden gleaming red. "Put it *down!*"

"Robbie, what the hell's—"

Hale sneered and shouted and fired, and Sandera didn't know why the man didn't run, why he just stood there like a target, like some kind of idiot cowboy, high noon in Hunter, the stupid son of a bitch; and he returned fire almost reluctantly and hit him high on the right leg but the man still didn't go down, he only fired again, once with each gun, still smiling, not even staggering, until the cruiser reached the intersection and Hale dropped to his knees and began shooting as fast as he could, driving Robbie to slam on the brakes and open the door and drop from his seat to the street, listening to glass shatter, hearing metal puncture, suddenly popping over the door to fire once, just as the man stumbled back to his feet.

The impact staggered Hale back two paces.

Sandera yelled, "Enough, Jimmy! You're hurt! Put it down, put it down!"

Hale closed his eyes.

Then Robbie saw the dark rosebud in his forehead, just above his left eye. "Oh shit," he whispered as Hale toppled onto his back, the hollow *crack* of skull meeting blacktop carried to him by the wind.

He waited.

Hale didn't move.

A leaf skipped from a maple and spiraled onto the young man's chest.

He waited.

The radio stuttered.

He reached in and took the mike, stared at it for a moment before switching off the loudspeaker and telling Pete Gorder to send an ambulance to Field and Grange because he'd just killed Jimmy Hale. Then he dropped to the seat and waited for the sirens.

"I'm so sorry," Glenn whispered into the summer-smell of Marj's hair. "Honest to god, love, I'm sorry."

Her cheek rested on his shoulder. "I didn't know. I swear I didn't know."

"I know. And everyone else will too."

"But Grover—"

"—will have a hard time designing a doghouse from now on. I swear to you, Marjory, he'll pay. I swear it."

She lifted her head.

He kissed her.

"Will you forgive me?" he said, his lips brushing hers.

"Yes."

"Do you believe me when I tell you that I'll do everything I can to make sure you won't be hurt?"

She nodded.

He kissed her.

She squeezed him until she wept.

When Lake Road passes under the traffic light on Springwood Avenue, its name changes to Old Farm Road in memory of what had been there before the town had grown. The blocks become longer, the street somewhat wider as it enters the first development established in town. The trees aren't quite as high as in the old part of Hunter, the shrubs more exact, the lawns more even and less inclined to weeds. The acreage for each place is impressive, however, and a white Dutch Colonial takes up most of one corner.

On the second floor, in back, the master bedroom is vast, and Kim Raddock used it as often as she dared without being called a whore. Besides being nobody's business but her own, it wasn't her fault, she believed, that she enjoyed sex now and then; it wasn't her fault that her former husband had dumped her and her daughter to live with a virtual child in Tennessee; it wasn't her fault that Nate Pigeon attracted her on a level she used to think was beneath her.

She preferred to call it primal.

And when she was slick with perspiration, her hair drenched, her legs aching, the sheets soaked and stained and half fallen to the floor, she gulped for air and pushed him off her. Gently. Very gently. His moods were hard to gauge, and when he was angry he tended to hurt her. No bruises. No punches. A grip here, a pinch there, a look that was more damaging than any fist he could use.

After much twisting and grunting, she bunched a pillow beneath her back and lit a cigarette.

Nate lay on his stomach, his head cradled on his arms.

"You know," he said, voice partially muffled, "one of these days you're gonna kill me."

She smiled at the top of his head. "No such luck, lover. You won't get away from me that easily."

He grunted; it might have been a laugh.

The room was white and gold, the king-size bed the same, and the white curtains on the floor-to-ceiling windows darkened as sunlight slipped away behind the clouds. The molded double doors that led to the hallway were closed. Cool air breezed down from hidden grates in the ceiling's corners.

She watched the smoke swirl away.

Nate groaned and stretched and cradled his head again.

"You have a hairy ass, you know that?" she said. And he was pale, always pale, never taking the sun, never going swimming, hating it when someone even mentioned sailing or boating or having a picnic on the Spit. "I mean, I think you have more hair on your cheeks than you do on your face."

He turned his head toward her. "Thanks. I think."

She inhaled, blew smoke, watched it swirl and vanish. "That's not a complaint. It's . . . it's you, you know? It's what makes you special."

"A hairy ass makes me special?" He closed his eyes briefly. "Swell. You can put that on my headstone."

She grabbed his shoulder, dug in her nails, and bared her teeth when he tried to pull away. "Don't," she said tightly. "Don't you dare talk about dying."

He pushed himself quickly up on one elbow. "Hey, Kim, take it easy." His free hand covered hers and removed it carefully from his shoulder. "I was only kidding." He blew on the red marks that puckered his skin. "Jesus."

She felt her lower lip begin to tremble, held it still with her teeth. "I'm sorry."

"It's okay."

The cigarette was stubbed out in a crystal ashtray, and she folded her arms over her chest, grabbing her shoulders, staring at the curtains. "I'm cold."

"I'll warm you up. Just give me a minute."

"No, Nate, I'm cold." A blanket had been thrust to the foot of the bed, and she tucked her feet under it, as gooseflesh pimpled her thighs. Her knees were red. Her stomach began to hurt. "I'm cold."

He sat up then, crossed his legs Indian-style, and reached out for her, but she shook her head and looked away. "I don't get it," he said. "You said you were cold."

"I feel like I'm dead," she whispered.

"Hey, Kim, knock it off."

She shook her head again, then stared at the white telephone on the nightstand. "I've been on that thing for hours. My ear is ready to fall off. Do you have any idea how many hours I've been on that thing?" She looked at him sideways. "Hundreds. It seems like hundreds. And do you know what they say? 'Sorry, Kim, I haven't seen her today.' 'Sorry, Mrs. Raddock, we're doing all we can, but she might have run off because she was afraid she'd get caught.'" A dry racking laugh. "Caught? My Beverly? Hell, those damned cops couldn't catch her if she robbed the bank naked in the middle of the day."

Nate eased away from her, one inch, another.

"I don't know where she is, you know. I haven't the faintest idea where my daughter is. And do you know something? The only time I cried is when I dropped that crap on Erskine's desk. And do you know why?"

Nate mumbled something, it may have been, "No."

"Because I was so goddamned *embarrassed!* Can you believe it? I was *embarrassed!*"

She could tell by the way he contrived not to meet her gaze that he was uncomfortable. She didn't care. She didn't care if he loved her (which she knew damned well he didn't), she didn't care if he only liked her (which she doubted and always forgot), and she didn't care if he was running from her bed straight to Loretta Frennel's (which she knew damned well he was). He thought he was using her, using her money, using her house, which only proved how asinine a vain and stupid man could be.

She lowered her arms and shifted to sit in front of him, her legs out, her gaze forcing him finally to lift his head and see her.

"Does that make me a slut?"

"What?" He was comical in his confusion. "What, crying because you're embarrassed?"

"No." She took his right hand, held it when he tugged, and pressed it to her breast. "Because I'm here in bed with you instead of looking for Bev."

He squirmed forward, straightening his legs, lifting hers until they rested across his thighs. "You can't be everywhere at once, Kim. You have to rest sometime or you'll be no good to anyone, least of all her."

She leaned into his hand, leaned close to his face, searching his eyes for sarcasm, testing his breath for hypocrisy before letting herself smile and sliding up his legs until she was able to squeeze his waist with her thighs and feel the perspiration run again.

"You're a real cold sonofabitch, you know that, Pigeon?"

Before he could answer she kissed him, as hard as she could, hearing his startled protest the moment she tasted his blood, leaning her head back to look him in the eyes and dare him to stop her now, dare him to pull away, dare him to tell her it was late and he had to get back to his goddamned dusty typewriter before he lost his goddamn inspiration, dare him to tell her that Beverly was all right when she knew damned well she was dead, out in the goddamn woods somewhere, probably raped and torn apart, and her mother was in her king-size silk-sheeted bed fucking a man who pretended to be a writer when all he was was a whore with a bankbook between his legs.

She didn't love him.

She didn't like him.

But right now she needed him, so she kissed him again, tenderly, longingly, until the double doors opened and someone gasped, then began to laugh.

Nate jumped as if an electric wire had touched his back, scrambling to yank the sheet over his lap.

Kim only stared, not sure if she should scream or cry.

"Well," Beverly said cheerfully, "do you mind if I come home?"

Kim continued to gape, flustered, embarrassed, finally leaping off the mattress and running to her daughter, who deftly swept up a nightgown from the vanity bench and tossed it into her arms.

"My god," Kim said, reaching out, drawing back, wishing to hell she could breathe. "My god, my god, where have you been? All this time . . . are you all right? Oh my god, Beverly Ann, are you all right?"

And she wept. And grinned. And didn't care what her daughter thought of the man cringing in the bed. Didn't care that the girl had been gone so long without calling. There were no scratches, no bruises, no bandages—

"Oh god, Beverly Ann, Jesus, what happened to you?"

Beverly laid her hands on her shoulders and kissed her

cheek, smiling broadly. "You get dressed first. I'll tell you all about it. I'll meet you downstairs." She looked at Nate. "Alone. I have a call to make."

"Okay, okay, whatever you say." Hating the tears she couldn't stop and the knot in her throat and the lead in her chest and the ice in her belly. "I'll be down in a second. You're calling the police?"

"No," Beverly said. "I have to call Bern. I . . . he'll be worried sick." She smiled softly. "I think he loves me. He has to know."

The doors closed without a sound.

Kim spun around and threw out her arms. "Jesus, Nate, she's back!"

Laughing, skipping, she raced across the room and threw herself onto the bed, knocking him onto his back. "Don't you dare get dressed," she whispered in his ear, tickling him, kissing him wherever her lips lighted. "Don't you dare move, you bastard, you hear me? Don't you dare move. I'll find out what the hell happened, and then I'll be right back. And then, you little prick, you're going to screw me to the wall."

Glenn held her until Gorder pounded on the door, yelling the news that Sandera had shot down Hale. Marjory backed away, eased around the desk and dropped into his chair while Glenn yanked on the knob and calmed the dispatcher down. He could hear Audrey whistling. Aster was on the telephone, covered the receiver and called out, "Beverly Raddock's home. She just walked in the door."

Glenn stared from one to the other, not sure if he should smile, remain sober, do a jig, collapse. Finally he took a deep breath and ordered Aster to Kim's house to find out what had happened, told Pete to send Plowright over to assist Robbie until he himself could get there, and backed into his office, shaking his head.

"Incredible," he said.

Marjory grinned up at him. "One of your banner days."

He wasn't sure. A man was dead, but a girl had returned from the all-but-dead in the minds of those who'd been searching for her. Nancy had her car. Bern would stop moping. And if Cheryl had hit a home run and Dory hadn't gotten into a fight with her, he couldn't think of anything left to complain about.

"I just don't believe it. I . . . just don't believe it." He reached over the desk for his gunbelt. "I'll have to go out for a while, hon."

"That's all right," she said. "I think . . . I don't know, but I think maybe Hawkwood deserves to die." Then she held up a warning finger. "It doesn't mean I won't stop trying, though, Glenn."

He grinned. "That's okay by me. If you had, I would have taken you straight to a shrink."

She laughed.

He winked. "Y'know, this is getting to be like one of Cheryl's happy dreams." And when Marj frowned puzzlement, he explained the advice he'd given her and Dory the other day, chuckling now at the simplicity of it.

"Fly?" Marj said. "You dream that you fly?"

"Did," he corrected, and grabbed up his hat. "But it doesn't matter. If it works, who cares? At least they'll be getting their sleep."

Marj picked up a pencil, tapped it against her chin. "Will you be long?"

"I doubt it."

"Mind if I wait?"

"I'll be busy when I get back."

"I don't care."

He blew her a kiss. "Then stick around. I'll hurry."

And thought *damn but I love her* as he stepped into the outer office just as the door slammed behind Aster.

"Happy dreams?" Gorder said, close to smirking.

"Pete, it isn't nice to eavesdrop."

Gorder spread his hands. "Who's eavesdropping? You were practically shouting." He laughed and put a match to his cigar. "Besides, that isn't all so farfetched, y'know."

"What isn't?" he asked, knowing he shouldn't, hoping to forestall a lecture by moving toward the exit.

"Controlling your moods and stuff with dreams," the dispatcher said, raising his voice. "'Ain't you never had a dream that came true?"

"Not so I remember," he answered.

something bad

"Audrey, did Ollworth come for his kid yet?"

"No," she said.

"Call him again. If he isn't here in five minutes, throw the bum in the gutter."

"Well, they do," Gorder insisted as the radio hissed to life. "And sometimes they come true before they come true."

Glenn exchanged amused looks with Audrey—

something bad, daddy

—and hurried around the side to his car in the back lot. Marj was at the window, and he waved as he got in, blew her another kiss, and saluted as he left.

He'd been wishing for a normal day, a normal start to the weekend, but the way things had turned out, abnormal wasn't turning out so bad either.

Mars stood at the front door and barked, lowered his head and growled, backed away, barked again.

Trace stood in the kitchen doorway, an unloaded shotgun in his hands. "What?"

The dog bared its fangs, and barked once.

"What?" he demanded.

Slowly Mars turned and looked at him, turned back to the door and sat down. And barked.

Loretta marched into the hospital, glowering at the receptionist, daring her to stop her as she veered through the lobby to the corridor that would take her to Hugh. Enough was enough. Doctor Milrosse could huff and blather all he wanted, but she was taking her husband home. If all he was going to do was lie there, eating money, breathing money, taking up space, she could manage just as well in their own house. Besides, Hugh was terrified of hospitals, and staying a week in one couldn't be doing him a damn bit a good. Probably it was making him worse. Giving him dreams. Giving him ideas about death and dying and making him weaker than he would be if he were in her care. It couldn't be good for him. It damned well wasn't good for him, and as she rounded the corner and headed for the nurse's station, her heels sounded like whip-cracks, her fingers began to snap, and Doctor Milrosse himself looked up and smiled just as she reached him, handed her a sheet of paper before she could say a word, and told her that all was well at last, that Hugh was already dressed and waiting for her in his room. She almost argued, almost accused him of lying, instead snatched the release form from his hand and continued to march, not caring that the nurses glared at her for the noise, not bothering to check the other patients as she usually did, to see which had survived, which had moved, which beds had been stripped to make room for someone else. And at the door she paused, took a breath, and pushed in, and knew she had to be dizzy from the heat or too furious to see straight or too astonished to believe her senses—he stood at the window, fifteen pounds lighter, his clothes slightly baggy, his face leaner, his arms and chest more muscular, his smile more tender when he suggested they hurry because it damned sure looked like rain.

"Hugh?"

He took her shoulder, drew her close, held her snugly and whispered in her ear, darted a tongue at her lobe that made her squirm and giggle and throw her arms around his neck and draw his lips to hers, kissing him harder and more fervently than she'd done in months, drawing back in amazement when she felt how ready he already was and kidding him about losing it before they got home. He grinned. He kissed her again. He suggested that if they didn't hurry, either the rain would dampen his ardor forever or he'd have to lock the door and let the tight-assed nurses in this place hear a thing or two, or three, or four. And Loretta, somewhat lightheaded from her swing from rage to delight, held him more tightly, snuggling her cheek against his while she thought of all the time she'd wasted with assholes like Nate Pigeon, feeling an abrupt wash of remorse bring tears and let them loose, feeling an abrupt prayer for redemption bring sobs that nearly choked her, feeling his arms and his breath and his hands and his legs and pulling away, breathless, to shake her head and grin when he asked her if she were all right, reassure him that she never felt better in her life and they'd better not linger or tightass Milrosse would think of another reason why Hugh should spend just one more night, in observation, on the machines. Hugh agreed. Loretta kissed him on both cheeks, wiped the tears from her face with the backs of her hands, and turned toward the door just as her husband said, "Did he come yet, Loretta?"

Nancy lay on the hammock with her hands cupped behind her head, her legs dangling to either side, rocking her gently. From Bern's window she could hear raucous music, deliberately cranked up to annoy her. But today she didn't mind. Mom had just called with the good news about Beverly, there had been an actual honest to god shootout in town, and tonight Brady Jones was going to call her for a date. It had to be for a date. And though she was nervous, she couldn't quite hold on to the fact that it was real, that he'd really talked to her and asked her permission, for heaven's sake, to get back in touch.

If she was going to be honest about it, it made no sense.

If she was going to be more honest about it, she hadn't even thought of him for well over a year. When he'd attended the high school, he had just . . . been there. A not quite hunk who really didn't interest her except that once in a while she would run into him in the school hall and remember his name. Then he was gone, and forgotten, and not even Bern had talked about him since.

So why did *he* want to see *her?*

There had to be a catch.

Maybe Thorny had barfed up some lies about her, slimy lies about her, telling him she did it, all the time, with anyone, something like that. She wouldn't be surprised. Thorny was capable of just about anything when he couldn't get what he wanted. But if that was true, it didn't say much for Brady, did it. Wrong. It said tons about Brady Jones, and none of it good.

No. She didn't think that was true because nothing Brady had said or done the other day sent her warning signals, and she knew she was getting damned good at recognizing them. Vorssen, the pig, gave her more practice than she wanted.

The music was turned down; she could hear her brother singing. Bad. Godawful. She giggled and shouted, "Are you dying or what?"

"Drop," he yelled back.

"You wish."

"Damn right."

So why in god's name did Brady Jones want to see her?

She gave up and rocked herself, watched the lake darken from sky blue to cloud gray. The wind had settled itself to a steady cool breeze that chilled her pleasantly. Tiny waves more like ripples moved away from the dock toward the Spit. The sailboats sped now, bellies filled and hulls leaving white wakes that rocked the float at the Spit, and she could imagine herself on the deck of one, stretched out, cool and warm at the same time, rocking side to side.

God.

Oh god.

"You want something to drink?"

She started and nearly toppled from the hammock, glared at her brother standing at the screen door. "No, I do not want something to drink, thank you."

"Whoa!" he said, backing away. "Sorry I asked."

"Don't be."

"Hey, what the hell's wrong with you?" He came out then and punched at the sky. "It's a great day, right? You got that thing—"

"Car, you creep."

"—and Bev's back okay and the bad guys are lying all over the streets of Hunter. What the hell more could you want?"

"You going over to see her?"

He shrugged, scanned the water with feigned nonchalance. "I don't know. Maybe. Gotta call first, though. Her mother's probably reaming her out for . . . whatever. Later. Maybe after supper."

She nodded knowingly. "Sure."

"Aunt Susan wants to know what we want for dinner."

Her eyes closed. "Oh please, give me a break. Let's talk Mom and Dad into taking us out instead."

She heard him laugh, heard him cross the porch to the far side. When she looked he had perched on the railing, heels hooked to steady him.

"You got a problem?"

"I don't know," he said.

"Boy, you sure don't know much, do you?"

He leaned back, rocked forward. "Nance, Aunt Susan told me you might go out tonight or something."

"Yeah, so?"

He laughed shortly. "Well, I was just nosy, that's all."

"Mind your own business."

"She told me you were going with Brady Jones, for god's sake."

She planted a foot on the floor to stop the hammock's motion and sat up, swung her left leg over and stared. "What's the matter with that?"

"Hey, c'mon, Nance."

"No." She stood. "I want to know what's wrong with that? Not that it's any of your business."

"Jesus," he said and looked away to the lake, looked back at her sideways. "I mean, that's an okay joke for Aunt Susan, I guess, but I know better, okay?"

She wanted to yell at him, chose to stomp inside instead and march into the kitchen. Aunt Susan wasn't there, but there were pots and a frying pan lined up on the counter. A jar of olives, a jar of sweet pickles, two jars of mustard. Her stomach lurched, but she decided that Bern would be on his own tonight. Whatever all this was for would serve him right.

In fact, she thought as she left the kitchen and headed for the staircase, she might even have a couple of suggestions for her aunt as to Bern's favorite foods.

At the top step she paused when she heard the screen door open and close and felt her brother staring up at her.

"What, damnit?" she said without looking around.

"Nance, I already told her about Brady."

She did turn then and grabbed the railing. "Oh really? And what did you tell her, smartass?"

"Nancy, it was in the paper, for Christ's sake!"

"What? What?"

He moved to the stairs and cupped the newel post with both hands. "He's dead. Don't you remember? He's dead."

She forced a harsh laugh. "Right." And would have continued on to her room had it not been for the way he looked at her—sad and fearful at the same time, as if he thought she was going crazy. It wasn't an act. She knew him too well. Just as she knew that Brady couldn't have died without her knowing it because she knew him in high school, and . . . that was two years ago.

"Can't be," she said, the words sprouting barbs that caught in her throat.

Bern started up toward her, but she waved him away.

"Can't be. I mean, it can't be, Bern. I *saw* him. I *talked* with him. Jesus, he rode me home on my bike, for Christ's sake."

It was his turn to sputter, to be doubtful, but a decisive shake of his head seemed to clear his mind. "Nance, he was killed in an automobile accident just before the end of his freshman year. He was buried out there." Slowly he lowered himself to the bottom step. "Why the hell," he said quietly, "do you think I don't want a damned car?"

A laugh escaped before she could stop it; a hand clamped against her mouth; her legs carried her back to the wall where she leaned, heavily, until her knees grew too weak to hold her up. She slid to the floor, could just see the top of his head down there, at the bottom.

"Bern, I talked to him on Wednesday."

He didn't move.

"He rode me back on my bike."

The head moved, only slightly.

"Cheryl and Dory saw him too." She shaded her eyes with one hand. "Dory wanted to know if I'd kissed him."

She watched him push himself up, backward, one step at a time, until he could see her; then he turned and rested his back against the wall, grabbed his knees with his hands as he stared at the banister.

"Maybe," he said, "it was the day."

Perplexed, she frowned.

"I mean, it was pretty bad, right? Vorssen made grab-ass at you, remember? You were pretty shook. I mean . . . you could have . . ." He didn't turn, but she saw his face, saw it twist as if he could twist sense of something that made none to him. "It could have been the day."

"I wasn't hallucinating or whatever," she said, confusion replaced by an unreasonable anger. "I touched him, okay? Goddamnit, I touched him!"

"Touch him all you want," he told her calmly. "Touch him all you want, he's still dead."

She waved her hands at him angrily and scrambled to her feet. "You're trying to mess my mind up, that's what you're doing," she snapped. "You're trying . . . I'll call his parents, damnit." She glared at him. "That'll do it, won't it? I call his parents and then you stop messing with my mind!"

"God, Nance," he said wearily, "they moved a year ago. They even gave the house to Mom to sell."

"Oh sure, right," she said. "Sure. And Mom . . ." She dropped onto the top step, stared down at the door. "Jesus." She swallowed and hugged herself. "Jesus, they used to live—"

"—in the Lincoln Log place," he finished for her. "Yeah."

She listened to the wind then, and felt it slip into the house, curl around her ankles, touch the round of her calves. "Bern," she whispered, "I *touched* him."

There was thunder, faint and distant.

Loretta felt as if she were going to fly.

One minute she was in her husband's arms, weeping in relief as he made verbal love to her and laughed and told her he adored her, and the next minute she was in the hallway, the sweat from the sun still drying on her arms and back, her eyes still working to adjust from the afternoon's glare.

A touch of heat stroke, she thought; that's all it is, a touch of heat stroke. Wishful thinking. Prayer. Wanting him back so badly that for a moment she'd had him, and all her sins forgiven.

And now she felt as if she were going to fly. As Doctor Milrosse explained so maddeningly patiently that Hugh had entered a sudden, inexplicable critical phase of his unknown ailment, her head filled with helium, her arms puffed and chilled, and her legs demanded release from the burden of holding her up. The man was lying. He had to be lying. If there had been no heart attack, no stroke, how the hell could he be critical, for god's sake? And Milrosse finally lowered his head and told her he didn't know. It happened sometimes, that's all, and he didn't know why and he didn't know how and they were, she had to believe him, doing all they could to bring him back. But she didn't believe him. She pushed him aside and strode into the room, still feeling like flying, and saw her husband in his bed. Tubes. The hiss of artificial breathing. Pallor. Bruises where the needles had struck and sucked and struck again. Swollen hands, wattled neck, the top of the green hospital gown pulled askew to expose a portion of his chest. Milrosse stepped in behind her. She felt him. She didn't turn. She walked to the side of the bed and barely heard the doctor explain that intravenous feeding often caused such swelling, that lack of exercise often resulted in such bruising, that he wished to hell he knew what the hell was wrong because only that morning Hugh had sat up and made a laughing pass at one of the nurses. Loretta spun around, fists at her waist, and she told him that her husband never, *ever*, made passes at other women.

The young doctor's eyes widened.

Loretta nodded sharply. "So tell me another, Doc."

His lips quivered.

She sneered and turned around.

And Hugh's left hand was there. Right there. Poised at her breast. IV tube dangling and swaying and surgical tape stained and swollen fingers grasping and she caught her breath and held it until the panic she abruptly felt subsided into relief. She took the hand gently and didn't flinch when it was cold.

"He knows I'm here," she said quietly.

"Mrs. Frennel." Cautious footsteps on the tile floor. "Mrs. Frennel, I think you'd better leave now. I'm going to have to do some tests and—"

"You're crazy." She leaned over. Hugh's eyes were still closed. "He knows I'm here."

"Mrs. Frennel, please. I'm going to need time to examine him, alone."

She refused, shaking her head curtly. She kissed the bulging knuckles and pressed the hand against her chest. "Hugh?" she whispered. "Hugh, it's me, baby. I'm here. It's all right, I'm here."

Milrosse stood at the foot of the bed. "Mrs. Frennel, I'm going to have to insist."

"Insist all you want, hon, I'm not leaving him again until he can walk out."

Hugh's eyelids danced, and opened, and Loretta smiled and cocked her head, and gasped when the hand broke from her grasp and snared her neck and pulled her down until she could smell his flesh and the medicine and the dry foul breath that slipped between his chapped and peeling lips.

"Hugh, honey, please, you're hurting me."

Milrosse hurried around the other side of the bed and reached for the arm to pull it away.

"Hugh, please, honey, please."

Hugh stared at her.

Milrosse called for a nurse and orderly, reached again and grabbed the arm, and yanked.

Loretta kept on smiling. Hugh was half awake, half dreaming, that's all it was, he was in the middle of a nightmare and didn't know it was her and as soon as he recognized her he'd stop trying to choke her. But it was hard to take a breath, and hard not to hit him, and harder still when he jerked his arm and she sprawled over him, yelling, kicking the IV stand against the wall, feeling Milrosse's hand beneath her, still gripping Hugh's arm and pinned now, pushing at her, kneeling on the bed, calling louder for assistance, while she felt again the urge to fly because it was, as she stared into her husband's dead eyes, the only way she was going to get out of this place alive.

"Hugh," she gasped.

And Hugh bit her mouth.

The brown car coasted to a stop, sputtered, and Glenn sat for a few seconds to summon calm before he left it, reached in and grabbed his hat, slapped it on, and looked around.

What sunlight remained as the clouds continued to thicken make the area less bright than sickly, the rooflines unnaturally sharp, the flowers unnaturally vivid; and the steady breeze had strengthened to a light and steady wind, underscoring the neighborhood's curious silence with a constant snakelike hissing from the foliage above him. Leaves killed by the heat crept along the pavement. Behind him, on Springwood, a car horn sounded, another responded.

The intersection had been blocked off in all directions by patrol cars parked at uneven angles across the streets, roof lights mutely flashing, deputies standing beside them to warn off the small knots of people drifting down the sidewalks, across the lawns. An ambulance from

Hunter General idled in the center, its back doors open, an attendant in the front seat, smoking a cigarette.

Glenn prayed there had been no complications. There should be excitement, buzzing, chatter, movement. Yet it was almost as if no one here knew what to do, how to behave. Like extras on a movie set, waiting for directions.

But the wind only blew and the people only drifted and a twig snapped under his boot, louder than it should have.

At last he spotted Sandera, leaning against the side of the ambulance with head down and bare, apparently listening to lank and ginger-haired Hank Plowright standing in front of him, lips and hands moving. Only Plowright noticed Glenn's approach, and he came toward him quickly, one hand on his gun, the other tucked in his hip pocket.

"Hank," Glenn greeted, and scanned the blacktop for the body.

"Sheriff."

"What's going on?"

The deputy winced. "Well, nothing, sir. We, uh, we decided to wait for you before . . . well, before we cleaned things up. That's okay, right?"

Glenn managed not to sigh aloud. Plowright had been on the force for only a year, too young and eager to make much of an impression other than that of a puppy who demanded its right to tangle up your feet. For him, problems of empty ticket books were on a par with robbing one of the local banks.

Plowright finally gestured toward the ambulance. "Hale's in there."

Glenn said nothing, eased past the man with a *good work* smile and walked over to the vehicle. Inside was a stretcher covered with a sheet stained with blood at head and waist. An intern sat beside it, looked up and nodded.

"Dead?" Glenn asked.

"Couldn't be more," the man answered. "Your man's kinda shook, though."

Glenn backed away and closed the doors carefully, moved around to the side and stood beside Sandera, who, when he glanced up, couldn't have been more pale had he been dead. "What's the problem, Robbie?" he asked gently.

Sandera yanked on the brim on his hat. "I killed him, Glenn. Jesus. I shot the sonofabitch three times. Here"—he stabbed his thigh—"here"—he jabbed his shoulder—"and goddamnit, here!" He pressed a thumb against his forehead before dropping his hand to his side.

Glenn saw the deputy's cruiser, windshield nearly shattered, hood pocked, left headlamp shattered. "He shot back?"

"He shot first."

"You all right?"

"Never hit me." He shuddered violently, straightened and grabbed Glenn's arm, pulled him to the front of the ambulance and pointed wordlessly at the ground, at spatters of dark blood, and a small pool of it to one side, a leaf trapped in its center. "He fell right there, Glenn. Right goddamn there. Jesus Christ, I shot him."

This was no time for speeches and bromides, so Glenn

touched his shoulder once, a signal to stay and stay calm, and walked slowly around the space left clear by the vehicles, knowing he was being watched, doing his best not to play to the crowds he heard whispering, once or twice calling softly. He resisted gazing at the trees, moved instead to the battered cruiser and poked his head inside. Blinked slowly. Stood, and grabbed at his hat to protect it from a sudden gust.

Sandera was a good man. He knew that. And he knew that good men didn't have gunfights every day, not even in Philadelphia, with shadows in the middle of the afternoon. Shadows that fought back. Shadows that bled. No cop of his acquaintance, either small town or big city, enjoyed using his weapon; that crap was saved for television and movies and the special effects men who had never seen a man die.

Hell, he thought a little sadly, and returned to Sandera. "C'mon, let's go back to the office."

The deputy looked at him, eyes pinched in a squint.

"Hank," Glenn summoned, lowering his voice as he headed for his car, "it's time to clear this mess up. Make sure Hawk has all the necessary pictures, talk to as many people as you can. See if you can find someone who saw Hale, saw where he came from. Maybe you can find out where he was hiding. Go house to house. Check the yards and garages, storage sheds, you know what I mean. And get somebody—no, go with the ambulance yourself. Make sure Hale gets to the morgue. Call me when you get there."

Plowright nodded enthusiastically, stammered something Glenn didn't understand, and damn near came to attention as he threw a sharp salute and hurried off.

Glenn watched him for a moment, not sure if he should smile, then beckoned to Robbie, who pushed off the ambulance as if he were an old man.

And when they were in the car, Glenn spotted John Wortan in the crowd, pushing back his cap to scratch at his head. His hand froze on the key, and he swallowed when Sandera slammed the door hard.

"Sheriff," Robbie said, "I shot him."

"It was self-defense, Robbie."

"Yeah. Yeah."

He turned the key, slapped the wheel, and recklessly maneuvered the car about until he could turn around. As he drove, he held up a hand for silence, glanced in the rear view mirror and saw the ambulance crawl through the congestion. Its lights were off. It stopped when Wortan stepped up to it and said something to the driver.

"I shot him."

"Deer," Glenn said.

"What?" Sandera gaped, astounded. "What the hell are you talking about? You trying to say this is like shooting a goddamn deer? You think a goddamn deer shot my vehicle full of holes? You—"

"No," Glenn interrupted, voice low and steady. "No, I didn't mean that."

"Then what are you talking about?"

He wasn't sure. And he didn't try to explain.

When he pulled up in at the parking lot behind his office, he could see someone sitting in his chair. Marjory. Damn, he'd forgotten about Marj waiting for him. He opened the door, got out, leaned his elbows on the roof and waited for Sandera. Then Glenn told him about the deer he had seen in the back of the farmer's truck. The conversation. Then the diner and the denial.

Color had returned in blotches to the man's face, and he shrugged. "So what does that have to do with the price of apples and my . . . Hale?"

"I don't know," he answered truthfully. "Beats me, but I don't know."

Sandera groaned and said, "I need a drink."

Glenn grinned and suggested they talk first, take the episode through step by step so their report would be coherent, all bases covered. Get it on paper. Cold paper. And forestalled a sputtered protest by walking away, listening to the man follow, stepping inside just as Marj left his office. As soon as she saw the look on his face, she ducked back inside and reappeared with her purse. He lifted an eyebrow. She glanced pointedly at Robbie as the deputy passed without acknowledging her, and Glenn lifted his hands.

The breeze became a wind that slapped against the window.

"I'm going to get the kids," she told him, touching his arm, kissing his cheek. "Cheryl's probably having fits already."

"Why?"

"Didn't you hear the thunder?"

He hadn't. He shook his head.

"Dory's probably teased her to tears by now."

He heard the long scrape of a chair across his office floor. "Okay," he said. "I'll get home as soon as I can."

Her look made him uneasy. "Anything wrong?"

He felt Audrey and Pete watching. "Not really," he

said, keeping his voice down. "Robbie's just shot his first man." He kissed her quickly. "I'll talk to him a while. And there's a ton of paperwork. You head on home, save the kids from the storm. I'll call, let you know when I'm free."

He patted the small of her back for reassurance, and waited until she was outside before he hurried into the office, sat down, and said, "Robbie, before you say anything, let me tell you you're not in trouble. It was self-defense, and this isn't one of those paranoid places where we have guys running around, trying to pin things on their own. Hale was a psycho. A killer. For god's sake, the man beat his own parents to death after raping his mother."

Sandera leaned back in the chair, legs stretched out, hands limp in his lap. He stared at the ceiling. "You ever shoot a man, Glenn?"

"No," he admitted. "I've had the gun out, I've popped a few in the air, but I've never . . . no."

Sandera pulled at his mustache, hard, harder, until he winced and dropped his hand. "It shits."

"You could have been killed yourself."

"I know. It still shits."

No kidding, he thought.

The room darkened swiftly, greylight relieved only when the ceiling lights in the outer office were switched on. They sank Robbie's face in shadow, but he could see the younger man start when thunder muttered, and muttered again.

He reached into a drawer and pulled out several blank forms he pushed across the desk. "Here."

The deputy looked at them, looked at Glenn.

"You fill them out, you go home, you do what you have to do. You come back on Monday."

"I'm not a baby, Glenn," Sandera said resentfully.

"No kidding." He tapped the papers. "That's why you get to fill these out before you leave."

A typewriter clacked; the radio sputtered.

"Right," Sandera said with a ghost of a grin. He scooped up the forms and rose, picked up his hat and walked carefully to the door. A look of gratitude over his shoulder Glenn acknowledged with a wink.

The telephone rang.

"Got it!" he called, and snatched up the receiver. "Sheriff's office, Erskine here."

"Sheriff, would you mind telling me just what the hell is going on down there?"

Glenn stared at the receiver. He recognized the voice—it was Don Milrosse from Hunter General, who because he lacked seniority had been put in charge of the morgue, such as it was. The man took his duties seriously, even though he seldom had to exercise them.

"Doctor," he said, "I'm afraid I don't—"

Milrosse wasn't listening. "I've got one semi-hysterical woman here whose husband can't make up his mind to die, a farmhand who's been chewed up by a baler for Christ's sake, the roads are packed with idiots coming here for the weekend just asking for accidents, and I can't afford to have one of my ambulances tied up for nothing."

Glenn covered the mouthpiece. "Robbie, in here!" He removed his hand. "Look, Doc, I don't have the slightest idea—"

"What are you people thinking of, anyway?"

259

"Doc," he said sternly. "Doc, if you would tell me what's wrong, I'll give you an answer, okay?"

Sandera paused on the threshold, a form in one hand, pen in another. Glenn waved him in, then said, "What? Repeat that, please. I didn't get it."

Milrosse snorted. "Of course not. And you're not getting another ambulance, either, until I'm positive there's someone to put in it."

Glenn stiffened. "There was someone in it, Doc. Jimmy Hale. And he was dead."

"I say again, Sheriff, there was no one in the ambulance when it arrived. No corpse. No injured victim. No blood. Just a poor slob in one of your uniforms who looks like he's ready for one hell of a long vacation. He says you sent him here. You have that much manpower, Sheriff, that you can waste a deputy's time like that?"

"Now hang on, Doc," Glenn said, "there's something wrong here. I saw—"

"Damn right there's something wrong. And as soon as I get things cleared up here, I'm going to find out exactly what it is, and then I'm going to have your goddamned badge!"

Glenn opened his mouth to retort, scowled when the receiver slammed down on the other end, and threw his own into its cradle. "Pete!" he yelled. Then, to Sandera, "Plowright has screwed up." Gorder lumbered into the office, cigar snapping. "Get out to the hospital and find out what the hell happened to Hale's body. Milrosse says it never got there. Plowright claims I ordered him to ride back in an empty ambulance." He glared. "Find out, and bring me someone's scalp."

"I'll go," Sandera offered instantly.

"You stay." He waited until Pete left, bellowing at Audrey to take the radio, then pushed back his chair and turned so he could see the parking lot. The tree was in a frenzy, lashing at the wind, spilling leaves and twigs onto the blacktop and cars. Night's come early, he thought, and hoped Marj had reached the kids. Then he stood, shoving the chair away.

"Watch the phones," he ordered as he left the office.

"Hey, Glenn!"

"Watch the phones," he repeated. "I'm going out for a minute. I'll be right back." He paused at the door. "Do those forms right, Robbie. I'm going to use them to hang someone's ass."

He didn't take his car.

He trotted down to the corner, hesitated only a second and swung right, deliberately holding back from a dead run, refusing to think about anything but not tripping until he reached Field Street three blocks later. Then he stopped. Held his sides and gulped for air. Blinked a stinging drop of perspiration from his eye and walked west as fast as he could. Another three blocks, and he stepped off the pavement, wiped his face with a palm, glared at the sky, and stood in the middle of the empty intersection.

There was no blood.

None at all.

He hunkered down and traced the street's rough surface with one finger before kneeling.

No stains.

None at all.

The blacktop wasn't porous enough to have absorbed the blood he'd seen less than half an hour ago. And there was no sign that some queasy homeowner had washed it away with a hose.

He had seen it. He had smelled it. And now it was gone.

Impossible.

deer?

He started back for the office.

what deer you talking about, Glenn?

And when he hurried inside and slammed the door behind him, Audrey swiveled around the radio and Sandera stood in his doorway.

He tried to tell them what he'd found, what he hadn't found, and turned instead to the window. He opened the blinds and looked out at the street.

"Glenn?" Robbie said.

"I . . ." He was cold. Much too cold.

The telephone rang.

Don't answer it, he thought; just . . . don't answer it.

Sandera opened the flap and came through the gap. "Glenn, you gotta tell me what's wrong."

Nothing is wrong, he thought, except things aren't right. Things that can't be, are; things that were, aren't any longer.

The telephone rang.

"It's raining," he said.

A faint drizzle, barely seen, that stained the sidewalks dark brown and raised a stench from the tarmac. It struck the window with drops barely seen, startled pedestrians into holding up a palm or checking the lowering clouds or lingering in a doorway just to see if they weren't dreaming. The traffic didn't hurry. Windshield wipers remained in their wells more often than not.

Windshields abruptly streaked with color as the street-lamps flickered on and neon buzzed on and speckles of reflections began to gather in the street.

Sandera stood beside him. "You went to the corner?"

He nodded.

"And?"

Glenn's inhalation was halting, a struggle that ended when he opened his mouth deliberately wide and rocked his jaw side to side. "Nothing. I didn't see anything." He took hold of the cord and pulled the blinds up. Then he looked at Robbie. "I didn't see the blood."

Robbie said it without speaking: *impossible.*

"Sheriff?" Audrey said. "Sheriff, it's your wife."

"Later," he said dully. "Tell her I'll call her back later."

A trio of young women scurried past the office, heads bowed against the wind.

"Sheriff, I think you'd better take it."

Across the street, standing with his back to the window of a stationery store, was Reverend Zachiah, head bare and face in shadow. Glenn almost waved, but a station wagon intervened, and Audrey called him again.

The station wagon passed; the cleric was gone.

"Later, damnit!"

When she didn't respond, he looked impatiently over his shoulder.

"She says it's important," Audrey explained apologetically, pointing at a telephone on one of the desks. "Really important." Another apology, this time a shrug.

Sandera held his arm, let it go, and he walked slowly to the desk, picked up the receiver, and said, "Marj, I've got—"

"Glenn!"

He almost dropped it, held it with both hands. "What."

"Cheryl . . . Dory . . ."

"What? Where are they? What happened?"

"I don't know." He could hear the fight against weeping. "I don't know. Nothing happened. I don't know. I . . ."

Muffled voices then, and Bern came on the line.

"Dad?"

"Right here, pal. What's going on?"

"Dad?"

God, he thought, and sat on the desk's corner, shaking his head angrily when Sandera and Audrey looked anxiously at him. He could hear fear in his son's voice, something a great deal more than concern. In the background he heard Nancy; it sounded as if she was calling someone's name.

"Bern, what the hell—"

"Dad, it's crazy here," Bern said rapidly. "We can't find Pint and Dory, and Nancy says . . . Jesus, Nancy says she's seen a ghost."

"He's *not* a ghost!" Glenn heard his daughter shriek.

"Brady Jones, Dad," Bern said quietly. "She says she talked with Brady Jones."

Glenn rubbed his forehead, shoved the hand through his hair back over his ear. "Look, where are your sisters?"

"I don't know. Dad, you gotta get home. Now! Things are—"

The receiver changed hands again.

"Glenn?" It was Marj. "Glenn, I've called all over.

They weren't at the field, they didn't play ball like they were supposed to. Nobody's seen them all day. Glenn—"

"I'll be right there," he said.

"Glenn, please—"

"Damnit, I'll be right there!"

He hung up, sagged, gripped his knees and held them.

The telephone rang, and he jumped off the desk, backed away from it to the counter, then ran into his office for his hat and jacket. When he returned, Sandera was already ready to leave, and Audrey looked terrified.

"What!" he demanded.

"Sweet," she said, the receiver hard against her chest. "He wants to know . . . he wants to know what he's supposed to tell Mrs. Raddock about her daughter."

"But she's back," Sandera reminded her.

Audrey shook her head. "Sweet . . ." She held the receiver out, pleading, and Glenn grabbed it from her.

"Aster," he snarled, "what the bloody hell is going on out there?"

All he heard was a dial tone.

All he saw was a flash of lightning before thunder ripped above the building like a sheet tearing in the wind.

After that, there was nothing.

All the lights flared, and died.

Bern lay on his bed and listened to the storm.

Nancy and his mother were downstairs, feeding on each other's growing hysteria, and he couldn't take it any more. All they'd done since calling his father was yell at him, at each other, pacing through the lightning-fed rooms until, suddenly, the electricity failed and they'd screamed and clutched each other, and he'd fled.

The sheet was clammy.

Lightning bleached the posters he'd taped to his walls.

He listened for the rain, frowned when he heard none, but he didn't get up. There was no way he was going to go downstairs again, not until his father came home. He didn't know what to do, didn't know what to say, and the look in his mother's eyes had scared him to death.

He propped himself against the headboard, left foot tapping the wall nervously, right leg hanging off the mattress, swinging, kicking, swinging.

He ought to get up. He ought to throw on a coat, get a flashlight, and go find Cheryl and Dory. He'd forgotten all about their hiking expedition until his mother had said something about not finding them at the field. He tried to tell her when the phone lines went down, but she wouldn't listen. And Nancy was no better, babbling on and on about Brady Jones and losing her mind. He ought to get up. Pint was out there in the storm, probably near the ridge, screaming at every lightning bolt, shrieking at each peal of thunder, and Dory would be no help at all. No help. He was the only one. He ought to get up.

He did.

And he stood at the window, averting his face from the next flare of blue-white that let him see the whitecaps on the lake, the waves slapping against the dock, the trees that had lost all their color and had become solid black.

The door opened, hinges squeaking, as thunder deafened him, made him hunch his shoulders.

Aunt Susan came in. "Are you all right?"

A dark figure, and small, the white of her white blouse and shorts phosphorescent without casting a glow.

"Yeah," he said shakily. "It got a little hairy down there, that's all."

"They're afraid," she answered softly, and took another step. "I'd forgotten what these storms were like out here." She hugged herself and shivered. "Brutal."

"Sometimes, I guess." He lowered himself to the sill, felt the cold of the pane behind him. "The wind's up, though. It won't last long."

"Scary," she said.

He nodded. "Yeah, some."

"Very," she insisted.

He lifted a hand and nearly slipped off his perch. Her laugh was quiet, and friendly, and he could see her glancing around, examining the room. But he couldn't see her face. It was midnight outside, six hours before its time, and when she nudged his foot with a toe, he started, not realizing how close she'd come.

But he still couldn't see her face.

Thunder.

"At least," she said with a quick laugh, "I'm not on the road. I'd probably run up a tree."

He answered her laugh with one of his own, forced, uneasy, as she moved to stand beside him and look out toward the lake.

"God," she whispered.

He stared at the open doorway.

Lightning.

He closed his eyes.

Thunder.

She said, "It's times like this, you know, when I miss Wesley the most." Her hand floated, hovered, rested on his shoulder. "When storms like this came up, he used to laugh at me, talk to me like I was a kid or something. Every time. He would tell me, every time, that thunder can't hurt me, and as long as I don't stand in the middle of a field or stay in the water, I won't get hit by lightning." The hand gripped, and relaxed. Her voice quavered. "Christ, it isn't easy."

He had to look at her then, and exhaled sharply, felt his mouth remain open—while her left hand held his shoulder, her right had been unbuttoning her blouse. White skin and a line of shadow. A shimmering as her chest rose, and fell, and rose and caught, and fell. She still faced the lake, her profile steady as she shrugged the blouse off her right shoulder, used her right hand to slide it off her left.

Oh god, he thought, and couldn't move. He tried to push off the sill, but he couldn't move. And he couldn't take his gaze from the darklight that made her breasts seem larger, fuller, the sheen of perspiration on her skin more like moonlight than lightning when the lightning flashed again and she said, "It's not easy." Softly. Very softly. As her head turned slowly, and slowly she licked her upper lip and slowly shifted her hand from his shoulder to his chest and slowly worked at the top button until it was free and her hand was on his skin and he shivered and closed his eyes, and stiffened when she pressed into his side, his arm between her breasts, and her breath warm and sliding across his neck, his cheek, the lobe of his ear.

"Aunt Susan." A croak.

Her thigh moved against the hand he used to grip the sill's damp lip, moved across it, into it, pinching flesh against wood, until her left leg nudged it way between his and she pulled her right leg after it.

He couldn't see her face.

He swallowed. "Aunt Susan." And stared over her head at the doorway. He didn't dare look down. He didn't dare call out. If his mother saw him . . . if Nancy saw him . . . he didn't dare move and he didn't dare look and he bit the inside of his cheek as hard as he could when her other hand joined the first inside his shirt, unbuttoned to his waist though he couldn't remember when, and his stomach muscles jumped when her thumbs brushed across them, and his right knee jerked, and his throat filled with something that burned but not badly. "Aunt Susan, it's . . ."

She leaned into him, and he could feel her breasts against him.

Rain snapped at the window.

She seemed to stumble, and he grabbed her shoulders to prevent her from falling, snatched his hands away when she sighed, put them back on her upper arms and held her, tried to pin her, but couldn't push her away.

Her lips touched the hollow of his throat.

He could smell her hair, almost taste it, and a strand lightly tickled the underside of his chin.

"You don't know," she whispered, hands slipping around his sides, fingers spreading across his back. "You won't know for a long time, Bern."

"Know . . ." He swallowed. "Know what?"

She leaned her head back.

He couldn't see her face.

"What it's like." Her eyes. He could see her eyes, glistening as if they were diamonds, or filled with tears, or smiling.

He managed to shake his head. "I guess not."

Her tongue touched him; he started.

A whisper: "Do you make love with your girlfriend? Do you, Bern? Do you make love?"

Jesus. Oh Jesus. Please, Jesus, don't let this.

"I . . . no."

He could feel her breasts.

He could feel her stomach.

Rain lashed against the window.

She brought her left hand into the open and ran a finger down his chest, swirled it across his navel, ran it up again to his chin. "Never?"

Thunder.

He closed his eyes.

Jesus, please.

A whisper: "No."

The heel of her hand pressed against his buckle, and slid downward along the length of his zipper until she was able to cup him, and hold him, and take a deep breath that made him moan without wanting to, and shift without meaning to, and open his eyes at the next bolt that exploded on the ridge just above the black rock.

And he saw her face.

And screamed.

Kim stood in the open doorway, her negligee poor protection against the storm-cold wind that slammed inside, pressed the silk against her body, rattled a lampshade and flipped a magazine's pages. The rain wasn't quite a downpour, yet hard enough to thrum on the roof and bounce from the steps onto her bare feet. The entire block was dark, and she didn't doubt the whole town was as well. Nate Pigeon's car had vanished in the gloom, and she glared at the place where she'd last seen it, then glared at the sky and dared it to rain harder. Prayed that the cop who'd disrupted her celebration with her lover had somehow fallen into the creek, which would already be swollen by now, deep enough to drown the dumb son of a bitch.

She massaged her upper arms.

Nate had bolted the moment the deputy had left, mumbling something about seeing her later. Next week. He'd call. See you around.

She saw someone coming toward her through the rain.

A step back, and a one-eyed squint, and a man strode across the lawn, bent against the storm. For a moment she thought the cop had returned to apologize for getting her hopes up about Bev. Then the wind shifted direction, the rain parted, and she saw that he had no uniform, only a suit jacket drenched and dark, his pink shirt virtually invisible, white collar without tie.

He didn't look up.

She backed into the house and closed the door, reached out to turn the bolt, and leapt to one side when the door smashed open and the man stood there in the rain.

"What the hell do you want?" she demanded. "Get the hell out of here!"

He shook his head, raked back his hair. "Hello, Mrs. Raddock," he said. "Remember me?"

* * *

Glenn charged through the door, Sandera right behind him, and they were met by Marj and Nancy, holding candles. Before either could say a word, he heard Bern scream and flung himself up the stairs and around the corner. Too fast. He hit the opposite wall and had to throw out a hand to keep his balance. As he did, Bern staggered out of his bedroom, shirt open, feet bare. When he saw Glenn, he sagged against the frame and covered his face with his hands.

"Bern," Glenn said anxiously. He glanced into the room, let lightning show him it was empty. "Bern, you okay?"

Footsteps behind him.

"Yeah," Bern said, lifting his face, blinking hard. "Yeah."

Marj brought a candle, protecting its flame with a cupped hand. "What?" she asked timidly.

"A dream," Glenn told her. "Looks like he had a bad dream, that's all, don't panic." Then he took her elbow gently and led her back to the stairs. "Throw some cold water on your face, son," he said without looking around. "Change your shirt and come on down."

He heard a mumbled, "Right," and steadied his arm around Marj's waist. She leaned into him and trembled. He held her tighter. And once in the living room, he sat her on the couch before telling Nancy to dig up all the candles she could, Robbie would help her, he wanted light in here, as much light as they could muster. And something warm to drink.

"Aunt Susan's in the kitchen," Nancy said as she left. "She's already put the kettle on."

"Dory," Marj said weakly.

"It's okay," he assured her. "First I find out what's happened, then we'll go find them."

She looked up at him, cheeks hollowed by the candlelight, eyes red-rimmed and getting swollen. "You're thinking like a cop, Glenn. God, they're your daughters."

"At this point, thinking like a father isn't going to find them," he told her, hoping he didn't sound as cold as the words had felt on his lips. "For a change, having a cop for an old man may do them some good." He smiled. She made a poor attempt to respond. "It'll be okay. We'll—"

Lightning.

Marjory whimpered.

In less than five minutes there were candlesticks and saucers, two lunch plates and an old silver tray, and the light was strong and golden and the shadows on the walls had not been born in the wind. Marj and Nancy sat on the couch, Sandera and Bern stood by the door, and Susan bustled silently in and out of the room carrying steaming cups of tea, of coffee, and one cup of hot chocolate she'd made for herself.

Glenn wanted to scream at the time it took to get them settled, more than once started for the door to begin the search for the children without them. But each time he did, he looked at his wife and grabbed the reins and held himself and held, until the screaming faded.

"All right," he said at last. "One at a time. Too much time has been wasted already, so don't make a production, okay?"

"Glenn," Marjory cautioned.

He nodded. "Sorry. Just . . . tell me."

Lightning.

And she did, explaining how they were to be at the field, playing ball, then at home for supper. Nothing unusual, until she'd driven there to pick them up and found the field deserted. She didn't worry. There were friends. But none of the friends had seen them, not at all, not all day.

"That's because they weren't there," said Bern, pushing off the wall to stand behind the couch.

"I know that," she snapped. "Honestly, Bernard, haven't you been listening?"

"I mean, because they went hiking," he snapped back, glaring down at the top of her head.

She twisted around. "Hiking? What are you talking about? They didn't go hiking, for god's sake."

"Bern," Glenn said quietly, "how do you know?"

"They didn't!" Marj insisted.

"I saw them," Bern said. "This afternoon. After I got home."

Glenn listened then while the boy told them what Cheryl and Dory had said, and watched his wife swing from rage to terror, watched Bern grow more distressed as he realized his sisters had tricked him, had lied. And when he was finished, Glenn held up a palm before Marj could speak, held it while he closed his eyes and tried to force himself to think. But all that happened was an image of his children walking through the storm, trees falling around them, branches lashing at their heads. He grunted. The hand became a fist.

Happy dreams, he thought.

"Jesus Christ," he said aloud. Then he said to Sandera, "Robbie, make sure the first aid kit's still in the car, will you, and bring it here. Marj, check the bathrooms for one." When she leapt up, eyes wide as a startled deer's, he took her arms and whispered, "Just in case, okay? Just in case."

She nodded jerkily.

He smiled as best he could and let her go. "And change into something warm," he called, knowing nothing he could say would keep her in the house. "Bern, those old blankets in the garage. Get them. We may need them."

"What about me?" Susan asked.

"The telephone," he began.

"They're down," she reminded him. Then she looked to the window and saw the storm. "Maybe . . ."

He couldn't help a grin. "Maybe you should stay here. In case the phones come back and you can call around again. And have warm soup, food, dry clothes, stuff like that ready when we get back, okay?"

Her gratitude at once annoyed and relieved him, and she vanished into the hallway, popped back and blew him a kiss he returned with a simple nod.

"Daddy?"

He sat beside Nancy and hugged her around the shoulders. "Don't worry, we'll find them. If I know Dory, they haven't gotten very far. I'll bet they're holed up—"

"Daddy, what about Brady?"

It was her voice more than the words that made him look at her just as Sandera returned, a plastic raincoat over one arm—her face was taut with fear, near to breaking, and the violent shudders that rocked her against him made him groan in silence.

"Darling," he said, "Brady's—"

She pushed him away and backed into the corner, legs curled, clutching her ankles. "I touched him!" she said. "Goddamnit, I *touched* him!"

And Sandera said, "Jimmy Hale."

And Glenn thought *deer* just as Bern slammed the door open and said, "Dad, those cots? You know, the ones we kept under the blankets?"

He didn't speak.

Candlelight danced, streaks of dark on the walls that looked not at all like shadows.

"They're gone, Dad. They weren't there."

Enough, Glenn pleaded as he pushed heavily to his feet; dear God, enough, I can't think, I can't—

Marjory stood at the foot of the staircase, a first aid kit in one hand, the other pulling at her throat.

"What?" he asked, and gestured angrily at Bern to close the door before all the candles were blown out.

"I'm not sure," she said. She'd changed into jeans and a sweater, hiking boots on her feet, obviously changing her mind about remaining in the house during the search. "That bottle of sleeping pills . . ." She swayed, and Bern grabbed her. "The bottle's not there, Glenn. It was nearly full. Now it's gone."

The telephone rang.

He could see them then, falling apart in stages around him, cracks in facades and cracks in voices and hands beginning to scrub hands raw. He turned his back on them. He stared at the candles, shunted panic to a side-street, filled his lungs and held it. All right, he thought. All right. All right. One step. One step. Cheryl and Dory have a place somewhere. They have the pills. They're trying to make things better by dreaming better things.

Jesus Christ, Erskine, you're out of your goddamn mind.

He lowered his head and breathed through his mouth, one breath at a time, quick, shallow, slower, deeper. He swallowed a taste of acid and turned back to them, hoping his expression was one of confident command.

Susan came to the doorway, looked around and said, "That was for Nancy."

Nancy cowered, knees against her chest. "Who was it?"

"I don't know, sweetheart. He said to remind you about your date tonight, and then we were cut off." She shrugged nervously. "I thought the lines were down."

And Nancy screamed, and Marj ran to her and grabbed her and pulled her face into her shoulder while she wept and beat the armrest with a loose and weak fist.

Glenn looked at Sandera. "A nightmare," he said. "Today's turned into a goddamn nightmare."

"Get them back," Marj implored him over Nancy's sobbing. "Dear god, Glenn, get them back."

"It's Pint," Bern said then.

Scornfully, Glenn dismissed him with a glance, and told Susan to show Sandera where the flashlights were. They'd need them. All of them. In the woods it would be dark, too dark to see in spite of the lightning. And he called after them to bring all the slickers and raincoats they could find. And hats, if there were any. Anything else they could think of.

"Dad," Bern insisted, moving hesitantly around the couch.

"Marj, you're going to have to stay with Nancy."

Marj resisted, finally nodded when Nancy tried to curl and climb into her lap.

"Dad, listen to me!"

"Damnit, Bernard—"

Bern grabbed his arm, hard. "Damnit, it's Pint!"

something bad, daddy

They're all nuts, he thought, briefly finding despair; my god, they're . . .

what the hell deer you talking about, glenn

"Happy dreams," his son whispered, leading him to the window, rapping a pane with a knuckle. "Remember?"

"Sure," he said. He waved at the storm. "This is all her doing, right? We're in a dream, right? None of this is happening, right?" He yanked his arm free and glared. "What the hell are you talking about?"

deer you talking about

He shook his head. No. No, I am real and this is real and we're wasting time because Cheryl and Dory are out there right now in a goddamn—

Sandera flanked him on the other side. "Glenn," he said, keeping his voice low, glancing back at the women huddled on the couch. "Glenn, I shot Hale in the head. You saw him in the ambulance." He grabbed his elbow, shook it once, let it go. "He was *dead*, Glenn, now he's gone."

The telephone rang.

Nancy whimpered.

Glenn wanted to scream himself, to bring sanity back

to his house on the lake; but all he could do was push the two away from him and stalk into the hall, to the table midway toward the kitchen where the telephone sat.

And rang.

And Susan stood in the kitchen doorway, shadowed, arms up and palms pressed against the frame. She was naked. She was smiling.

There was lightning—her face was a skull, charred and smoking.

There was thunder, and she was at the table in her tennis whites, afraid to touch the receiver, hand out and snatched back and out again, until he eased past her and picked it up.

The line was dead.

A moan: "Oh god." He sagged against the wall and set the heels of his hands against his eyes, gripped his head. "Oh god." And lowered his hands and looked at his sister-in-law. "I just saw you naked," he said flatly.

"Too late," she answered with a quivering smile. "You lost that chance a long time ago."

"Sue, I'm not kidding."

Movement to his right, but he was too drained to move away, and nearly slumped to the floor when Marjory slid out of the dark, candlelight behind her. She seemed composed, and he wondered; she seemed calm, and he doubted. And he heard his own voice crack when he said, "I don't know . . . I don't know what's going on."

She said, "I think Bern is right."

"Marjory, for—"

She hushed him with her fingers, then ordered Susan into the kitchen to start getting the food together, took his hand and brought him back to the living room where, as Bern rolled up the blankets and Sandera handed out flashlights and rain gear, she reminded him of the nightmares, and Cheryl's earnestness in wishing things could be better, for her, for them all.

Happy dreams.

Marj tied a scarf over her head and nodded when Sandera told her quickly about Hale and the deer, and she suggested that Cheryl was trying to create a new place of her own, where she was a famous ballplayer and her older sister had a boyfriend and her father had no bad guys left who could hurt him. Bev had run away because Bev had hurt her brother.

"It can't happen," he told her, desperately wanting to believe it. "You can't change reality just by dreaming the change. It's impossible."

"You told them about your flying."

"My god, it's a trick, that's all. It's a stupid trick to get me to sleep." And he laughed as if trying to humor himself back to the way it had been this morning, when Hale had been disposed of and Beverly Raddock had returned and "Oh Jesus," he said, and thought: it was a trick.

Thunder.

He stared out the window.

Happy dreams.

something bad, daddy

"She knew," he told them, galvanizing himself, slapping on his hat. "I don't know how, but she knew Hale was coming." No; impossible. "And wherever she is, that"—and he pointed at the storm—"is scaring her half to death." Which brings Hale back from the dead, and sends Beverly off again, and who the hell knows what else?

Bern struggled into a poncho, swore when his arms didn't immediately find their holes. "Dad," he said, "how—"

"I don't know," he admitted. "Maybe we're just as nuts as we sound. But what else explains what's going on?"

Bern waved him silent. "That's not what I meant. I believe it. I think I do. But . . . so how do we tell what's real and what's not?"

Glenn didn't know, didn't want to think about it, wanted only to find his daughters and get them safely home. Once that was done, he would consider it all again. But not now.

The telephone rang.

"Don't answer it!" Nancy yelled, and pleaded with her mother not to leave her, not to go. Marjory soothed her then, caressed her hair, kissed her cheeks, reminded her that Susan would still be here as she helped the girl to her feet. Glenn and the others followed them into the kitchen, tested the flashlights, and listened as Bern told them again what Cheryl and Dory had told him that afternoon.

A secret place, Glenn decided; kids always have a secret place, and that's where they went. Maybe a cave in the hillside, or something they'd built on their own. He wouldn't be surprised. Cheryl was clever enough, and Dory strong enough, that a mansion wouldn't be beyond their capabilities.

Right.

He grinned mirthlessly.

He opened the kitchen door, closed it and told Robbie to check in with Audrey before they let the storm take them.

"Glenn, we're wasting time," Marj scolded.

"Just a minute, that's all," he said, tapping a hand against his leg, a foot on the floor, watching Nancy follow Susan around as if she were afraid her aunt would vanish.

Then Sandera returned on the run, shaking his head, handing over to Bern the first aid kit he carried. "I gotta get back," he said breathlessly.

"What?" Glenn demanded.

Sandera glanced at the others, and said, "Pete just found Mrs. Raddock. She's . . ." He looked around again. "She's dead, Glenn. Murdered."

"Oh shit," Glenn muttered. He should go; he was the sheriff. He should stay; he was a father. Sandera's expression gave him his answer. "Okay. Go. And tell Audrey to have the others keep an eye out for my daughters. Do not try to take Hale on your own, all right?"

"Hale?"

"Well, who the hell do you think it was?"

Sandera left with a hasty salute.

And Glenn automatically took a step to follow, slapped his hip, and said, "All right, let's go." There was no need to say anything else. He had no doubt that he would find the girls and find them safe; what he didn't know was what else he would find, out there in a world whose new god was a frightened child, a thought he immediately rejected with an angry grunt as he marched across the yard, gasping at the rain that lashed his face. He couldn't think like that. He didn't dare, neither for his sanity nor for his children. Think like a cop is what he had to do; anything else would lead him to disaster.

At the back he paused, beckoned the others to lean their heads toward him. "We don't have to stay together," he said loudly, above the wind. "We'll never find them if we're bunched up. But don't get out of sight of the flashlights, okay? As long as we can see them, we'll be fine. And when you find them, scream like hell."

Marjory nodded, leaned over and kissed him.

Bern only looked up at the slope, dark and changing, and wished he hadn't let his sisters go. It was stupid, him believing a story like that, and on an ordinary day he would have called them on it. Not that it mattered now, he thought glumly as he thrashed into the underbrush and felt the wet leaves and needles steal traction from his feet; not that it mattered.

His mother was to his left, his father already farther on and higher. He used the flashlight like a spear, stabbing into the brush even though he knew they weren't there, slicing through the foliage in hopes of finding a treehouse or platform Cheryl had knocked together from old wood.

Lightning crackled like dry wood on the hearth, and instantly there was thunder that made him hunch his shoulders, rolling across the hills, echoing and doubling back. The force of the rain neutralized whatever protection the leaves might have offered, and water more like ice found gaps in his collar and froze his spine, burned his chest. It was difficult to breathe, and he soon found himself gasping, spitting, continually wiping his eyes clear even though the poncho's hood had a beak that should have helped him.

He wasn't sure he completely understood all his mother had said about Cheryl and Dory and their dreams. But he believed it. He had been with his aunt in his bedroom, seducing him, while she'd been down in the kitchen. He had seen the blackened skull where her face should have been.

A fallen log tripped him. He fell to his hands and knees, and swore when the flashlight trapped his fingers beneath it. The light caught the rain, slashes of dead white.

Unless she really had been there. And had returned to the kitchen only after he'd shouted. Real upstairs, real downstairs; it made him dizzy trying to think.

"Cheryl!" One hand cupped the side of his mouth. "Pint! Dory!"

He went to his knees again when a bed of leaves slid out from under him, and he rolled onto his back, close to weeping with frustration. When a voice called his name, he answered and pushed onto his knees, saw a beam of pocked light waving and responded with his own.

He stood.

He swayed and climbed on, grabbing for branches to pull him upward, hissing at the sting and burn on the cold skin on his palms.

"Dory!"

Beverly.

A pine cone thudded against his back and he whirled, swinging his free arm wide.

God, was she back or wasn't she?

Lightning, distant, barely illuminating the trees.

Automatically he began to count the seconds to the thunder, reached three before it came, sounding somewhere behind him. The storm was sailing east.

"Cheryl, c'mon, it's me!"

A heavy tangle of laurel; he knelt down, jabbed the lower branches, knowing the kids weren't there, they couldn't be, not in this rain, but not wanting to be the one who had missed them if they were.

His name again, and he waved his light to prove he was still there, still moving, still all right. Then, when he saw the beam again, he realized he was being signaled. He ran. A foot against the bole of a whipping birch launched him upward and to his left, listening to the dull crackle of plastic around his ears, grunting when a branch lashed the backs of his knees. He fell again and crawled a dozen paces before standing. And running again. Seeing at last his mother leaning hard against a tree that was nothing more than a bole and a single branch.

"What?" he shouted.

She turned, saw him, and pointed to a spot above her.

When he reached her, he realized she'd been stopped by the creek bed, even now carrying only a desultory trickle of water.

"Does that lead somewhere?" she asked. "I can't get your father's attention."

"No, not really," he said. "It cuts across here for a while, then flattens out. There's nothing there."

"Oh god," she said, vainly dried her face with a forearm. "Oh god."

"Mom, are you okay?"

She nodded, and hoped he wouldn't see the lie. Her stomach was filled with bile, her throat dry from calling, and if she tried to stand now she would collapse, she knew it, and nothing was going to prevent her from climbing this goddamn hill. Nothing. Not even if her heart stopped.

"I'm all right," she told her son. "Just a little pooped, that's all. Not used to it."

"It's a bitch," he agreed.

She smiled, squinted up the slope and said, "Is the ridge much farther?" The dark had taken the trees, the increasingly infrequent lightning had taken away most of her reference points, and only the angle of the ground told her which direction she was moving.

"A hundred yards, maybe more," he answered. "I'm not sure."

She put a hand against his arm and pushed gently. "Go. I'll be okay."

His hesitation came close to breaking her, but she pushed him a second time and pushed herself clear of the tree, feet apart and knees locked until he finally smiled and moved away, following the edge of the depression. She watched him for a while, then used her flashlight to cut her a trail down the shallow bank and up the other side.

Her scarf was sodden, no protection at all, her hands so numb with wet and cold that a touch of a twig, a snap of a leaf made her grimace and want to cry. Her feet were numb and close to hurting. She could feel her nose running, could feel the occasional tear that ran with the rain down her cheeks and dripped and ran from her chin.

She sneezed.

Glenn was far on her left, his flashlight's beam winking at her as it touched a bole, swept a branch, and more than once she wanted to forge over there and let him hold her, if only so she wouldn't feel so alone. If only so she wouldn't think about today and Cheryl and happy dreams and nightmares.

It couldn't be, of course, and it was.

Stepping on a rock she stumbled, cried out at the fat needle that stabbed up her calf and toppled her into a cage of white birch, where she clung to the slippery bark until the pain faded.

It couldn't be; like the day Susan called her to give her the bad news—that their father had died quietly in his sleep the night before. Mother was already gone, a decade ago. Now she was alone, and she couldn't imagine it, couldn't believe that so much of what defined her past was no longer with her. It was, at first, inconceivable; it was, at first, terrifying, even though she was a parent herself, well past the age when a scrape or a bruise would have her crying on her father's shoulder.

It couldn't be, and it was.

As a child's innocent wish and will affected what was real, or what, until now, she'd always believed was real.

Suppose—no, she ordered as she whipped aside a shrub. Think like that and you'll never get out of bed in the morning.

Thunder without lightning.

She blinked the water from her eyes and saw the ridge just ahead, open, easier going, and she scrambled up the slope to reach it, to stand upright, to look at the sky and demand to know where her daughters were.

She was cold.

She wanted to go home.

She felt her skin turn to ice as she staggered south along the narrow trail, and saw Glenn waiting for her, arms at his sides, water pouring from his hat—a dark defeated figure against the clouds that showed streaks of sickly white and patches of leprous grey.

They embraced.

He shook his head.

They turned when Bern called them, saw him running, saw him fall.

Marj broke away and stumbled back toward him, dropped to her knees as Bern pushed himself up and grinned at her stupidly.

"I know where she is," he said, through the blood that ran from the gash in his brow.

Loretta felt the doctor's hand on her shoulder as she stood at the foot of the bed and stared at her husband.

"I'm sorry, Mrs. Frennel," Milrosse said. "He just never regained consciousness."

When the doorbell rang and someone pounding on the door echoed through the house, Nancy grabbed a carving knife from its place in a kitchen drawer and told her aunt not to answer it, please, don't go.

Susan glanced down the hall, trying to smile.

"Please," Nancy begged.

The doorbell rang.

"Nancy, we can't just . . . suppose it's that deputy?"

Nancy shook her head wildly. It wasn't Sandera. She knew it wasn't. He was out in the storm, trying to catch

. . . someone. She couldn't remember. Someone bad. And when Aunt Susan started for the hall, she raced ahead and blocked the way. With the knife.

"Nancy, for heaven's sake," Susan said sharply.

The doorbell, and the pounding.

"I'll go," she said.

No, she thought; don't answer it, it's Brady and he's going to take you away and he's dead don't answer it, use your head and don't go.

She stood in front of the door, sensing her aunt hovering in the hall.

Don't answer it.

The knife was warm in her grip, and she took hold of the knob, turned it, stepped away quickly as she yanked the door in.

"Oh thank god!" Beverly cried. "Thank god some-one's home!"

Trace prowled the kitchen restlessly, knocking a plate from the counter when his elbow passed too close, kicking aside a chair when it got in his way. He didn't care. The floor was strewn with filth, but it didn't matter. The bastard was coming. He knew it in the way the storm howled and thundered over the house, the way the rain found all the cracks in the roof and had stained the wallpaper in his bedroom, in the bathroom, and collected in quivering puddles on the floor in the upstairs hall.

Mars knew it too. The Great Dane sat in the middle of the living room, facing the front window, muzzle trembling, saliva in droplets falling to the rug. Every few seconds he would shift his weight from one paw to another, and growl so softly the sound was swallowed by the thunder.

Trace checked the rifle, the shotgun, made sure they were both loaded. Three times an hour he checked every window in the house to make sure they were locked, the curtains and drapes drawn. Every five minutes he tried to sit and wait, heel jumping, hands kneading, tongue testing the air as if he were a serpent. But it did him no good. Sit, thunder, stand and prowl; and watch the black dog stare at the window.

Any minute now.

Any minute that sonofabitch would try to get in, would try to kill him, and Trace was ready. He'd not tried to understand why the bastard had gone free, why all those high fancy lawyers and faggot judges had let him loose. Who cares? Out was out, and free was free, and dead was going to be dead damn soon if he had anything to say about it, and by Christ he would because he wasn't about to stand around like some limp-wristed, knee-jerk, bleeding heart and let Jimmy in and try to talk to him and understand him and give him a chance to redeem himself in the eyes of the law and the eyes of the Lord. The eyes were blind. Jimmy had poked them out and laughed in the doing.

Trace paused at the back door, checked to be sure the boards he'd nailed across it still held. They were damp. Lightning flickered around the edges, touched his undershirt with silver.

His arms were bare. The shirt he'd put on earlier in the day had long since been discarded—the sleeves were too tight, they didn't give him enough room, enough quickness, and he'd stripped it off, paying no heed to the way his skin turned clammy and the sweat stank and the muscles of his scrawny arms remained on the verge of cramping whenever he lifted more than a grimy hand.

Mars growled.

Trace hurried into the front room and stood to one side of the drapes, carefully pulled aside an edge and looked out at the street.

The rain had become a downpour, the wind shoving it aslant, and the gutters flooded and rushed like rapids as the storm drains on the corner became blocked with fallen leaves and twigs. The air was slightly lighter, but he still had to squint to see the house opposite, and the man walking head down, bent into the wind, passing beneath a willow and pausing, looking up, looking straight at him, looking down and moving on.

Trace grunted derision. He wasn't surprised that a preacher would be out on a day like today. They were nuts. All of them. Grinning about God as if God were their best friend, while all the time God was wiring electricity to the doorknobs and wielding bats against skulls and letting bastards like his grandson walk free in the world while his child was trapped in a sodden grave by Marda Creek. Stupid bastard. Sonofabitch. Not enough sense to come in out of the rain.

He grinned.

He turned to Mars and chuckled.

His cheek pressed against the pane as he strained to see the far corner, turned his head to look west and nearly pulled the drapes down from their rod.

"Stand," he whispered harshly.

Mars bared his teeth and stood, and was silent.

Men moved over there, furtively onto porches, one

ducking behind a hedge, and he was damned sure he'd spotted that spic with the mustache driving past in a car that didn't belong to the cops. They moved so fast, were gone so quickly, he was ready to believe it was the drumming rain, the soughing wind, that had tricked his eyes; grey ghosts, mocking phantoms, pretending to protect him when they couldn't even keep a fucking kid in jail.

The car drove quickly by the house left to right.

A growl of his own, and Trace tried to see the other end of the block, but a mist had risen from the street, from the gutter, and if other men were there as well, they were invisible—grey ghosts and mocking phantoms.

Mars growled and turned his head.

The ghosts were real.

Jimmy was on his way, and Trace released the drape and sprinted for the kitchen when he heard the crash of jars below his feet, in the cellar.

The ghosts were real.

And Mars bounded to the cellar door and started barking, and clawing at the wood, and snarling at the knob, and backing away, still snarling, when the knob began to turn.

Sandera cursed vigorously under his breath as he made his way cautiously across the back yard of the house that backed onto Trace's. It was bad enough he'd been so anxious that he'd forgotten his poncho; now he had to cut through a goddamned mine field of rusted appliances, bedsprings, the skeletons of discarded chairs. There were ordinances against things like this, and as soon as he was sure the old man was still safe, he was going to come back and write up a few dozen tickets.

He stifled a sneeze.

Lightning blinded him for a moment.

He squinted through the rain at the high, thick evergreen shrubs that served as a fence between the two properties and hoped to hell he'd be able to find some shelter in all that tangle.

And hesitated when he heard the unmistakable blast of a shotgun.

Shit! he thought, and ran.

A second discharge, a high-pitched screaming wail, and he threw himself at the natural fence shoulder first, broke through so easily he stumbled and nearly fell. Then he charged up to the back door and wasted no time knocking. He raised a foot, he lashed out, and the door splintered off its top hinge. Almost immediately he was inside and crouched, his gun out and sweeping side to side.

He froze, and whispered, "Dear Jesus," in the few seconds it took to understand what he saw:

a hallway was directly ahead, and in it sprawled the biggest dog he'd ever seen. It was covered and punctured by splinters from a ravaged cellar door, and most of its head was nothing more than running blood;

the kitchen itself was a shambles, and off to his right was a table. Trace lay on it, on his stomach, and over him stood a man in a torn pink shirt, who turned and grinned and lifted the bloody knife he held in his left hand.

I killed you, Sandera thought, wiping his face with a forearm; Jesus God, I already killed you!

Jimmy Hale glanced down at the body of his grandfather and said, "Three down, one to go."

Sandera fired.

With a grunt, Hale twisted away and dropped the knife as the bullet passed through his upper arm. "Damn," he said, and reached for the fallen blade.

Still without issuing a warning, Sandera fired again, knocking the man against the counter, spilling pots and pans to the floor. Hale gasped, straightened, then tried to stagger toward him, arm outstretched, fingers arched into trembling claws.

"Aw Jesus," Robbie whispered, and pulled the trigger as fast as he could, not aiming, just shooting, until the gun was empty and the front door was bashed in and what seemed like a score of cops rushed into the room, all shouting.

"I killed him," he whispered as he sagged against the doorframe.

"No shit," said Sweet Aster. "Looks like you blew off his fucking head."

"I killed him."

Aster put an arm around his shoulder.

"He's dead, Sweet. I killed him."

"Right," the man said, and led him to the back door. "So let's get back to the station, huh? We'll get you some dry clothes, give the sheriff a call."

Sandera nodded. "I killed him." Then he looked up and said, "Do you really think he's dead?"

Under a sky now shedding strips of cloud the cabin looked too small, canted in the back, dark-stained and abandoned. Around it the grassless earth had turned to mud; an old tree, several times lightning-blasted, had fallen into the clearing, the great bulb of its netted roots washed by the storm.

Glenn jammed his flashlight into a pocket and moved as swiftly as he could toward the front, Marj and Bern on either side, none of them speaking, all of them gasping, half bent, half shambling. He wanted to ask his son what this place was, how he knew about it, but thunder, too distant to be more than a disgruntled rumbling, forestalled him, and he decided that questions would have to wait. The moment he'd broken free of the woods he'd thought of the pills taken from the house, and he could see it in Marj's eyes: *how many had they taken?*

The door wouldn't give.

He stepped back and kicked it just above the latch, kicked it a second time and fell into his son's arms when it gave way. And they stood there. In the rain. Looking in.

Marj was the first to move, and he didn't stop her. He followed behind Bern, glancing around as he stepped in, at once grateful for the respite the cabin provided from the storm, and hating the man who'd built it and thus gave his children the shelter that had no doubt fanned their plans. The walls oozed water like sap, there were too many puddles to avoid, and snuggled close against a piecework fireplace were the cots, and Cheryl and Dory, lying on their stomachs, blankets and pillows half covering their heads.

Wrappers from cupcakes and candy were crumpled on the floor; two cans of soda, a pile of chocolate crumbs.

"Jesus," he said quietly.

Marj instantly went to Dory, yanked the blanket

aside, and turned her over, lifted her with a hand behind her head. She whispered, "Wake up, darling, wake up, it's Mommy, wake up."

Glenn went to Cheryl.

"Oh lord, Pint," he said, gently removing the blanket and taking her in his arms as he took her place on the cot. "Oh lord, you're a dope." He kissed the child's hair, her cheek, and slapped her lightly several times. "Come on, Pint, let's wake up, come on, the Braves are waiting."

Movement shifted his gaze to Bern, who stood in front of him, holding out his hand.

Glenn closed his eyes.

Dory moaned, and Marjory laughed and said, "Sleepy head, get it going, c'mon, darling, let's get it going."

The amber bottle was empty.

Glenn looked up. "How far is the road?"

"A couple of minutes. Not far." Bern pointed toward the door.

"Go. Flag someone down, get to a telephone, call the hospital and the office. Get someone up here. Now!"

"Dad?"

Glenn's hand was on Cheryl's chest, and he couldn't feel her heartbeat. "Go!" he ordered, and Bern was gone without a word.

Dory moaned.

Glenn's hand wouldn't stop shaking as he searched for a pulse, held her closer and listened for her heart, and heard nothing but the waning. The bottle lay on the floor. How many? he wondered; Jesus God, how many?

"Move it, Doreen," Marjory said, scolding, pleading, laughing at the same time. "Let's go, honey." She stood, the girl too large for her arms and not large at all, as she paced the cabin briskly, one hand slapping Dory's face hard, then harder, grinning at Glenn and winking and telling him, "Thank God," before saying, "Dory, come on, sweetheart, come on, come on."

On one of her passes she opened the door and let the wind in.

During another she tried to stand Dory up, but the child's legs still wouldn't hold her, though her arms grabbed Marj's waist.

He flopped Cheryl onto her stomach across his thighs and pried her mouth open with one hand, slid a forefinger over her tongue. "Toss it," he urged. "Damnit, Cheryl, toss it."

There was no shudder, no gagging, no reaction at all.

He stood as Marj said, "Glenn, what's the matter?" and carried the child into the open air. Held her away from him at arm's length and shook her once, shook her again, slammed her against his chest and started walking toward the path he saw leading west from the clearing.

"Glenn!"

He turned. Marj stood in the doorway, Dory still in her arms.

"Glenn!" It was a wail, and a beseeching, and she tried to run and nearly fell.

He slapped Cheryl's face and bent her double and slapped her again, used the finger again as deep as his knuckles would let it go; no reaction, none at all.

"Glenn!" was a shriek he heard as if it had been muffled by a pillow, a shriek he ignored as he stumbled with his daughter through the weeds and mud and saw the downward turn and took it and stumbled on. Glaring

at the face turned up to the rain, demanding it stop fooling, the party's over, the game's undone, and if she didn't answer him and answer him now he was going to give her a tanning she hadn't had in years.

"Glenn," from beside him, Marj peering fearfully at Cheryl from over Dory's shoulder.

"I don't know," he said at last.

And Dory threw up down her mother's back, began to cry, began to struggle. Marj lowered her gently to the ground, but Glenn kept on walking, talking to Cheryl, threatening her, telling her what an idiot she was for doing such a thing, how could she, did she think she was magic, did she think she had some power?

"Cheryl," he snapped. "Goddamnit, Cheryl, wake up!"

Another slap, and the rain stopped, and the wind died, and his left foot slid over the top of a rock and he fell backward, pressing his elbows close to his side, holding tightly to the girl who didn't move when he landed and there was fire and there was screaming and something in his chest exploded just before he heard the siren.

"Glenn, please," he heard a moment later. "Glenn, please, let her go."

He couldn't see, but he felt a tugging and a prodding and someone tried to pry his hands apart and someone tried to take his child; he couldn't see, but he could fight and he would not let her go; he couldn't see, and she was gone, yet his chest still held her weight and he shook his head, clenched his teeth, when someone tried to make him stand, tried to get him to his knees, tried to force his eyes open by pulling his eyebrows up.

"Please, Glenn, please."

All the way into the dark where nothing waited and nothing watched and nothing warmed him and nothing fed him, and nothing made sense when his eyes finally opened and he saw the pale green ceiling and through the window saw the stars and saw Marjory on the bed, by his hip, his hand in hers. Her face was long and pale, her hair disheveled, a thin white blanket around her shoulders.

Her eyes were dry, but she'd been crying.

"Oh god," he said.

And Marj whispered, "You tried."

VI

The dream, when it comes . . .

. . . the spectered shadow of a cloud . . .

THE sun was white, the water flaring, the dock too warm to touch without caution.

He sat on the edge with his trousers rolled up to his knees, his battered grey hat tugged low across his brow, and watched the ducks circle a blossoming lily pad in the cove. Far behind him, in the driveway, Susan's car throbbed its impatience, backfired, and muttered and was finally switched off.

There was no silence.

A jay scolded deep inside a maple's crown, there were boisterous swimmers off the Spit, and the reeds and weeds along the shoreline rustled dryly in the breeze; a pickup stuttered past, a cyclist with a radio, three girls on the road laughed and pushed and chattered; a crow called and a dog howled and sparrows fussed back on the lawn.

In his hand he held a red-streaked pebble he tossed up once in a while, judging it, weighing, until at last he laid it beside him on the last plank and nudged it with his thumb. Watched it wobble toward the edge. Snapped out his right hand, and missed it, and it fell, and the splash that it made shook his head and made him sigh.

Slow; too slow.

Christ, he thought, don't you know another song?

He moved his feet and felt the water cold against his skin. A finger like a wiper took the sweat from his forehead and flicked it into the lake. A pain in his stomach made him stiffen before it passed, and he knew he hadn't felt it, that it wasn't there, it wasn't real.

Old; too damned old.

"Dad?"

Laboriously his head swiveled, shoulders and neck protesting, and from the shadow beneath his hat brim he saw Bern on the road, Dory beside him, Beverly just behind, her face still marked with fading bruises and lacerations.

"Hi," he said.

Bern shifted uncomfortably side to side. "We're going. You sure you don't want to come?"

"I can see them just fine from here," he said, using his thumb to point to the Spit, and the beach where the Labor Day fireworks would be float-based this year. His son would be gone in a few days, plenty of time for goodbyes without the intrusion of strangers.

"You'll miss the party, Daddy," Dory protested. She wore a dark blue baseball cap, and orange shorts. "Lots of garbage food." She grinned and performed a quick and silly dance step. "We can eat 'til we barf."

Disgusted, her brother shoved her into Beverly's side. Glenn adjusted his hat lower. "No offense, but I'll pass. You guys go ahead, have a good time."

Bev waved shyly, and he smiled, and turned back to the water before the smile became a grimace and the grimace became a snarl.

Is she real, he asked the pearls that rose and fell on the water's surface; if you're so goddamned smart, can you answer that for me?

Jimmy Hale had abducted her when she'd picked him up on the road outside of town, beat her senseless with his fists and used her car to take him to her house. Kim had been raped, and strangled, then bludgeoned with the flat end of a hatchet he'd found in the garage. Bev had awakened, hot-wired the car, and in her half-deranged condition had driven away to find Bern. And found Nancy instead, who almost killed her with a knife.

But damnit, who is she?

A child on probation and about to lose her best friend, a small part of a smaller part of his mind answered softly, making him sigh. She had freely, even gladly, admitted holding the things Thorny had stolen from all those houses, but a lenient judge and Glenn's plea had kept her from a cell when it had been surmised that it had been Hale who'd left the messages on the wall and in Loretta's car.

The ducks signaled softly to each other and, single file, took their leave.

He watched them, then shifted his gaze back to his feet, distorted and swollen beneath the surface, even as he moved them to try to see them more clearly. His arms became rigid; he lifted himself from the dock and swung back and forth, seven times before he tired.

Slow; old.

The hill let loose its shadow, and the sun turned white to red, and a swarm of gnats mobbed the air until the bass began to feed and a bat swept from the trees and the stars came out without a moon.

His stomach grumbled.

He kicked the water.

Colored bulbs strung through the trees on the Spit reflected dimly on the lake; a bonfire on the sand; figures without shape or sex blended into shadow.

On the far side of the lake he noticed a spinning flash of red and blue that marked a cruiser on the road, moving slowly, without sirens, probably giving some kids a ride to the party. Sweet Aster, he decided; Plowright wouldn't have the nerve, and Pete was at the station, and Robbie was out with Susan, he had no idea where they'd gone.

A throat cleared behind him.

He lifted a shoulder to show that he'd heard.

Marj sat beside him, and did a great deal of unnecessary fussing with a small picnic basket covered with white linen. She flipped aside the linen and placed a bottle of wine and two glasses on the dock between them. There were sandwiches in there as well, and two salads covered with clear plastic wrapping. "The back of your neck is red as a beet," she chided gently, pushing her hair from her eyes as she peered across the lake. "You'll pay for that in the morning."

The house lights were out behind them, the late rising moon not yet ready to work, and in the dark he could barely see her, and saw her perfectly, every detail, braille without a touch.

"I want to quit," he said abruptly.

She laughed and punched his arm.

"I'm serious."

She laughed again. "Shut your mouth."

"Now wait a minute," he began.

She cut him off with a painful jab to his bicep, another to his hip. "I said shut your mouth, Erskine. You want me to get the spoon?" A loud exhalation, her hands slapped to her bare thighs, a survey of the cove and the lake and the boats gathering near the Spit. "I got a call from New York today. The corporation is going to leave me out of the lawsuit. Grover's on his own, the son of a bitch." She looked at him, unrepentant. "I hope he fries."

"At least," he said, trying to catch her spirit, "Suncrest didn't go under."

"Nope. At least not yet."

"It won't," he told her. "If it did, you and I wouldn't have anything to fight about anymore."

"Don't you believe it, Sheriff," she contradicted with a broad wink. "I'm not quite ready to get all that dull."

A firecracker popped and echoed.

Something large splashed in and out of the water at the back of the cove.

He wanted to ask her then how she could do it, laugh and drink and tease him, and get up every morning and not want to cut her throat, or rage through the forest, or tear the house down with her bare and bleeding hands; he wanted to ask her about her mourning, why she'd surrendered it so soon, why she'd accepted the grave and headstone and not lost her mind. And knew instantly it wasn't so, that he wasn't being at all fair. At odd times at night she wept without sound; at odd moments during the day she wept without drying the tears; when she saw Dory with Cheryl's cap on he'd seen her clench her fists so not to scream. She lost weight. She cut her hair. She let Susan do all the cooking and, for a while, Susan had managed all the cleaning as well.

"I should have known how," he confessed, hearing splashing and yelling and laughing from the Spit.

A few seconds passed before she touched him, let him go. "I shouldn't have had the bottle."

He grunted. He refused to continue the litany he had created, and for which she voiced all the proper responses. He should have done this and she should have done that, and why didn't they try this, and if only they had done that, and the flagellation had been such that at the end of July Bern had finally lost his temper and threatened to move out because he couldn't stand it any longer, they were killing the house and him and why the hell didn't they just stop it and let themselves alone?

Glenn had almost hit him.

Marjory had left the room.

And Nancy had called from the hospital to ask if anyone remembered that she was there, and awfully lonely, none of the doctors were any fun at all.

She was still there, improving daily, and Glenn had visited her that afternoon and promised to bring her home the first thing Monday morning. Her therapy had been declared successful by men who hadn't been there.

"I'm not crazy," she had told him. "I'm not crazy anymore."

"Jesus," he'd answered, and embraced her for an hour, stroked her hair, rocked her tenderly, and didn't think it was the time to tell her that Thorny's family attorney had somehow finagled him probation. If Glenn and Gorder had anything to say about it, Ollworth would be like Nate Pigeon before the autumn was done—gone and not missed, forgotten except in lying stories only fools told over drinks.

"Do you know what I'm afraid of?" Marj said, pouring them each a glass of wine.

He knew—dear god, how he knew—but he said, "No, what?"

She sipped; she wouldn't finish. "I keep thinking, and I know that's it's crazy, but I keep wondering if Cheryl . . . that she isn't . . . wasn't the only one who could do it." She looked at him; despite the night he saw the need. "Suppose there's someone else? Suppose it isn't over?"

Suppose, her expression asked, *it wasn't Cheryl but Dory?*

He put the glass aside and took her in his arms. It was the only thing that kept him sane—during the days through his leave of absence combined with vacation time, during the evening when he yawned and was afraid to fall asleep, and especially when he looked in at Dory and was tempted to shake her awake, to kill the dreams she might be having.

"Hale is dead," he reminded her.

"How do you know?"

He hugged her tighter. "Faith, my love. Faith. Right now, it's the only way."

The first rocket exploded above them, a green umbrella of sparks drifting down onto the lake.

When she nodded, he kissed her, and knew that all he had to do was believe it all himself. Which he supposed he would, given time, and the insistence of his son and the return of Nancy, and the stubbornness of Dory to find herself a boyfriend, and the godawful food Susan would prepare until she left.

The second rocket was a screamer, the third and fourth in swift succession had Marjory applauding, and he laughed when small soft arms suddenly wrapped around his neck and Cheryl whispered in his ear, "Daddy, all that noise is scary."

CHARLES L. GRANT

NEW VOICES IN HORROR